PRAISE FOR CLAIRE McGOWAN:

'A knockout new talent you s
—Lee Child

'A brilliant, breathless thriller that kept me guessing to the last shocking page.'
—Erin Kelly, *Sunday Times* bestselling author of
He Said/She Said

'Absorbing, timely, and beautifully written, *What You Did* is a superior psychological thriller from a major talent.'
—Mark Edwards, bestselling author of *The Retreat* and
In Her Shadow

'*What You Did* is a triumph, a gripping story of the secrets and lies that can underpin even the closest friendships. Put some time aside—this is one you'll want to read in a single sitting.'
—Kevin Wignall, bestselling author of *A Death in Sweden* and
The Traitor's Story

'Hitting the rare sweet spot between a satisfying read and a real page turner, this brilliantly written book deserves to fly high.'
—Cass Green, bestselling author of *In a Cottage In a Wood*

'McGowan writes utterly convincingly in three very different voices and she knows how to tell a cracking story. She will go far.'
—*Daily Mail*

'One of the very best novels I've read in a long while . . . astonishing, powerful and immensely satisfying.'
—Peter James

THE
OTHER
WIFE

THE
OTHER
WIFE

CLAIRE MᶜGOWAN

THOMAS & MERCER

Text copyright © 2019 by Claire McGowan
All rights reserved.

Published by Thomas & Mercer, Seattle

www.apub.com

Amazon, the Amazon logo, and Thomas & Mercer are trademarks of Amazon.com, Inc., or its affiliates.

ISBN-13: 9781542093156
ISBN-10: 1542093155

Cover design by Heike Schüssler

Printed in the United States of America

THE
OTHER
WIFE

Fire spreads fast.

She had not realised just how fast, but already orange flames are licking the roof of the large house, black smoke pouring from every window and door. She's running, slipping, the grass wet with dew beneath her. The dogs run beside her, a blur of fur and barks. They know something is wrong, but they can't understand just how bad it is. She's not sure she's understood it herself yet. She can smell it already, thick and choking, and imagines how it is inside the house. Smoke, and heat, and terror. No way out.

She reaches the top of the hill, the glint of the sea in the distance, the moon turning dark water silver, and stops. There will be no escaping the house now, she can see that. A feeling expands in her chest – is it relief maybe, or excitement even, mixed in with the fear? It's gone up like a matchstick. She should run to the nearest house, shriek at them to call the fire brigade, stumble out her explanation of a late-night dog walk, couldn't sleep, such terrible guilt at being safe. Then it will be over. But as she stands, waiting just a moment more, frozen, she sees something that will lodge in her memory for ever – a white face, at a high window. Sebby's window.

He has managed to open it a crack, though he can hardly reach the catch, and she can hear his cry, carried on a breath of ash and flame, a sound she will never forget. Her name, screamed in terror. *Help me! Help me!*

Without a second thought, she runs towards the flames.

PART ONE

Nora

The first time I saw her, I was struck by how sad she looked. Given my own situation, I was surprised by that. What did she have to be sad about? If anyone should have been sad it was me, moving into the tiny, spidery cottage, my furniture packed away in storage. The money gone, the big house. Everything gone.

It was when I first viewed the cottage, a still-warm day in October. The agent – a young man with too much aftershave, whose name was Gavin – had driven me in his little branded Fiat. His upselling was so tiresome. I wanted to tell him I'd already made my mind up to take it, as he went on about peace and tranquillity and getting away from it all. The cottage was one of three, set down a narrow country lane several miles from the M25. Sevenoaks was the nearest town, and it wasn't that near. There was nothing else for miles, not a single building. Once they had been staff cottages, tied to the big ruined estate a few fields over. Holly Cottage was empty, half-derelict. Ivy Cottage was the one I'd be renting. Willow Cottage was the one she lived in. 'You'll have neighbours,' said Gavin cheerfully. 'Nice young couple. Bought the place, ooh, about six months ago.'

I said nothing. I wasn't sure I was up to meeting them yet. It felt too soon, after everything. But I admit I was curious, and had my eyes peeled as we passed their cottage. They'd made some inroads in their garden, but I could tell they were city people. They'd planted all the wrong things, delicate flowers that wouldn't survive the first cold snap; a poor attempt at growbags, which I could see were being ravaged by slugs.

As the car swept past, Gavin driving too fast for the narrow country road, I saw movement at the window, and a woman inside the house, shading her eyes to look at us. Her gaze was strange – hungry, somehow. She had fire-engine red hair, a shade that couldn't be natural, and her face was pale.

'That's the wife,' said Gavin. 'Came down from London. Escaping the rat race, you know. They did the whole place up – fancy alarm system, underfloor heating.' In that moment, I felt sorry for her. Maybe because these city transplants never understood what real country life meant. Maybe it was her air of boredom, sadness. Fear, even. Maybe the way her eyes followed me as I got out of the Fiat and walked up the narrow weed-choked path to Ivy Cottage. As if she was desperate to talk to someone, anyone at all. I felt I should wave, or greet her in some way, but shyness held me back. There would be time for that later.

Inside, Ivy Cottage was damp and dark, unrenovated for years. The bathroom was unfashionable lime green, and a vine poked its way through a crack in the kitchen window. In every way it was inferior to the place I'd lived in for the past ten years. But I couldn't live there any more, so I had to move forward. 'I'll take it,' I said, and felt a small dart of enjoyment at the surprise Gavin tried to hide in his face.

I didn't speak to her that day, but I guessed even then that we'd be getting to know each other quite well.

Two weeks later, I arrived with a removals van. It had been a busy fortnight, getting ready to move. Packing up, renting a storage unit – it was expensive but I couldn't bear to let them go, all my beautiful things. I'd needed to hire removals men, buy boxes, pack, divert my post, cancel the services. It was exhausting, and used up the last of my money. It was still a shock having to think about that, not just whip out my debit card and dip into the ever-flowing river of cash I'd thought I had.

On the last day, I locked up the house – my beautiful house – and posted the key through the letter box. For a moment I wanted to kick the door in, take it back. I imagined new people moving in, entering a blank space of white walls and wooden floors, filling it with noise and colour and life. Most likely it would sell to a family with children, a house that size, and my heart gave an old familiar throb at the thought, the two upstairs rooms that were still just spares or studies, never nurseries, never the children's rooms.

It couldn't be helped. I was only forty-two – there was still a chance. I had to hold on to that.

With all the busyness, I hadn't had time to think about her, the red-haired woman who would be my neighbour. It wasn't until the van was pulling down the tiny lane, with difficulty – we got stuck under branches several times – that it hit me. I'd meet her soon. Maybe today.

Suzi

The noise of the van made me jump from where I was slumped on the sofa, surrounded by tissues and half-drunk cups of tea. You would hardly know me in this state, flattened by a dull crushing misery, or else hectic with terror, so much that I can't sit down, and I pace the living room making plans. How I might get away. Where I could go. Every time the phone rang or my mobile buzzed, my heart leaped up. I could feel it gasping in my chest, sluicing adrenaline into my veins. If anyone knew the situation I was in, they would think *How have you let this happen? How could you be so stupid?* I'd have said the same, before it was me.

So when I heard the van, I was on my feet, head crowding with my excuses already. *It's not true. I didn't mean it. I'm sorry.* Poppet had run to the door at the sound, his nails skittering on the slate floor, barking foolishly. We had so little traffic here; we didn't get milk delivered and Nick had routed most of the post to his office. It must be him home early, and I wasn't dressed and hadn't started dinner. What would he say? Or maybe it was something else. *Her.* But no, it was a removals van, and I remembered seeing the estate agent's car one day a few weeks before, someone coming to view the cottage. I never imagined they'd take it. A woman was being helped down from the cab by a stout removals man. She was in her forties, dressed in a gilet and proper country-style green wellies. Her hair was long and dark, grey showing through at the crown, and I could see from a distance she wore no make-up, like me. Perhaps she'd had the same thought: there was no one to see us out here.

Before all this, I had really tried. A large part of me was relieved to have left the situation at work, and everything with Damian, if not London itself. For the first few weeks it was like a mini-break, waking up with the eaves of the cottage over my head, the cheeps of birds outside. I'd put on my Hunter wellies and Joules quilted jacket and some kind of snood Nick's mum had got me for Christmas – which made me think, retrospectively, maybe she'd known? Maybe everyone had known we were moving except me? When Nick came home I'd make sure to be cooking or cleaning or wrangling the various tradesmen who'd transformed the crumbling cottage into a shiny modern box, complete with wine cellar and studio and music room for the guitars Nick supposedly played, which had dust in the frets he hadn't touched them for so long. I could honestly tell my friends I was busy, a renovation goddess like Sarah Beeny.

I am well jel, tapped Claudia, from the back of a taxi. When I thought of her, zipping along to some glam restaurant, where they'd take her nice, impractical coat and offer her a drink, I was so *jel* I could feel the bile rise up in my throat. But if you admit to friends how unhappy you are, you have to admit it to yourself as well.

Nowadays, things have changed. When Nick goes to work each morning and my wifely smile rusts over, I let myself think of all the things I put out of my mind when he's home. I take the jumper from under the bed. I hadn't washed it – thank God, I hadn't washed it. I look at myself in the mirror, my lying naked body – *how could you be so stupid* – and pull the jumper over my head, and for a second, so sweet and painful I nearly burst, I'm surrounded by you again. Most days I pray, obscurely, not sure who or what to, to change the past, to go back to how things were. *Please, let me turn back time. Give me another chance.*

That morning, the van arriving shocked me out of it, made me take an honest look at myself, how pathetic I was, what a mess. I wiped the snot and tears from my face and realised I was standing there in your old jumper, unshowered. Shame washed over me, a familiar feeling by now. What would Nick say if he could see me? What would you say, for that matter? I decided I'd better get cleaned up and meet my new neighbour.

That was the first time I saw her. Even though there was no threat I felt jittery with terror, shaking with it. Sometimes, since you'd gone, I was so afraid I could feel my heart beating inside me, like the wings of some terrible bird.

Elle

Years ago, when Elle was still a teenager, her mother had told her it was important to get ready before your husband came in the door. Freshen up, brush your hair, change your clothes. Tidy away any cooking mess or laundry sitting out. Greet him with a smile on your face, ask about his day.

Elle had laughed at it, privately sure that she would never even have a husband. She'd be too busy soaking up the applause after a sold-out concert, roses raining down on her as she bowed on stage. She'd wear a red silk dress and brush her long hair so it flowed over her shoulder like a river. She would never get married, or if she did, it would be to some adoring rich man, who would worship her and never expect her to roughen her magical hands with housework.

But here she was, almost thirty years later, and her mother had been right after all. It did matter, the way he saw you when he first came in the door. If you were fresh and smiling or if you were complaining, moaning that he hadn't taken the bins out or fixed the leaking tap in the downstairs bathroom. Sometimes she would arrange herself to make it look like she hadn't tried at all. Draping herself in a chair, hair brushed out in a shining curtain, a book in her hands, a glass of wine beside her. The book would not have been read, the wine would not have been her first. But he didn't know that. Appearance was everything – she'd learned that over the years, if nothing else.

Where are you? Where are you?

Now she sat, too nervous to maintain her tableau, watching the clock tick on. Nine o'clock. He was never normally so late. Maybe he'd gone for a drink with someone from work. They drank so much, the doctors; hardly surprising, the stress they were under. She made it a point never to nag, even when the dinner she'd cooked was dried up in the oven. She'd just smile and apologise, offer to make an omelette or call for a takeaway.

Why hadn't he messaged? She held her phone tight in her hands, leaving sweaty smears on the screen. Nothing. What a difference it would make, to see the little message window turn black, or the dots that meant he was typing. To know he was safe, and coming back to her. She'd already been on all the news websites, searching for words like *accident, crash, taken to hospital.* She would be ashamed if he knew how often she did this, how easily panic set in. He worked at the hospital, for goodness' sake, they'd have called her right away if anything had happened.

Her knuckles had gone white. Carefully, she set the phone down, then sprang up to see if anything needed doing. She straightened the cushion she'd been sitting against, the exact duck-egg shade as the vase on the sideboard. Flicked some specks of dust from the windowsill. Not that any dirt was allowed to settle. Some nights when she couldn't sleep, she could almost hear the dust falling, the spiders spinning their webs, the grease building up in the kitchen. She would get up, pull on rubber gloves in the dark.

She went into the kitchen and turned the heat down on the chicken casserole she had cooking – she usually tried to make things that wouldn't spoil if he was late. Rinsed the sink out for the fourth time. Arranged the tea towels. It was dangerous, being alone like this. Too much silence for thoughts to creep into. Flames, licking up a brick wall. A face at a window.

Where are you? Why haven't you called? Where ARE you?

Then, just as it felt unbearable, just as she was sure she needed to hold her hand under the scalding tap, or against the burner on the hob – anything to distract herself – she heard the blessed, blessed sound of tyres on gravel. He was home!

She ran to the door as he was unlocking it. Safe, whole, home to her. She flew into his arms. 'Thank God! I was so worried!'

'Hey, hey, what's this? I'm not even very late.'

'It's just – you didn't call and I . . .'

He pulled away, putting his hands on her shoulders. 'Elle-belle, we talked about this. I can't always leave on time, or get to my phone.'

She nodded, trembling. Shame was pouring into her like a sluice gate. 'I'm sorry, darling. I just love you so much. I worry!'

He was gentle. 'I know. But everything's fine. Darling, you aren't going funny again, are you?'

She avoided his gaze. 'Of course not. I just worry.'

'Well, I'm here now. How about some dinner for a hungry man?'

'Of course.' Her head was already clearing, filling with what she needed to do. Turn up the casserole, make a salad, slice the bread, pour wine for him. Make sure the bottle she'd opened wasn't too empty and if it was, hide it and open a fresh one, pour out one glass to make it look like that was all she'd had. 'Was it a terrible day?'

'The usual disaster zone.' He couldn't tell her what he did all day, she knew that. Patient confidentiality. Her heart swelled with pride for him. Saving lives, ushering children into the world. Stitching women back together as they lay, broken and bloody. And here he was, coming back to her. The least she could do was make sure he had a welcoming home to return to.

'Sit down, darling.' She massaged his shoulders, trying to ease him into a chair. 'You must be so tired. I'll bring you a drink. Whisky? Or wine?'

He stayed standing, gently pushing her away. 'I need a shower first. That hospital smell.' A nightly ritual, it helped him relax.

'Of course. There's fresh towels and that soap you like.'

He paused at the foot of the stairs, smiling at her with tired eyes. 'What would I do without you? I'll be down in a minute.'

She heard him go upstairs, and once again she looped the living room, making sure nothing was out of place, everything was neat and clean and tidy. Perfect.

She could almost see her mother smiling at her – not that she had smiled much while she was around. *You learned at last.* Elle liked to think she would look at her daughter now – her spotless house in the nicer part of Guildford, her handsome doctor husband, her French cookery and elegant clothes – and she would at last approve.

Suzi

I'd wondered if I should bring her something, but I wasn't the kind of woman who had cakes lying around in Tupperware or punnets of home-grown strawberries. I'd just go and say hello. I put on my too-clean Hunters and jeans under the jumper – I didn't feel ready to take it off, not yet – and made sure to tidy up, in case Nick came home early again. I set the dishwasher running, a silent whoosh behind brushed chrome. I adjusted the underfloor heating as it was far too hot, although when I checked the thermostat was set at eighteen, and outside the November weather had turned, all the warmth leached from it. This house seemed to keep everything in.

Nick had left his breakfast dishes on the table, of course, a new habit since we'd moved here. I had broached once or twice the fact I was now doing all the cooking, cleaning, washing and housework. He'd looked at me in astonishment, grinding pepper all over the stew I'd laboured on. 'But I've been working all day.'

I'd felt the helpless rage rise up in me – he'd always worked all day, and yet in London we'd shared everything, stopping by the shops, running a sponge over the shower. 'I'm working too.'

'Hardly.'

I didn't answer. I was supposed to be studying for my art thera-pist certificate, as well as painting, but we both knew I had done neither for weeks.

I was almost excited, I realised, as my feet made deep prints in the autumn mud. It was the first time in days I'd seen anyone but Nick. The dog was frantic at the door. *Walkies! People!* I wished I felt such enthusiasm for life. I couldn't find his lead – I never put it back in the right place – so I tied him with a scarf. There were three movers altogether. They must have been family because the younger men had the same burly width and curly hair as the older one.

'Hello!' I was dragged across the lane, the dog almost strangling himself with joy at seeing someone other than me. The older man regarded me, chewing gum. 'I'm the neighbour – is someone moving in? Exciting!' I was already trying to flatten my vowels, be more working class, not Mrs Hunter Wellies and Joules Gilet.

He was hefting a chest of drawers, his muscles rippling under tattoos. 'In there,' he said laconically. 'You wanna get that dog a lead.'

What was it about pets that meant you got advice from random strangers all the time?

'Be careful with that, will you?' A posh voice, cool and controlled. I turned. The woman was on the doorstep, holding a small plant in a pot. 'It's quite valuable. Please don't scrape it.' The man gave me what I thought was a class-conscious eye roll and I glowed. I wasn't the middle-class bitch here! I might own truffle oil but I was just like him!

She was older than me, eyes sinking under crow's feet, hair greying. She looked me over, and I saw her frown, perhaps at my unsuitable clothes, or maybe at Poppet, who was being a nightmare.

'Hello,' I said. 'I'm next door. Have you moved in?'

'Moving.' She was looking at the yapping, straining dog. 'Is that a scarf?'

'Oh, I couldn't find his lead, and he's such a bad dog, he'd be on the road in seconds.' Poppet had been a deep trial to me from the very beginning, when I'd been stuck at home with him as a puppy, unable even to step outside – they couldn't go out at all for the first two weeks, who knew? I'd begged Nick to let me go out for air, ten minutes even.

'But the pupster will be lonely,' he'd said, putting on his work jacket, something as simple as going to an office making me jealous. I had realised at that point that Poppet was now the number two priority in our family, and I had slipped to third.

The woman bent to him now, and very firmly said, 'Sit *down*.' And he did, ears flattened.

'That's amazing.'

'Just firmness. I grew up around dogs.' She crouched down, stroking his silky ears. He gazed up with deep adoration. 'They're so guileless. Not like people. He's a lurcher, is he?'

'Yeah.' How did people do that, tell just by looking? Really, I knew nothing about dogs.

She put out a hand. 'Nora Halscombe.'

I grasped it, fumbling with the dog. Her skin was surprisingly calloused. 'Hi, Nora. This is Poppet. Daft name, daft dog. I just wanted to say hello. There's only us, you know. It can be very isolated down here.' Again, the penetrating gaze. I felt a craven urge to do something and bent to lift a packing case the men had left by the stone path. 'I'll get this, you must be swamped.'

I felt her hand encircle my wrist, cool and oddly strong. 'No,' she said. 'Please don't. Not in your condition.'

I must have turned pale, and for a moment I felt the same cold dread flush through me like a weir, as it had every day since it happened. 'I didn't think I showed much yet.' The baggy jumper should have hidden it, surely.

'Oh, I know the signs.'

It felt too intimate, like when complete strangers come up behind you and tuck in the label of your shirt. The truth hit me like a bucket of cold water – I was almost six months pregnant.

What would happen when the baby came – surely I couldn't keep this up, this tightrope-act I walked every day? What would I do? I tried to change the subject back to her. 'Is it just you living here? Are you married?'

I could tell I'd made a terrible mistake by the way her face stiffened. 'I'm a widow,' she said finally. 'I wanted to be out of the house as soon as possible. Well, that's not entirely it. I had to move – money, you know. My husband was the one with the career.'

'I'm sorry. I shouldn't have asked.' Tears filled my eyes, to my deep horror and shame. 'God, I'm sorry, I – I lost someone close recently. It was – well, I'm still getting used to it.' Why had I said that? It wasn't the same kind of loss, even if it felt like it. My opinion of myself went even lower.

Nora's face was still frozen. 'A change will help, I'm sure.'

'I hope you'll be happy here.' I was screwing up my eyes to keep the tears in. 'Perhaps you'd like to come for dinner one time.' Supper, I should have said – she'd call it supper. 'I'm learning to cook. So far it's mostly burning, but you never know!' I turned to go. 'Oh, and if you meet Nick, that's my husband, perhaps you wouldn't mention what I said – you know, about the loss. It might upset him.'

'Of course.' She smiled. 'I'm good at keeping secrets, Suzi.'

It was only when I'd fumbled with the alarm – Nick said I had to set it every time, even just to pop out, but I was always scared I'd get the code wrong – and shut the door and started chopping onions for the recipe he'd left out that I realised I hadn't actually told her my name.

Nora

I'd been sure I would meet Suzi that first day, with just the two houses on this isolated road. And sure enough, I was still unpacking when she wandered over, dragging a lurcher pulling hard on an improvised lead. I did hate to see untrained dogs like that. Her hair was loosely plaited, strands of it falling over her face, and under her jacket she wore what looked like a man's jumper. I peered closer – yes, it was a man's jumper. I began to feel nervous. What would she be like?

I made myself smile at her, despite everything, as she stood talking to Brian, the head removals man. She wore no make-up but she was beautiful, and beside her I felt so old and dried-up, though there couldn't have been more than ten years between us. A widow. That's what I was. The word itself aged me, as did the loss.

It was only as I got nearer, and she lifted her hand in a greeting, that I saw something I hadn't prepared for at all. She was pregnant. And at once I found myself all at sea again, poleaxed with a pain so great I could hardly stand up.

I'd thought I was ready for the next step. Maybe I was wrong.

After Suzi went, I spent the rest of the day unpacking, trying to make the small damp place feel like home. It had been cleaned before I moved in, but not to my standards, so I had to leave the furniture in the middle of the room while I sponged skirting boards and dusted cobwebs. It went round and round in my head – she was pregnant. There would be a baby. Could I still be here, in that case? What did it mean for me? I had been so certain, but the knowledge made me falter in my plans. The cottage was so small, so ugly. And it was hard to get used to the silence out here, the fields that stretched out in every direction, the only noise the vague hum of the M25. The sense that nothing human was nearby, just bare trees, frozen ground.

Except Suzi, of course. My new neighbour. Standing at my own darkened window, I glimpsed her behind the sealed glass of their renovated cottage. It reminded me of Uplands, when I used to look out the glass panel of my room door at the other girls, who for all their feralness had a camaraderie of sorts. No one wanted to be friends with me, the possibly deranged posh girl. Ivy Cottage, that was the name of my house. Ivy that creeps, and clings. An invasive weed. And Suzi's was Willow, willow that droops and bows, melancholy.

I shivered, envious of Suzi's thick windows – the panes here let in draughts of cold air, and I'd had to wedge a rug against the door, it was so cold. When it got dark – before four already, so early – I came out of my unpacking daze and found myself alone in a damp, cold, cheerless house. I had no food in. I hadn't set up my lamps and candles or television, or figured out how to use the heating. I'd hesitated over putting my husband's picture out, and in the end decided to keep it in a drawer by my bed. I didn't need it out, reminding me every second. Besides, it might upset Suzi if she saw it. I'd seen her face when I mentioned I was a widow.

Overwhelmed, I sat down on the stairs, with their old patterned carpet. *What am I doing here?* I couldn't answer it. They say grief is close to madness. Perhaps I was mad. The noise of my phone ringing made me jump; it sounded so loud in the silence. 'Hello?'

It was Eddie, the lawyer I'd used since I was sixteen. The only person still around who'd known me when I was a child. A short, wheezy man, close to retirement; I was so happy to hear his voice I almost cried. 'I don't have good news, I'm afraid,' he said, when he'd finished asking about the cottage (I lied, said it was charming).

'Oh.' It seemed like a long time since anyone had good news for me. I wasn't sure it was possible any more. 'The money?'

'The forensic accounting didn't turn up anything. No secret accounts or trusts. It looks as if it really is gone. And as you know, the life insurance was cancelled last year. I'm so sorry, dear.'

I hadn't believed it when he first told me. It didn't make any sense. 'No, no, there's plenty,' I'd insisted. I couldn't have said how much, but I'd always had the impression it was limitless for all the things I wanted. Comfortable. Not something I needed to worry about.

'I'm sorry. The accounts just seem to be . . . depleted. There's nothing there.'

It was an interesting word to choose. I felt that way myself – diminished. Drained. Empty. A husk of a person, in a husk of a house. All I had left was a certain wild pride, and a drive to keep on going, in case I looked down and saw the gaping abyss I was balanced over. 'Thank you, Eddie.' I hung up before he could hear me cry.

Suzi

I was a bit troubled by the thing with my name, but it was easy to explain to myself. Gavin the estate agent might have mentioned it to her, for example. I had to stop dwelling on things. Rumination, they call it in psychology. When your brain worries away at a minor thing until you wear a hole in yourself, like an unravelling jumper. The way I think about the last time I saw you, taking the memory out and rubbing it smooth as a stone. *We'll figure this out. But for now, don't make any waves. Go home.*

It isn't home, I'd said, made bold with fear. *Not with him.*

Soon. And you drove off in your Jaguar, leaving me by the side of the road in the September sunshine, the waving grass brushing my bare legs, my city sandals far too clean to have been for a proper country walk, so that I had to muddy them on my way home in case Nick suspected. I'd been so happy just then, despite the fear and the sick feeling of having to tell him. I didn't doubt you would come for me. But since then – almost two months now! – I hadn't heard a word. I'd replayed it a thousand times. Had I done something – said something – that changed everything so utterly? What was it? Meanwhile, my stomach was swelling like an opening flower in water. Something had to be done. But what?

Nick was late that night, after I went to Nora's. I'd taken to hovering by the front window when he was due, like a woebegone dog, hands on my belly. Not because I missed him. More because the clock had hit six, the hands balanced straight as a knife, and I knew if it tipped any further I'd tip with it. That night, he idled outside, locking the car. He must have been on the phone; I could hear his voice but not what he was saying. The low roll of his laugh, unfamiliar as thunder in a long summer. He was talking to a woman, I could tell. Someone in the office, probably, some bright young graduate. Loyal. Liked dogs and wellies and didn't crave the pound of tarmac under her heels. He was silent now. Off the phone. He still didn't come in. I went into the hallway and up to the door, right up close to the Farrow & Ball paint, pressing my bump into it along with my ear, and I imagined I could almost hear him breathe on the other side. What was he waiting for? Then suddenly he wrenched it open. I saw him like a stranger might, a middling-height man in a Superdry jacket, a shirt and tie, glasses steaming up in the cold. Brown hair, a nice rather than a striking face, or so I had once thought. 'What are you doing?'

'Oh! I just heard the car.' I wanted to ask, *who were you talking to*, but I wouldn't. I wouldn't turn into him. 'You're so late.' I trailed after him into the kitchen.

He looked at me in weary bafflement. 'But you used to be late all the time. Three a.m., one time you came back, in London. Remember?'

'It's different. I'm on my own here.' We were hovering close to the edge, so I turned away, tidying some dishes around the sink.

'You can go out too,' he said, taking off his coat. 'I'm not stopping you.'

I threw a mug into the sink. It didn't break and when Nick glanced over, I picked it back out again, shaking, as if my hand had slipped. I'd wished it would break. That was why people threw

23

things in arguments. It wasn't rage. It was the need to show the other person that, however things looked from the outside, something was broken and jagged. 'I can't, can I? You have the car, the station's miles away.'

'There's cabs,' he said mildly, switching on the TV. I hated him at that moment. Saying *there's cabs* was like saying, *there's a key*, when you're locked up inside a cell and it's hanging on the wall outside. It was too expensive to get a cab, they often wouldn't come out to us, or couldn't find us, and anyway, where would I go? I had no friends round here. I was still too ashamed to face any work people, and too worried my other friends would see right through me – Suzi with her cottage and rural idyll and giving up work. I couldn't admit I had been wrong about all of it.

I decided to try again. I had to make the effort, heal the gaping wound between us, the one I had opened. 'Did you see we have a new neighbour?' I asked, my voice forced into cheeriness.

'Oh. Yeah.' He was looking in the fridge now, though I'd spent hours making a lasagne. He asked me to cook, left me recipes, and then he stood and shovelled down cheese singles. 'Strange someone wanted to live here.'

'Apart from us, you mean?' It came out tartly, and he gave me that weary look again. There was a pause, and I reset to pleasant breezy wife. 'It's a lady on her own. She seemed nice. Bit posh.'

He shut the fridge. 'Is dinner almost ready? I'll go in the music room if not, I want to lay down some tracks.'

When we got married, Claudia had given me a comedy book called *Instructions for Wives*. It was from the fifties. It said things like, before he comes in, make sure you look fresh and pretty, tidy round the house and so on. It was one of those ironic 'look how far we've come' gifts. Some days, as I sat clock-watching and worrying if my stew with venison would be OK, I wondered how much of a joke it was, really.

When I served the lasagne, Nick put a forkful in his mouth and made a face. 'Is this the recipe I left?'

'Sort of. I modified it.'

'It's a bit too salty. Not good for the baby.' He regarded me with a kind of exasperation, like an under-performing employee. The baby, who already dictated our lives, was only the size of a butternut squash. But I wouldn't say that. I'd back down, because there were too many landmines around me and I was trapped. And he was right. He had done all this for me, so much, and look how I'd repaid him. The sting of guilt was like salt in a wound. 'I bet you didn't walk Poppet today either, did you?'

How did he know? It was true that, after my meeting with Nora, I'd just given the dog a quick run up and down the road, not the hour Nick insisted on. 'I lost track of time, after all the excitement. I didn't feel up to it.'

'You're supposed to walk every day, Suzi. Never mind that you need it – the doctor said you shouldn't gain weight till the last trimester – but what about poor Poppet? It isn't fair otherwise.'

I hadn't even wanted bloody Poppet – another little surprise after the move – and here I was responsible for his entire wellbeing. 'OK.' I felt tears wobble in my voice. Thinking: *How did I get here? Who am I? Who is this man?* Amazing to think that only weeks ago I was sure I'd have left all this behind me. 'Anyway, I've invited her for dinner. The neighbour. Her husband's dead.' To my horror, when I said this, there was a catch in my throat, like when I'd spoken to Nora.

I tried to hide it but Nick was looking up from his phone, frowning. 'What's wrong?' He couldn't suspect. He might have already noticed my strange emotions, how red my eyes were when he got home. For a moment, terror ran through me like electricity. 'Well?' The one syllable seemed to ask so much. *Tell me the truth, Suzi. Tell me what's going on.*

Did he know?

I stammered, 'N-nothing. Hormones.' I should have said something like *I imagined it was you and it upset me*, but I couldn't bring myself to.

Luckily, I'd reminded him of the baby. He touched me at last, on the stomach, leaning around the table. 'Causing trouble for Mummy already, little one?' There was real tenderness in his voice, and as so often in marriage, we came to an unspoken truce.

For a moment, I thought about telling him. Dropping the load of guilt I'd been carrying, laying it down at his feet. We had loved each other, not so long ago. Maybe we could again. 'Nick . . .'

He got up. 'I'll make you some green tea. It's good for the baby.'

I really hated green tea.

'Lovely,' I said, putting aside all thoughts of telling him; that was clearly madness. Instead, I needed a plan. And soon.

Elle

She stood by the window, listening to the clock tick slowly on, eating away at her life. When he was with her, it was easy to believe he was working all these nights – he was a doctor, of course he did long hours. She missed him, but couldn't take him away from his important work, the lives he saved.

Alone, it was harder. He thought she was suspicious, always finding fault, but in fact the opposite was true. She did her best to blind herself, as long as possible. But on these long nights, just her and the house where not a speck of dust stirred, with only the TV and a wine bottle for company, sometimes she failed. Little voices began to whisper at her: *Where is he really? Is there someone else?*

Her treacherous mind would add up the evidence. Coming home late, hiding his phone, slipping it under the sofa cushions when she walked into the room. Sometimes at night she'd wake to find him gone from bed, and she'd wait till he came back, and he'd slide in saying he just got up to go to the bathroom or for water, but she knew he'd been gone for ten minutes, more. All so subtle. She could have been imagining it – it might not have crossed her mind if she'd been busy, if she'd had a job or other things in her life. If she still played the piano, instead of only dusting it each week. If she'd had a child. Where would he have met a woman even? Some pretty nurse, a drugs rep, a girl from the shop where he bought his coffee? She thought of the conference he'd been on a few months ago, an overnight stay in a hotel near Heathrow. So boring, he'd told her. Not worth discussing. *Who is she? Is she pretty is she young is she nice? How did it begin? How long?* They had started again, the litany of thoughts. However much she tried to banish them by alphabetising the books or cleaning out the cupboards or polishing the silver, they wouldn't go away.

You stupid girl. It's all your fault.

Was it just in her head? That was it, the possibility she could never discount. The fact that she could not trust her own mind. It whispered things, it distorted the facts. It was not reliable.

As she stood, lights swung on to the driveway, tyres crunching on gravel. He was home, but her heart did not lighten as usual. She watched him sit in his car, doing something on his phone. A smile lit up his face, one she never saw any more. Playful, sexy. Engaged. He never engaged with her now – she was like a cat he stroked in passing, absent-minded. He looked up, saw her watching, and waved. She forced herself to wave back. Had a flicker of guilt crossed his face? Or had she just imagined it?

He walked to the door and came in, and she breathed in the lemon of his aftershave. Such a handsome man, with his dark-rimmed glasses, his expensive shirt hugging a chest that was honed and muscled, even at forty. How lucky she was. 'Are you alright?'

'I just . . .' The chirpy denials wouldn't come to her tonight. 'You're so late. You're always late.'

He breathed out a long sigh, heaving his satchel on to the chair. 'Oh Elle. Not again.'

'Please, if you're – if there's someone, just promise you won't leave me?'

He grasped her arms, looked deep into her eyes. 'There's no one. Why can't you see that? I'm just so busy. These cuts, they mean we all have to work harder.'

Guilt washed over her. Complaining about her own trivial feelings, when he grappled with life and death. 'I'm sorry.'

'Are you taking those pills?'

She squirmed. 'They make me fuzzy.'

'It's for your own good, darling. We don't want another episode, do we?'

She looked away, and it took her a long time to be able to say, 'No. You're right. Are you hungry?'

The terrible thing was, she'd love him no less if it was true. As she drifted off that night, in the beautiful bedroom under the thick duvet and the smooth cotton sheets, she thought about the woman, who might not exist at all. She wondered about her name, what she looked like. If she was married too. If he might end it with her now that Elle suspected, if he'd bother to have that conversation, or simply stop getting in touch. 'Ghosting', it was called. She'd learned that term from a teen drama she'd watched on one of the nights he wasn't home. Disappearing from someone's life like the dead, with no apologies or explanations. She could see there might be a certain appeal in that.

In her craziest moments, when she woke at three and felt like the only person in the world, like a shipwrecked sailor on a deserted island, she would imagine talking to the woman, if she even existed. What she might say to her. How she might warn her off.

Suzi

The next morning, when Nick went to work, I did what I'd promised you I never would. I called your mobile.

It was a number I only had for emergencies, if I couldn't find you when we'd arranged to meet. It must never ring or sound with a text or call when she might be around, that had been made very clear to me. And yet you had gone – was I supposed to just accept it? The fact that you had, in all likelihood, ghosted me? With trembling hands, I went to the corner of the kitchen that sometimes had reception, hit the number – saved for no particular reason under *Lucy P* – before I could think too much about the ramifications, and heard an electronic voice. *The number you have dialled has not been recognised.* Had you changed it, in case I tried this very thing?

What could I do now? Throwing the phone down on the counter in frustration, I went into my 'studio' – what Nick had called it when he set it up for me. I hadn't said I wanted one, but then I hadn't said I wanted to move to the country or get a dog or give up work, so I suppose it didn't matter. It had been built during the frenzy of alterations that saw the new windows and doors go in, the underfloor heating, the old cellar dug out for wine and Nick's 'music room'. 'Try the chair.' Nick had rocked it for me back then, showing me the studio. 'It's won design awards. I know you think office chairs are hideous.'

It was almost heart-breaking, this remembering of things I'd said years back. Like a new lover, not a husband of three years. Guilt was like a stone on my chest. Now, I sat down on the expensive chair, uncomfortably far away because of my bump, and turned on the computer he'd bought me. I started, as always, by clicking through every story on the local news. There was nothing. A domestic violence case in Medway, but that was a woman murdered, strangled by her ex-husband. A child attacked by a dog in Hastings; a terrible thing, that made me shut down the window with shaking hands. No accidents, no raging house fire that killed a local man, no pile-up on the M25 – nothing to explain your silence. No sign of your name, anywhere, even though I'd trawled the staff lists of every hospital nearby. Sometimes, in my more crazy moments, I imagined you'd died on your way home, that last day. I knew this was stupid. It was just so hard to take in, when the last thing you said to me was, *don't worry, we'll be together*. Soon, all the prints you'd left on my life – a hair caught in my scarf, the marks of your fingers on my phone screen when you picked it up once – those would all be gone, as if I'd never known you at all. Like a ghost.

I had googled your name a few times too, despite the danger – it was easy to find out what someone had searched for, I knew. I had even, though it was stupid given I didn't know her name, looked for *Sean Sullivan wife*. Because sometimes, when I got really crazy indeed, and the fear and sadness were replaced by pure rage, I thought about finding her and telling her. Turning up outside your house, showing her the hoarded messages in the secret account, and bringing it all tumbling down. Of course, Nick would know then too. I'd be burning my life to the ground along with yours. I had no money, no job, and I was pregnant. It made no sense.

But that didn't stop me thinking it.

Nick and I had moved here as part of our new life. London had broken us and we'd broken each other, and it was starting to feel as if our MDF-filled flat in Shoreditch, traffic thundering outside and sirens going all night, was like being walled in together. I was working, he was working. I drank too much cheap white wine with colleagues in darkened bars, and eventually it seemed normal to stay out with certain of these colleagues instead of going home to recrimination and silence. It was make or break, and we decided make. So when he came home one night and said I was to take the next day off, I acquiesced.

He must have been planning it for a while. A new job with Kent County Council – I didn't even know he'd applied – and a cottage outside Sevenoaks. It looked like something from a fairy story, by which I mean full of sweetmeats and dark magic. As if guilty about what he was selling us, the estate agent pointed out the patchy mobile reception, the fact the road often flooded. 'The nearest station is five miles,' he said, looking doubtfully at my heeled boots. 'So if you need to get to London, it's not that easy.'

'We won't be in London,' said Nick firmly. I remember him standing there on that mild spring day, in sensible walking shoes, the North Face jacket that I secretly hated. 'Suzi's going to give up work.'

I was such a fool. Even with all this new machismo, the secret job, the proposed move, it wasn't until this point I realised he might know about Damian.

You remember I told you about Damian.

We never discussed it, as crazy as that sounds, Nick and I. It was buried in the ground between us, a landmine ready to go off. I couldn't even ask, because I wasn't sure what he knew, and if I was wrong, I'd be handing myself in to him. And here's the thing – when someone gives you an ultimatum, it's often a relief, after all that confusion, to no longer have any choice. So without me actually agreeing to it or any discussion at all, I was giving my notice and pretending I wanted to grow rhubarb in the countryside. My friends expressed happiness, in voices stretched with fear. What if someone made them move to the country too?

On the day we left our flat, hired van loaded up, I watched London dissolve into a succession of warehouses and blank suburbs, melting into green fields. When we arrived there was a stack of books on the table with titles like: *Improving Your Fertility. What to Expect Before You're Expecting. Kitchen Gardening for Beginners.* The heavy door sealed shut, and I wondered if I'd ever get out again.

Music. I heard music. I lifted my head from the computer, slowly, puzzled. It was faint, but growing louder. A pop-up on the screen? I tried shutting down Chrome, but it continued. Had I left the radio on? No, I hadn't had it on that morning. I wandered into the kitchen in search of the sound. Nick had forgotten his phone, maybe, or his iPad. We really had too many gadgets in this house. My own phone was charging on the side, the battery always drained these days. I'd have to buy a new one eventually, I knew, but some stupid sentiment made me cling to this one, the phone I'd used to contact you.

I paused by the voice-activated speaker, the tiny object that controlled everything in the house. The music was coming from there. And it was a song I knew. The one you had played to me that first night in the hotel, your eyes searching mine, an embarrassment of emotion between us. You'd sent me a link to it after, when you were still chasing me. 'Stay With Me' by Sam Smith. Full of yearning, and pain. Just the way I felt about you, but I hadn't put it on. Had I?

With trembling hands, I turned it off. The electronic voice said, 'Hello, Suzi,' and, viciously, I yanked its cable out of the wall. I had never wanted one in the first place, spying on me. But I had to be careful. With everything that was going on, it was harder and harder not to spiral out of control.

You didn't really believe in weaknesses of the mind. When I told you of my intention to be an art therapist, you'd laughed. 'Put it this way, if you came to me with a leg hanging off, would you want me to give you a pencil?'

'It's not the same thing!'

'Course it is. Mental ill-health is a chemical imbalance – which doctors can help with – or it's just feeling sorry for yourself. People should get out for a run, do some hard work.'

I'd looked disapproving. 'What about the heart? Doesn't that matter?'

'Ever seen a human heart? It's all tubes and blood. It's like a tyre. If it's leaking, you patch it up. Job done.'

I wished you were here now to tell me this. Because my heart was leaking, and broken, and I couldn't seem to find any way to fix it.

Nora

After our first meeting, I didn't see Suzi again for a day or two. I watched from my living room as her husband went to work and came back, as Suzi left the house to stare in puzzlement at her dying plants, or to drag the dog on a too-short walk. She glanced at Ivy Cottage as she passed, but didn't come over, and I wondered how to speak to her again. My luck was in when, the next day, she locked herself out of the house. From my windows I saw her pacing in her front garden, agitated, the dog straining on his lead, and threw open the door. 'Everything OK?'

'Oh God, I'm such an idiot. I keep getting the alarm code wrong. There's a call-out fee if it goes off, so I'm scared to try again.'

'So you can't get in?'

She threw her hands up. 'Not till Nick texts me the code.'

'Do wait over here, please – it's so cold. We can have tea?'

She hesitated. 'Thank you. I don't know if I said, but I'm Suzi.' Later, I would turn that line over in my head, looking for hidden meaning.

As she sat in my living room, I noticed she had her phone in the pocket of her cardigan, and kept fingering it as we spoke. Waiting for a call, clearly, or a text. One that hadn't come, and I didn't think it was Nick's. She was so nervy too – she jumped when a tree branch scratched the window, spilling tea on her jeans. 'Crap!

I'm sorry. It's the pregnancy, it's made me so clumsy.' At least she'd opened up about that now – foolish to try to hide it, when it was so obvious. I wondered if she was the kind of person who was good at pretending things weren't real.

There was so much I wanted to ask her now she was here, inside my house, but nerves made me tongue-tied. I was so curious to meet the husband. She talked about him a lot during our tea. 'Nick hates it when I forget to start dinner.' 'Nick's always on at me to shut the gate, in case the dog gets out.' 'Nick says Poppet needs at least an hour's walk a day, but it's so hard in the frost. I'm afraid I'll slip.' The opening was there. I was standing in the kitchen doorway, drying a china cup with a tea towel. It had been my mother's set, a wedding present, printed with small blue cornflowers.

I said, 'I could come with you, if you like. I've been meaning to walk more. And that way I could fetch help, if anything happened.'

She reacted with too much pleasure. 'Amazing! I would love that. I'm such a disaster, really, I need someone to make me go.'

For some reason, Suzi had thoroughly internalised the message that she wasn't good enough. That she was bad somehow. I wanted to find out if that was true. 'How are you feeling, with the pregnancy?'

She put her hands on her stomach. 'Pretty good, now the sickness has stopped. It was so unexpected. We tried in London, but I guess I never really thought it would work.' She blushed slightly. 'And now – well, it's happening. I can't get my head around it.'

'Nick must be pleased,' I probed.

Her face paled and I wondered why. 'He's thrilled. He worries I don't eat right during the day, or I'll slip in the fields or something.' And yet he'd got her a dog that she had to walk for an hour a day. I found that interesting.

'It must be hard, out here alone,' I said, and she bit her lip, and I thought she was going to tell me something, and I almost had the crazy urge to tell her things back, explain what had brought me here and what had happened to me. Loneliness can make you do mad things. And I thought Suzi was lonely, maybe even lonelier than me. At least I was used to it.

Suddenly she leaped to her feet, phone in hand. I wondered if it had gone off, though I knew it wouldn't be the message she was hoping for. That would never come. But then I heard the sound of a car in the lane, slowing down as if to stop. It was rare enough that it must be Nick. 'Crap! It's almost five! He's early!' Fumbling, she set her cup down, splashing brown liquid against the wall. 'I'm sorry, Nora. I need to explain about the alarm. He'll do his nut!' Fumbling, she wrapped her scarf round her neck. 'Oh God, I'm so forgetful. I meant to ask if you'd join us for dinner on Saturday?'

I made a show of thinking about it, even though I didn't and wouldn't have any other plans. The chance to see inside their house, meet the husband – of course I wouldn't turn that down. 'That would be nice, thank you. Can I bring anything?' That middle-class call and response. Then she would say, 'Just yourself,' and of course I would bring something anyway.

Suzi played her part, then said, 'Great! Looking forward to it. You can meet Nick properly.' Then she ran across the road, not looking to see if there was traffic – there rarely was, but even so – and I thought how light and energetic she was, even pregnant, even sad and afraid. The fire of her hair stood out about the autumn leaves and the hanging shadows of the lane. I saw her run to greet the husband, her hand gesticulations. I imagined what she was telling him – excuses about being locked out, probably. He wasn't at all what I'd expected. A slight man, barely five foot eight, with a square face and short hair. He wore a Superdry jacket over suit trousers, a tie. The kind of man you'd walk past in the street and hardly notice, and yet Suzi was so afraid of him she'd practically flung her cup down to go to him. Very interesting.

I wiped up the splash of tea turning a pale brown on my white wall. Already I was starting to find out so much about the people next door. I was right – this move had helped me. As my mother used to say, a change is as good as a rest.

Suzi

Saturday arrived, and I found I was so strangely nervous. I kept getting that lurch in my stomach like when you have to do something part of you is dreading. I didn't know why. I thought about Nora's loss again, my own illicit grief pressing hard against the walls in my chest. A glass of wine would have helped, but that was a no-go. Nick was already cross at me for getting locked out yet again, the third time since we'd moved here. I couldn't seem to remember the code, or maybe I'd hit the wrong keys with my cold, pregnant fingers.

As Saturday wore on, we were both weirdly jumpy. We had even dressed up, pathetically, me in a black maternity dress and tights, Nick in a navy shirt and trousers I hadn't seen before. They fitted him well, and I noticed in an abstract way that he had lost weight, gained muscle. All those gym trips, keeping him out even longer, while I stewed at home, getting fatter by the day.

When we first moved we'd had a few people down to stay, and it was only then I'd realised how isolated we were, not a house or shop for miles about, only the empty cottages and fields in every direction. Claudia had said she couldn't sleep, it was so quiet – I'd found her reading the paper in the kitchen at 5 a.m. 'I'm sorry you had a bad night,' I said, a little defensive.

'It's OK, love,' she'd said. 'Some of us just aren't made for the country. I miss the traffic and the choking fumes!'

But I didn't think I was made for it either.

As seven drew near, I found Nick and I were snapping at each other, as if we were going to be inspected.

'Did you put out clean—?'

'Of course, I'm not stupid.'

He jumped up suddenly. 'What if she has allergies? I mean, so many people don't eat wheat or dairy now . . .'

'She said she ate everything.' We almost couldn't look at each other. As if our whole life were suddenly going to be put under scrutiny.

We were so quiet we heard her footsteps on the driveway, bang on time at seven. Nick rushed forward – I put up my hand to stop him. It's just weird if you think people have been sitting there in silence waiting for you. I went to the door myself, holding my bump self-consciously under one hand. I put on a smile to open the door to her. 'Nora! So pleased you could make it.'

She entered, wiping her walking boots on the mat. I wondered why she'd worn them for the short journey over, and I saw they were dirty, as if she'd gone scrambling about the fields first. She didn't say anything for a moment, just looked round the hallway.

'This is Nick,' I said, ushering her into the living room.

She gazed at him keenly. 'Hello. Nick.'

'Our new neighbour!' Nick moved clumsily to take her hand. 'Um . . . can I take your . . . ?' He gestured for her coat, a waxed Barbour, and they sort of got tangled up together. I closed my eyes briefly at the awkwardness.

'Do sit down.' I lunged forward. 'There's olives . . . crisps . . . eh, and dinner will be ready soon.'

'Thank you.' She didn't sit. 'These are for you. I thought you wouldn't be drinking, so perhaps alcohol wouldn't be right.' It was a punnet of apples, small and sweet and fresh, water still clinging to them.

I saw Nick nodding, pleased. When I'd first told him I was pregnant, shaking with guilt, terrified he would add up the dates and know the truth, he'd put Operation Baby into action. Immediately I was banned from any alcohol, even a sip. 'But surely I could have a bit,' I'd said weakly, watching him pour an open bottle of wine down the sink.

Nick had slammed the bottle into the recycling bin with what for him was a lot of force. 'Would you feed it a glass of wine when it was born? Everything you drink goes right into the baby. You ought to know that.' Not only booze but also fish, seafood, nuts, caffeine, soft cheese and plastics were on the banned list.

I took the apples. 'How lovely! From your garden?'

'I found them when I moved in. Creeping up between the stones of the wall.' Nora gave an odd, stiff smile as she lowered herself to the sofa. 'Thank you for inviting me.'

'Not at all. You just moved in?' Nick sat down opposite Nora as I poured wine, looking longingly at the silky red liquid.

'Yes, I lost my husband recently.' She said that with a strange intonation, as if he had simply disappeared down the back of the sofa and might turn up again.

'I'm so sorry.' Nick lowered his voice respectfully.

'And how long have you two been married?' She looked between us, her keen gaze like a searchlight.

'Oh – about three years, is it, love?' I smiled at him. We were good at doing what happy couples did. Maybe no one was really happy. Maybe everyone was just copying it off TV and films.

'Three years in March.'

Nora said, 'And you're expecting. How lovely. People used to rush right in, of course, but it's nice to wait for a few years, isn't it?'

'Er . . . yes.' Nick filled my silence. 'We're very excited. It's the first grandchild for both our families, so it's very . . . exciting.' I wanted to scream at him to find a different word.

'A boy or a girl?'

He looked at me quickly – *Who is this woman? Why have you put me through this?* – 'We don't know. We asked them not to tell us.'

She drank her wine quickly, greedily. It occurred to me that maybe she was nervous too. 'Of course. Too little mystery in the world.'

Nick cleared his throat. I brought over the olives and we arranged ourselves around them, grateful for any little prop. 'So where were you before, Nora?'

'Oh, just in town. We had a big house there, but on my own it seemed too empty. I've always liked cottages.'

'Yes, we just fell in love with it here, didn't we, Suze? I always dreamed of living in an old house.'

It's a strange experience, hearing your spouse talk to a complete stranger. You want to shout out, *That isn't true! You never told me that!* Like a test you don't understand why you're failing.

'So what took you out of London?' Nora said. Nick gave her the usual spiel – we wanted space for our kids to grow up, to breathe clean air, slower pace of life – but she kept staring at me. 'Did you mind giving up your job, Suzi?'

'Oh! Not really – I've got time to paint, and that's what I always wanted.' I was saying my lines as expected. Nick was watching. My director. It was true I used to complain all the time about my boss, the tampon and cornflakes ads I designed, the lack of time for painting. But I liked the salary and boozy lunches and being able to sink thirty quid on wine if I felt like it. I'd long suspected I wasn't cut out for the privations of the artist's life. Suddenly, under Nora's frank gaze, I found myself wanting to be honest. 'It has been a big change, actually. It's hard.'

'Sometimes a change is what's needed,' said Nick, his eyes fixed on me. 'Suze was going down a bad path in London.' I looked up sharply. He wouldn't, would he? 'Drinking too much, staying out late with colleagues. Weren't you, baby?' He reached out and tousled my hair, a little too roughly.

I stood up, on the pretence of looking for more olives. 'You know how it is. London culture.'

Nick laughed. 'And yet I was there too, Nora, and I never stayed out late.'

'He's a home bird,' I said, aiming for affectionately teasing, and missing.

'One of us had to be.'

More silence, and I began to curl my fingers into a fist, it was so unbearable.

'Might I use your bathroom?' said Nora, no doubt wanting to get away from the knife-cut tension in the room.

'Of course, let me show you.' Nick got up.

'I'll just . . . check on dinner.' In the kitchen, I realised I was shaking. I was thinking about Damian again, when I'd tried not to for so long. Had that been Nick's intention, to throw me off balance?

I felt air brush my neck – Nick had followed me into the kitchen. 'Isn't it ready yet? Our guest will be hungry.'

Tears pricked my eyes as I opened the Aga door, still getting used to the way I could no longer bend at the waist. A bloody Aga! I'd never wanted that. 'What was that about?' It was risky, but I was too angry to let it go.

'What?'

'All that Suzi's a drunk, Suzi stayed out late crap. I moved here, didn't I? I haven't been anywhere in months, have I?'

Nick looked at me, and for a second I almost didn't recognise him. His voice was cold. 'If you find it so hard to be here with me – your husband – then maybe you need to have a rethink about your life.' I was so close to crying. I opened the Aga door again, just to hide my face. He said, 'Serve it up soon, please, it's late.'

A direct order. That was where we'd got to now. I removed the casserole dish, the steam scorching my face, and it was almost welcome. For a moment I thought about laying my wrist on the hot iron oven, just to feel something else.

You had gone. I needed to face it, now it had been so long, and not a word from you. I couldn't be in denial any more. I was a married woman in my thirties and I'd been ghosted. A stupid, faithless woman. I shouldn't have told you about the baby. I realised that now, but what choice did I have? You would surely have noticed at some point. So I'd done it, and you'd panicked. You had gone back to her, and I'd be stuck with Nick and my ruined life and a baby that probably wasn't his. Of course, my vulnerability was also my trump card. Your child, your DNA, easy to prove. It almost took my breath away, how easily we can destroy each other, when we're in love. If you weren't coming back, I had two choices. Your phone number was not in service, I didn't know where you lived, and my search of local hospital websites had not thrown you up. Either I tracked you down, made you acknowledge me, somehow found a way to forgive you for these weeks of silence. Or I moved to plan B. Making sure I never got caught.

As I ladled the cassoulet on to plates, mechanically running through a checklist – water, bread, vegetables, plates – I realised Nora had not come back from the bathroom. I slipped off the oven gloves and opened the door to the hallway. My studio door was ajar, and from the kitchen I could see Nora standing in it, looking about her with a slightly puzzled air. I called, 'Did you get lost?'

I could have sworn she jumped. 'I'm so sorry, I took a wrong turn.' She came towards me, and then there was the bustle of sitting down to eat, and I soon forgot about it and returned to my own inner torment, the question that had been going round and round in my mind since you disappeared: *What the hell am I going to do?*

Alison

FEBRUARY – THREE MONTHS LATER

The body lay under the snow for almost two months before it was found.

It happened sometimes in colder countries – Russia, Poland – though it was unusual still in England. But then everything about that winter had been unusual: the plummeting temperatures, the frequency of blizzards, the shock of people who thought they lived in a mild climate suddenly understanding about month-long freezes, snow tyres, pipe lagging.

It was still cold as DC Alison Hegarty stood at the side of the country lane, shivering under the unflattering duvet coat she'd had to buy several weeks into the onset of deep winter. 'Been here a while then?'

Her partner, DC Tom Khan, was bouncing up and down on the balls of his feet. 'Doc reckons so. It's frozen solid, look.'

Alison made herself look at the body in the recently melted snowdrift, which was being worked on by two CSIs, their white suits blending in with the patches of snow on the ground. The ice crystals in the eyelashes, the grey, ashy skin that put her greatly in mind of the contents of her mam's chest freezer up in Bolton. She knew she had to do this – it was part of her job. And this wasn't the first person to have frozen to death that winter; they'd already found two homeless men stuck to the pavements in Sevenoaks, a damning indictment of a town where just feet away people spunked sixty quid on their Christmas turkeys.

But that was different. They had not been murdered.

'How long'll it take to get it out?'

'Hours yet. Think of it like defrosting a freezer.' Tom made a chipping motion with both hands. He had moved down here from an East London beat, and liked to remind her he'd seen some terrible things.

Alison shivered even harder. 'Bloody hell, it's cold.'

'Winter is coming, mate. Well, it's here. Don't suppose there's a handy trucker's stop nearby?'

She shook her head in the Raisa Gorbachev-style fur hat she'd taken to wearing. Those Russian women, they knew how to deal with cold, and that was by throwing all sense of fashion out the window and essentially going out dressed as a bed. 'There's nothing nearby at all. Just those houses.'

She looked back longingly at the set of small cottages on either side of the country lane, a few yards down from where they stood. Nothing else for miles except fields and then the M25. This was a place you might pass on your way to somewhere, Gatwick or Heathrow maybe, and not even know it existed. It didn't have a name, it was so isolated. Not the kind of place she'd fancy living – she liked to be able to pop out for a pint of milk.

She thought fleetingly of knocking on the door of one of the cottages – especially the one that looked all mod cons, fancy sealed windows with tinted glass and a door that wouldn't be out of place on a vault – for tea and a warm-up of her frozen feet. But it wouldn't be right. Not until they'd questioned the occupants about the presence of a dead body mere yards from their doors.

'Come on,' she said, resigned. 'My mam uses the hairdryer to defrost her freezer. Maybe they can do something like that.'

Elle

'I'm sorry,' said the doctor. He was kind in the way private doctors were, knowing that each soothing word was earning them extra. 'There's no reason I can find for your infertility.'

She stared down hard at her hands, twisted in her lap. Her mother had always told her never to cry in public. Hold it in, save it for the locked bathroom, the edge of the towel bunched in your mouth to hide the noise from your husband. He should never see you cry, except prettily, with joy. When he proposed, when your children were born. 'There's really nothing?' She'd hoped for an easy answer, a simple fix to explain why month after month her body emptied itself, regular as clockwork.

Of course it's your fault. Why would any child want you as a mother?

'In about a third of cases, there's no reason for it. But there's always options. Adoption can bring a lot of joy—'

'No,' she said. 'My husband, he wouldn't want that. He'll want his own child.' They had discussed it, of course, when they met years ago, in the crush bar of the Royal Albert Hall, her aglow with a successful concert, him young and handsome, hardly able to tear his eyes from her. But back then, the idea of infertility or babies had seemed so far away. She'd voiced her concerns – her family history, the ethics of continuing her bloodline. He'd kissed her, her face cupped between his hands. *I only want you, my darling girl.*

She knew him better now. Having a child was not essential to him – he would never be the kind of father to change nappies or take time off for sports days – but he was also the kind of man who'd follow any woman who presented him with his own flesh and blood. The idea of being left for someone younger, someone untainted, was so crippling that Elle knew she had to get in first. If she was pregnant, if they had a child, he would never leave her. They'd be a family. And now here was the doctor telling her it maybe wasn't possible. They knew it wasn't him with the problem – he'd told her he got a girlfriend pregnant years ago, at university. She hadn't kept it, and sometimes, when Elle woke at night, she found herself wondering about that child. What it would have looked like. If it was a boy or a girl. A child that wasn't hers, but was his – that would be enough for her, maybe.

'There's IVF,' said the doctor soothingly, in those expensive tones. 'Perhaps your husband would be willing to try?' She thought of it, the indignity of cups and tests and the plastic sterility of it all. The planning. That wasn't him. He liked things to be passionate, spontaneous. Increasingly, he did not touch her at all in that way, simply stroking her hair and saying, *you must be very tired, darling.* But she wasn't. She wasn't tired.

'I'll talk to him,' she said, gathering up her Marc Jacobs tote. 'Thank you, doctor.' And as she walked out the door, she believed that she would. She'd cook him a wonderful dinner, light candles, open wine, and later on she would broach the idea of getting a little helping hand to start their family.

Suzi

Sometimes, lately, I felt like I was losing control of myself. It was just little things, like I found myself sweating, so I got up to turn down the thermostat, only to find it set way low, seventeen degrees, or I'd be shivering when the dial was up at twenty-two. As if the climate came from inside me.

There was more. The phone rang, and sometimes no one was on the other end, a dropped connection along the line. I went to bed early, exhausted, but woke up in the night, jittery with nerves. I'd hear a noise outside and run to the window, but nothing was ever there. Animals, most likely, something I wasn't used to after the city. I kept forgetting things too. I would set items down – my phone or a hairbrush or the glasses I was too vain to wear out of the house – and go back to where I was sure I'd left them, but they'd be somewhere else entirely. In my study, though I didn't remember being in there that day, or inside the fridge even. I'd told Nick about it, troubled, and he put it down to 'baby brain'.

'Nothing to worry about. Just shows the little mite is active!' He put his hand on my stomach, right up under my jumper and on my bare skin, and I pulled away. Maybe he was right. Certainly my brain had been a turbulent place since I lost you.

However, the Monday after our tense dinner party, I woke up to find Nick standing over me. Cold grey light poured in from the window, and I blinked. 'What time is it?'

'Seven.'

'Oh.' A deep exhaustion pulled me back into the warm duvet. 'I should rest, I think. It's so cold out.'

'Not today.' He stroked my head in a clinical, tender way. Like a nurse with a child. 'We've got an appointment.'

'What? Where?' But he was already leaving the room, turning the shower on for me. He wouldn't tell me where we were going as I ate bland porridge (no sugar allowed), or as I was marched to the car, my feet crunching on the frosty grass. I was grouchy. 'Nick, what the hell is this? Tell me where we're going.' Was there an antenatal appointment I'd forgotten?

He sighed, staring at the road ahead. 'I didn't think you'd go if I told you. It's nothing to worry about. They're just going to talk to you.'

A spike of alarm. 'Who?'

'The doctor.'

'What?' I gaped at the side of his head. 'You made me a doctor's appointment? Can you even do that for me?'

He shrugged. 'It's all online now. Seriously, don't you think you should see them? All this talk of music playing, the temperature, and the way you were on Saturday – sweetheart, I think you might need to talk to someone.'

I had nothing to say to that. It *was* weird, my mental state. Stress, maybe. Loss could also do odd things, I remembered that from my father dying. You'd see the person in a crowd, even start to call their name, before your brain caught up and reminded you it couldn't be them. But since I couldn't tell the doctor the truth, could they really help? 'What can they do for me? You can't take medication if you're pregnant, I'm sure.'

He kept driving. 'Nowadays it's safe to take some of them.' I found myself wondering – how did he know this? Had he been researching psychosis? Was that what was wrong with me?

I didn't feel I was losing my mind. But I wondered how it would sound if I said it all out loud to a professional, and I felt a flicker of alarm.

◆　◆　◆

It was unreal when it happened, the pregnancy. Nick and I had been trying for so long, noting every moment of heartburn or bloating and each twinge in my side. Even when the blood came on my thighs I'd convince myself it was a false period. Hope lets you see what you want. Hope blinds you. Then, when I met you, I realised I didn't want it after all, and I started fudging the dates to Nick – I made sure to only do the OPK tests when he was out, and I fed my ovulation apps with false data, skewing the fertile window. It was dangerous, sleeping with someone else and pretending you wanted a baby with your husband. I couldn't even say it wasn't the right time. We'd got the country cottage, I'd given up work. It was the right time and way past it.

One day, a month or two after we met, I decided to take a pregnancy test to quell my strange doubts, the odd cramp and feeling of constant hunger, the morning I looked at milk and wanted to retch, the chafe of swollen breasts against my bra. It couldn't be. I didn't get pregnant. Other women did, within a month or two of trying. I'd been trying for three years. Except trying wasn't the word any more. Enduring might be close, passive and miserable.

And there it was. I just sat looking at the test for ages, disbelieving. *It can't be. Oh my God. What what what.* I tried to count. There'd been Nick, of course, the obligatory monthly ordeal I was fairly sure was too late in the cycle. Then you. And we'd been careful – but not that careful. Nothing about this was really careful. Then it came to me, sitting on the toilet with my jeans round my ankles – I would tell you. I would see what you said. This could be our saving, both of us. A child. My heart swelled with fear and possibility. This was the way out of my life. I had been sure of it. But look at me now; I was even more trapped than before.

Nick had been so pleased when I said I was pregnant. I'd told him while passing through the room, trying to drop the words on to his lap without looking him in the eye: 'My period's late, by the way.'

He caught my arm. 'How late?'

'Um . . . not sure. A few weeks.' He would have figured it out soon, so I had to tell him, even before I'd found the courage to tell you. He watched me like a hawk. He'd notice if I didn't put tampons on the shopping list. You, I would not tell for another three months, as I hedged my bets and tried desperately to work out what to do.

Sometimes, when you think about the facts of your own life, or you speak them aloud to a friend, you catch yourself for a moment – *Is that really true?* There was me, feisty feminist Suzi, and I couldn't even buy tampons unnoticed because we had a joint account and I didn't earn and he did all the shopping because it was too far to walk to a shop and we only had one car, and even if we did online delivery he'd insist on checking the receipts for things they might have forgotten.

That morning, he drove to the shops to get the pregnancy test – he was late for work but he didn't even care. Flexitime, he said. First I'd heard of it. He stood over me while I peed on it and we waited. I already knew what it would say, but I was still praying hard, *please please please*, although I didn't know what I was praying for. A pink line. A fork in the road. A guillotine fall. These are the things that change your life.

◆ ◆ ◆

The doctor – a brisk middle-aged woman with unflattering plum lipstick and dog hairs on her skirt – was kind enough. 'I understand you're having some issues, Suzanne?'

Nick had come in with me. I wondered if I was allowed to ask that he leave the room. How would that look though? 'I'm fine,' I said, wearily. 'Just tired is all.'

'She sleeps all the time,' Nick said. 'I don't know why she'd be tired.' A tinge of concern hiding the fact this was another dig.

'Could be anaemia. Quite common in pregnancy. Schedule a blood test with the nurse on your way out.' I could see she wanted me off her hands, filed away, and that was fine with me. But not Nick.

'Then there's the confusion,' he said, taking my hand and threading his fingers through mine. 'She keeps forgetting the alarm code. She's hot, then cold, then hot again. Is that a pregnancy thing?'

'Can be hormones, yes.' The doctor was frowning now. I wondered if she had to tick some box about prenatal depression or whatever. Was that even a thing?

'Plus she's been . . . a bit ratty. Irrational, upset.'

'I am here, you know,' I muttered. The doctor gave me a sharp look and made a note about something.

'Again, hormones can lead to mood swings. It's quite common.'

Nick leaned forward earnestly. 'I'd love to know what I can do to help. She just seems so unhappy. She goes wandering off in the countryside for hours.'

I gaped at him. 'You told me to walk every day!'

'Just a gentle stroll, sweetheart. You're gone hours, sometimes.'

'But . . .' I subsided. Was this gaslighting? How could I explain that if I didn't go for long enough, he pulled me up on it?

55

'Don't overdo the exercise, especially in this trimester. If you're low on iron, you'll get tired very quickly.' She tapped at the computer. 'Let's do some blood work, test your thyroid and so on. Pregnancy can be a tough time. Maybe opening up to a friend would help.'

Sure, I'd just tell everyone that I'd slept with someone else and this might be his baby and now he'd buggered off. No problem. Nick was frowning. 'You don't think it's serious? She doesn't need, I don't know, antidepressants or anything?'

The look she gave him was enjoyable for me. A man, telling her how to treat her patient. 'It's too soon for that. Blood tests first, don't be afraid to rest, and like I said, talk to someone if you need it.' That was it, we were dismissed.

In the car, I sensed Nick brooding. 'Not much use, are they? What do we pay our taxes for?'

'You'd honestly rather pump me full of drugs before we know anything? The baby eats everything I eat, you know.' I parroted his words back to him and he scowled. 'Maybe I just need someone to talk to. Nora—'

'That's another thing. Who is this random woman? You've only just met, and already you're having heart to hearts with her?'

'I'm not—'

'I think there's something weird about her. I'd prefer you focused on the house, actually cooking a decent dinner, that kind of thing.'

I held my tongue until I could feel words piling up in me, like water in a stepped-on hose. My only friend here, barely a friend yet, and I wasn't allowed even that. Slowly, tears seeped out from my eyes and down my cheeks, and I wiped them on my cardigan sleeve. I never had tissues, of course.

Nick glanced over, sighed. 'You have to sort yourself out, Suzi. It's embarrassing, admitting I gave my wife everything she wanted and all she does is cry and complain.'

I said nothing. I didn't realise he knew how much I'd been crying. We drove the rest of the way home in silence. He pulled up outside the cottage. Willow Cottage, what a stupid twee name. I missed living at Flat 2C, Greenham Street, EC2. 'I have to get to work. Can I trust you to not set the alarm off?'

'I don't know,' I said, shuffling out. 'I don't know if you trust me at all.' My voice was thick with tears.

'Trust is earned,' he muttered, pulling off.

Instead of going into our house, I turned and went to Nora's. Of course she was there. She was always there. 'Oh, hello,' she said, coming round the side of Ivy Cottage. She was in dirty gardening clothes and looked flushed with effort. 'I wondered where you'd gone.'

'I wanted to take you up on your offer, if you don't mind,' I said. 'Come for a walk with me?'

Nora

I was making a start on the very neglected garden when Suzi came over, pleased to feel soil under my boots again and smell the rough dirt on my hands. Gardening was something they'd taught us at Uplands, a useful skill to come out of that hellhole. It was honest, and it helped calm the spiralling thoughts inside me. The plants couldn't hide what they were. Not like people. I could have told Suzi hers were already past help; she should have protected them at the first sign of frost.

I said yes to the walk, of course, slipping my key under a plant pot – since I was alone now, I had a fear of being locked out, with nowhere to go – and she went to get the dog, emerging in a tangle of lead and scarf and coat. I watched her set the alarm, bemused. 'You do that every time?'

'Oh! Yes, well, Nick insists.'

I said nothing. Country people would likely leave the door unlocked. I only didn't myself because I had things to hide. Perhaps Nick did too.

We trudged along the country lane then turned over a field, frozen grass crunching under my sensible boots and her impractical wellies. It was so quiet, no sound but our footsteps and the cry of faraway birds. Anything could happen out here, and no one would know.

I broke the silence. 'Thank you for having me over on Saturday. I hope you got my note.' I had posted one the next day, as I'd been taught, through the letter box. It had been an interesting dinner in the end. The husband had been nice – almost aggressively so. I could tell he thought of himself as a decent man, the kind who would never cheat or hit a woman, who recycled and swept his path of snow in the winter and gave to charities. I doubted he realised how much he put Suzi down, sneering at her painting and cooking attempts, the housewife role he'd thrown on her. Not for the first time, I tried to feel grateful I'd had another type of man. One who was never jealous, or passive-aggressive, or possessive. Even if he had his flaws in other ways. I would continue to watch Suzi and Nick, and see what I picked up. I had still not decided what to do.

Suzi looked embarrassed. 'Oh, really, there was no need, but thank you. Nora, I'm so sorry it was . . . That Nick and I had a bit of a barney.' She laughed without humour, the strain creaking in her voice. 'I don't know if you noticed. Silly, really – the stress of entertaining! We're hardly Nigella and Jamie.'

A barney was one way to describe the vicious sniping I'd seen, the coldness in his eyes when he dropped his hints. About what, I wasn't entirely sure. Suzi had been unfaithful before they left London, perhaps. Now was my chance. I said, 'You can talk to me, Suzi. I know we don't know each other that well. But it's just us out here. We have to support each other.'

She was wavering. My heart began to race. *Go on, Suzi. Tell me your secrets.* Although what would I say if she did?

'Oh, I'm fine, really. It's just the adjustment from work. I was in advertising – graphic design. I always said I hated it – the meetings, the office politics, the lipstick campaigns. But I guess I did like some parts of it. Seeing people, getting dressed up.' She gestured ironically at her clothes, old fraying jeans and the same man's jumper on top. It was dirty. She must rarely take it off. 'It's just

hard, making the change to full-time wife. I'm very lucky, really.'
If there was one thing I knew by now, it was the sound of a lie. I
heard it in her throat, the words she was trying to convince herself
were true. She hated it here. She hadn't wanted to move at all. 'Did
you work?' she asked, turning the subject away from herself.

I was quiet, wondering how to phrase it. 'My husband had an
important job. It seemed to make sense for me to stay at home.
But then we didn't have children, and I started to feel . . . invisible.'

'Like a ghost,' she said, and forced a laugh, but neither of us
found it funny.

'Yes. A ghost. That's a good way to put it.'

'You seem so young to be a widow. I'm sorry.'

'Forty-two.'

'That's no age nowadays.' I could see she was shocked I wasn't
older, that grief had aged me almost overnight.

I hesitated, thinking how to broach the subject. 'Suzi – are you
sure everything's alright? I don't mean to pry, but you just seem – I
don't know. Stressed?'

She thought about what to say for a long moment.

Tell me, I urged. *Go on, confide in me.*

Suzi sighed. 'Oh, it's just – it's hard sometimes, being stuck out
here.' She turned to me, earnest and open. 'I've lost so much. My
friends, my job. I don't know what I'm meant to do all day! Cook
and clean. But that's just drudgery, isn't it! I mean . . . some people
like it but . . .'

'You feel put upon,' I prompted. I so wanted her to feel she
could talk to me. It was clear there were things she was keeping to
herself, that were eating her up inside.

She bit her full lip. 'A little. Is that terrible? Nick works so
hard.'

'I've always thought it's easier to go out to work, in some ways.
At least you see people. Not just the same four walls.'

'Your husband,' she faltered, and I tensed. 'What was he like? What did he do? Do you mind me asking?'

I walked a few paces more. 'He was a manager. Nothing exciting. But he was – well, it's hard to describe someone you were so close to. He was full of life. Ambition. Dreams. I loved that about him.' I had been that way myself, once, before I lost it all.

She shook her head, as if breaking our connection. 'I shouldn't complain, really. I always wanted to have time to paint. But this place. I'm so worried about the winter. Do you think it will be awful?'

'It'll be fine,' I lied, thinking of the snow that often piled up in the narrow lanes round here. If Suzi was going to get away, she had even less time than she thought. Maybe it was up to me to help matters along a bit.

Suzi

It was restful, walking with Nora, my belly jutting out beneath my inadequate coat. She wore her old Barbour jacket, and sensible walking boots, and seemed to have no expectation we would talk as we set off over the frozen field, squelching in mud. I had the stupid dog with me, of course. I usually let him off the lead once we were away from the road. Sometimes he disappeared for ages, or even got lost in the bushes, and I would have to crawl about trying to find him and his pathetic wuffing. I worried what this meant for the baby, if I couldn't even get my dog to behave.

Every tree was bare, and my breath streamed out in front of me. I was glad of Nora's silence because my head was a mess. The visit to the doctor, the tension with Nick, your continued absence from my life. What was I going to do? I needed to make a plan, a way to find you, because I couldn't go on like this. But I was so afraid, of getting caught, of overturning my life, of what Nick would say if he knew. And always, at the bottom of everything, was a coating of guilt and shame. I had done this. I had brought this all on myself.

Our affair took me by surprise. Even after Damian, that awful drunkenness, the smell of piss soaking into my good handbag,

I didn't think I was the kind of person who'd do such a thing. Damian had been an accidental collision, like scraping your car into a gatepost. But you – no matter how much I excused it to myself, no matter how guilty I felt, it was deliberate. I knew exactly what I was doing, and still I walked into it open-eyed, like someone strolling through a doorway.

You told me afterwards that you weren't even going to have a drink that night. You were tired, bored with the medical conference and the tiny cups of coffee and the plates with the clip alongside for your glass. Seeing me in the hotel bar it was a spilt-second decision, the kind you make between breaths. The kind that changes your life without you even knowing.

Our bodies are wiser than we are. You knew this from your work – the effortless drip of hormones, the calibrated mechanisms in our brains. I think they took over for us. I was sitting alone at the bar, having the one gin and tonic I'd allowed myself. At twelve pounds a go, I knew Nick would query it, and I was still getting used to having no money of my own, a month after we'd moved to the cottage. I was still trying to make sense of what my life had become, a non-working wife in the country. Of the mess I'd left in my wake at my old job. Perhaps that was why I did what I did. You came over; we smiled in the mirror of the bar. I saw you reflected, a man of forty-ish but trim and fit, close-cropped dark hair, black-rimmed glasses, expensive suit. I sipped my drink self-consciously. You asked for a whisky, a fifteen-year-old Ardbeg, glancing at what I had, daring me into it though we hadn't yet spoken. Who was going to talk? I felt the moment stretch like elastic, and then I suddenly became afraid you wouldn't, as your chit came to sign – I took note of your room number, 255 – so I said, 'Good choice.'

You leaped on it. 'A whisky woman?'

I shrugged. 'Bourbon, really.' An exaggeration; at best it was my third-favourite drink.

'Good choice,' you echoed, raising your eyebrows. 'At the conference?' Looking at my lanyard. Or maybe at my breasts, which were in the same area.

'One of them. There's about three on at once.'

'Which are you?'

I did a little jokey wince. 'The child within – art therapy for repressed memories.' Surprising that Nick even let me go. Perhaps he felt he'd won an easy victory, getting me out of London, or maybe he saw it as my commitment to a new life, a new career. Or perhaps he'd just no idea what I was really like, what I could do if given my head. A horrible expression, that – it means letting loose the reins of a horse, knowing you can always pull it back if it goes too far.

You grimaced. 'Sounds messy.'

'Yes. You?'

'The pituitary gland – friend or foe?'

I laughed. You said later it was intoxicating, and all you wanted to do was make me laugh more.

'Actually, that's one of the keynotes,' you said. 'The event is called Endrocon. I'm a gynaecologist. No jokes, please.' You showed me your badge, the logo a drip of fluid, and the name Dr Andrew Holt. Of course, that wasn't your name, but I didn't find that out till later. Was it a warning sign even then, that you didn't correct my mistake?

'Andrew.'

You looked down. 'Oh! Yes.'

I refused to be impressed that you were a doctor. 'Is that hormones?' I wanted to show I knew the word endocrinology, despite my cheap print dress and the tattoo on my wrist. You lowered your eyes.

'Some women say everything is hormones.'

I smiled reluctantly. 'Some men say it's just cold in here.' There, I'd made an erection joke, we were definitely flirting. You looked again at my badge, lying over my chest, moving as I breathed.

'Suzanne.'

'Suzi.' We linked eyes. Yours were so blue, cold and pure as glacial lakes. I couldn't breathe, a sudden warmth spreading through my veins. It was all that clichéd and that fast. *I can't do this*, I thought. Not again. But, you know, it's so much easier the second time. Even the guilt felt familiar, worn-out, as if I only had so much capacity for it.

◆ ◆ ◆

'Suzi?' said Nora, as we tramped along the country lane.

'Oh, sorry, I was miles away.' I had to stop drifting off like this. I had to act like a normal person, an expectant mother. I had intended at first to tell her about the trip to the doctor, but realised I didn't know how to explain it. Whatever way I spun it, Nick came out like a concerned partner, and me like an unstable madwoman. 'The house is just over the hill.' I'd promised to show it to Nora, the ruins of the old country home our cottages had once been tied to. It had been bought by a hotel chain before the last recession, but never developed.

Within minutes of walking, the space and silence had done their work, and I could feel myself relax. It was so hard, trying to be normal around Nick. It was hard even when you were still around, waiting for the phone to ring with some revelation, waking at night poleaxed by guilt and panic. Worrying every time Nick got an email or text message, asking myself was I sure I'd wiped my iMac history and changed my password after he saw me keying it in that one time. Now, since you'd gone, I worried about other things. The baby coming, what would happen then. Who it would look like.

Remember when you surprised me on my walk that time? It was so risky. What if Nick had been with me? That was when the dog jumped up and ruined your trousers. Sorry. I almost didn't mind the idea of getting found out by then. It would mean she might let you go. I was braced for the fight with Nick. I'd even worked out what I might say: *You moved me here without asking, you made me quit work, you kept me a virtual prisoner . . .*

It was a nice fantasy, walking in the frosty woods, the dog's barks echoing in the silence. That you might be just around the corner, not gone from me. We made our way up to the house, and I began to look around. You could sometimes find things growing in the kitchen gardens. I'd brought a squash home to Nick once. 'Look! Foraging!'

'I don't know,' he'd said. 'Someone might get cross.'

'Er, who? It's not like a hotel chain are going to bother if I take a few bits of veg.'

It was the kind of fake-rebel act that Nick would have once said he loved about me. Funny how the things people love at first are the things they end up hating.

I had a look about the kitchen beds, while Nora went on ahead to inspect the ruined house. The greenhouses had cracks in the glass and missing panes, tools left about as if abandoned in a hurry. I found what I thought was rosemary poking through in one bed and rubbed it between my fingers, releasing the sweet smell. I ripped up a few stalks of it and put them in the pocket of my coat. There wasn't anything else, though I could see what looked like root vegetables coming through.

I wandered up to the house, the windows gaping blind, birds rustling in the walls. It was all impossibly romantic, *Rebecca* and *Jane Eyre* rolled into one. I peered into one of the windows, expecting to see it as usual, littered in ivy and branches and bird droppings, the floorboards rotting away.

Someone was there.

I staggered back – was it you? Come to find me? No, of course it was just Nora, standing still in the middle of a room, looking up at the sky.

'Nora!' I called, trying to hide the fear in my voice. 'You scared me.'

I could hear her feet crunching on fallen branches. I wondered how she'd got in. The door was usually shut, though I'd never tried it. Or perhaps she'd hopped through a window.

She was staring me in the face through the ruined wall. She seemed different – not as warm as on the afternoon I'd spent in her home, drinking tea, sharing confidences. Then she bent her head back, looking at the lid of the sky, white and flat. 'Do you know *The Tempest*?'

'Er . . . a little. From school.'

She said something that must have been a quote. 'The bit about the cloven pine . . . I always thought that a horrible image, don't you think? Trapped for ever. Looking up at a little bit of sky.'

I said nothing. My hands were cold and shaking, so I shoved them into my pockets.

Then she said, 'Suzi. When you asked me about – my husband. There's something I wanted to tell you. When we first met, he was . . . with another woman. I'm always ashamed to tell people that.'

Why was she telling me this? Did she know? 'Oh?' I managed to get out.

'I realise now I shouldn't be. Yes, we met in less than ideal circumstances, but that relationship was dead, and he and I – we were so happy until I lost him.' She was crying suddenly, her face twisted and ugly.

'I'm sorry.'

'You don't judge me?'

'No. Of course not.' *I'm the same, Nora. I'm the same.* I nearly told her then, and the yearning to speak the words was so strong I could almost feel them piling up in my mouth. But I had gone all this time telling no one, and I knew any leak could be catastrophic. All the same, I might have, because there is nothing so lonely as a secret you can't share, if I hadn't realised at that moment that Poppet was gone.

Elle

She'd been so good for years now about not wallowing in the past, but the appointment with the doctor had made her weak. All kinds of memories were returning, flashes slipping through the walls she'd built over the years.

Ellie! I'm frightened!

No, she wasn't going to think about Sebby. Or Mother, or Father. But all the same she found herself going into one of the spare rooms – a room that should have been filled with toys by now, soft pastels, chiming music boxes, plush fabrics – and taking down the box from the top of the fitted wardrobe. It was an old shoe box, from a pair of Jimmy Choos she had once worn on stage, always afraid she would trip as she made her way out. He would never look in there – he had no interest in what he called 'girly' things. Inside were photographs. A handful had survived, and when she fled Elle had swiped them, because now they were all she had. The only proof that these people had existed.

The pictures had the faded look of seventies shots. There was her mother as a young woman, so slim she would almost disappear if she turned sideways, stylish in flared trousers and a silk blouse, always with a cigarette in hand. One of her good days, when she laughed and smiled, flitted about the house like a butterfly. Invited people over, too many for the downstairs lounge, people from Elle's father's work and the village and anyone she'd ever met. Not one of the bad ones, where she screamed and threw things, the time she'd cut off Elle's hair while she slept because it was 'slutty', the time she'd shut the piano lid on her hands to stop the noise. Elle liked the cigarette one because it was proof, if anyone ever asked. *See, she smoked all the time. It's hardly a surprise what happened, is it?* Her father, whose face she could barely remember, so little had he been around. And Sebby, his dark eyes under a straight fringe, staring up at her. It was Sebby she ached for most. Too easy to imagine a little boy of her own, looking just like him, calling her Mummy. He would have been thirty-four now. Perhaps a father himself. Then a later picture, herself stiff and formal in a piano competition, long dark hair down her back. It would have been 1992. One of the last ever taken.

A noise made her jump. Was he back already? No, it was the noisy family next door, manoeuvring out one of their many cars, music blaring. She pursed her mouth in annoyance, and tidied the box away, creeping downstairs as guiltily as an addict. She hoped he would be home on time that night – she needed him close, to feel he was solid and alive and still hers. But seven o'clock came, and then eight, and then nine, and still she was alone.

Suzi

'Tell me again what happened,' Nick said, pacing in front of me, grim-faced. I wondered what time it was; somewhere around ten, I thought. The whole day lost in a panic.

I was on the sofa, my ankle propped up on a cushion. 'He just disappeared. I let him off the lead like always, but he was . . . gone. I don't know.' Tears pricked my eyes, yet more guilt. I had lost Nick's dog, on top of everything. Poor Poppet had done nothing but love us, adore us, and I'd lost him. 'Then I slipped and hurt myself. If Nora hadn't been there, I don't know what would have happened. I didn't even have my phone, it's died again.' Nick had been out searching for hours, calling Poppet's name, and had come back frozen and angry. Very angry with me. 'I'm sure he's just run off,' I pleaded. 'He'll find his way.'

I saw as Nick's face twisted that he genuinely cared for that idiot creature, more than he did for me it seemed, since he hadn't even asked how my ankle was, just was the baby alright. I found myself unexpectedly sad as well. The house was too quiet without Poppet's barking and panting, dashing across the floor avid to see me, even when I'd just been in the loo for two minutes. Surely he was just lost. He'd come back to us. 'Those will help find him, I know they will.' I nodded to a stack of Missing Dog posters on the table, which Nick had already printed up; a grainy phone shot of the dog, his eyes turned red by the flash, his tongue out. Idiot.

Nick rounded on me. 'There are gangs, you know. They steal dogs to order, sell them on.' He'd even rung the police. From the mood he'd been in when he hung up, I gathered they hadn't been as responsive as he'd hoped.

I could hardly countenance the idea of someone stealing Poppet. 'He'll be OK. Someone will have him.' Or else he'd been hit by a car, dying even now on some cold road, confused and frightened. I didn't want to think about that.

'Christ, it's late. I need to go to bed.' Nick ran his hands over his face. His dorky nylon rucksack already stood packed by the door. Water bottle, packed lunch, carry cup – he was such a model citizen. 'You'll be alright looking for Poppet on your own tomorrow? Wear proper shoes. You have to be more careful, you know – it's not just about you now.'

I shrugged. I didn't know the answer to that. It turned out there were varying degrees of alright.

That night, in bed, I found myself once again brooding about the first time we met, back in May. Not even that long ago, but it felt like years. The moment when a normal person, a happily married person, would have finished her drink and gone to bed, alone. So many choices I'd made that night, sending things one way and not the other. Ending up here, pregnant, afraid, stricken by a loss I couldn't even tell anyone about. Having the second drink that you offered me, for example. I was quite drunk by then. It was like being Shoreditch Suzi again, slumped over the table jawing about something, rubbing my leg against Damian's where no one could see, smoking outside in the cold and grasping his wrist to light my cigarette. She'd been fun, Shoreditch Suzi. In the end, after what happened, I'd hated her.

Then, going back to your room. The bar was empty and they'd cleared our table three times. You said something about a hip flask of something oak-aged and I got up with an embarrassing alacrity and we were in the lift. I remember leaning in towards you, drawn as if by wires, breathing you in, head spinning with the warmth of your skin, your aftershave. A feeling that was better than a drug, eroding all my guilt and shame.

Even the next morning I could have ended things, chalked it up to a drunken mistake. Another one, just like Damian. Instead, I went along with the slick advice you gave me, your firm kiss on my mouth like the stamp of a seal on a letter. 'Put my number in your phone,' you said. 'Use a woman's name, someone made up, and maybe an initial, like it's a work thing.'

I was sitting up in bed, still naked, a little wind-burned by the speed of your leaving. 'He won't look,' I said.

'They always look. Set up a secret email account and only use that – there's a browser you can download that deletes all data every time you click out. There's no need to get caught unless you're stupid.' You paused. 'Oh, and listen, my name's not Andrew.'

'What?' I didn't understand.

You laughed, not meeting my eyes, told me some story about a mixed-up booking, that Andrew was a colleague of yours at the hospital. 'When you saw my badge, I just went with it.'

'Why didn't you tell me?' I blinked in the cold morning light.

You shrugged. But I knew. You had not been sure you'd ever see me again, and it was convenient, having someone else's badge on. 'I'm sorry. My real name's Sean. I promise, it was just a mix-up. I have to go.' Even then, I had not heeded the warning signs.

I wanted you. And so I kept on walking, deeper and deeper into the sea.

That was an idea, wasn't it? I hadn't been able to find you on any of the hospital websites, but what about that supposed colleague of yours? What about looking for Dr Andrew Holt? At least, being pregnant, I had the perfect cover for investigating hospitals. Beside me, Nick drowsed so peacefully. The sleep of the innocent mind. Me, I hadn't slept properly in months, even before meeting you. And now was no different. Feeling the baby press on my bladder, I got up to pee, then crept downstairs, half-wondering if I might go online right now and look for you. But if Nick woke up, he'd want to know why. I couldn't risk it.

Downstairs, the house looked different in the dark, a hundred LED eyes watching me as I moved through the silent, tidy rooms. A show home was how he wanted it, not a real place where people lived. I couldn't imagine a baby messing up this space, and yet I could feel it inside me, growing day by day however much I denied it.

Suddenly, I became aware that I could hear something. Music again, but soft this time. The speaker. Some kind of lullaby, Brahms's maybe. Had I set this? Was there some button, some automatic setting that did all this? I didn't remember pushing it if so.

Suddenly, I thought back to the day before. The mad idea I'd had, that you could be there watching me, from the trees. It made no sense. Why would you disappear but leave me signs like this? I must have done it myself. But how? I went to the console, trying to turn it off – I barely knew how to work the thing. As the music stopped, I almost passed out at the sound of my name. 'Suzi. Suzi.' A soft whisper in the air.

What the *hell*? I looked around me wildly; where had it come from? It sounded like the corner of the kitchen, but there was no one there. Was it the speaker talking to me, an electronic voice? I stabbed at the thing, the green light bathing my face, hands shaking. Just some setting I didn't know about, some malfunction maybe, but all the same I found myself making a circuit of the house, testing every door and window. I wished we'd never got all this technology. Somehow, it just made me realise how alone I was.

Nora

I was worried, after what I said to her at the old house, that I'd scared Suzi off. Shown her too much of my real face, under the mask. It had been instinctive. I'd wanted to shout at her, tell her she couldn't just walk on to someone else's property and take things – I'd seen her inspecting the vegetables, slipping herbs into her pockets, and I had wanted for a second to slap her. But of course she knew nothing, probably didn't even understand the laws of trespass. A city girl.

I had to cut her some slack. Never mind the pregnancy: the biggest surprise since I'd come here was to realise I felt sorry for Suzi. There I was, widowed at forty-two, childless and likely to stay that way, broke and living in a tiny cottage. There she was, married, pregnant, obviously solvent, their cottage snug, tastefully extended. She still had the hope of a career in the arts, whereas I'd given mine up years ago. But all the same I pitied her. She was so afraid, so sad. On our walk, stepping along in the silent woods in companionable silence, I found myself wondering for a crazy second if she and I might actually become friends. But how could that be? I had to remember why I'd come here in the first place.

As it turned out there was no need to worry, because the moment at the old house was soon eclipsed by the dog going missing. We had looked and looked around the grounds, listening out for rustles in the bracken or telltale barking, but the animal seemed to have vanished off the face of the Earth – no surprise, since Suzi had still taken no steps towards training him. We looked for hours, a deep chill seeping into my bones. We searched on opposite sides of the road, calling into the trees, tramping as far in on the verges as we could. I could hear Suzi's voice in the cold air, rising up, a note of panic. 'Poppet. *Poppet!*' What a stupid name for a dog. I knew she would never find him like this but I had to at least make an effort, calling his name myself, kicking at the odd bush or hedgerow. Then I heard a scream go up – Suzi.

◆ ◆ ◆

It took me a while to find where she was. In the gloom of the winter afternoon, the overgrown woods of the old estate encroaching on either side, it would be easy to get lost. I followed the sound of her voice and found her slipped down into a narrow, deep ditch beside the road, clutching her ankle. 'Nora! Thank God. I fell over. These stupid wellies. Can you help me?'

For a moment, I hesitated. Suzi was helpless. Her pregnancy, plus the slipperiness of the muddy ground, meant she'd struggle to get up. It was possible no one would find her for a while out here. Even a rare passing car wouldn't hear her out the window. When Nick came home he'd look, but would he think to go this way?

'Nora!' A note of panic again. 'What are you . . .'

I snapped back to myself. 'Sorry. Just thinking of the best way to move you.' I braced myself, holding on to a tree branch, and squelched down the muddy side to help her to her feet. She had mud on her face and all along her jeans, and moving her was like dragging a dead weight. How vulnerable she was. If I hadn't been there, what would have happened to her?

I felt jittery with adrenaline afterwards. I had forgotten what I was capable of, all the different people that lurked inside of me.

Suzi

The next morning, exhausted after falling asleep around six, the birds already cheeping outside like the bloody Hallelujah Chorus, I was just finishing up my list of household chores, which somehow seemed to get longer every day, and worrying over everything like a dog with a bone, when the phone rang. Immediately, I was flooded with terror, as I had been every day since you went. Was this it, the one I'd been dreading? *Her*. Or another silent call, so unsettling.

'H-hello?'

'Hello, dear. Just calling to see how my grandbaby is?'

My heart calmed, then sank. 'Hi, Joan.'

Nick's mother, a widow of barely sixty with nothing to do beyond sudoku and haranguing the parish council about parking, called almost every day. Not to ask about me, but about the baby, who wasn't even born yet. What would she say, Joan with her *Radio Times* reader offers and her book club, if she knew what I was really like? For perhaps the thousandth time that week, I wondered how I'd ended up here. 'I was just thinking about Christmas, dear?' Fishing for an invitation, clearly. I could hardly think that far ahead, though I knew it was coming on fast. I was supposed to be with you now. Not making plans for another year with Joan going through the listings mags and circling every programme she wanted to watch, usually involving Alan Titchmarsh or Jane McDonald. This was not my life, and yet here I was stuck in it.

I felt jangly with nerves, moving back and forward between contradictory opinions like closing one eye and opening the other. Who was doing these things, the phone calls, the music, taking Poppet? You? But why? You wouldn't. Would you? Were they even real, or was I imagining them, trapped in my own frazzled, lonely mind? I had to find out. Joan's call had reminded me time would not stop just because I couldn't decide what to do. With every step I took, I could feel the baby move with me. This was happening. I needed to act.

First, I checked my secret email account, the one you'd suggested I set up just for you. There was nothing there, just my own plaintive requests for you to call me. Then I went to Google and opened a private browser window to type in your name. It felt wrong somehow – I had never said it out loud, because nobody knew about you. I searched for *Sean Sullivan*, but there was nothing. Well, there were hits, of course – Sullivan was a very common name – but I trawled through several, realising they weren't you. Likewise with Facebook. I knew you had an account, because you'd mentioned a few times how annoying you found various behaviours, like people boasting about their run times, or pictures of their kids on the first day of school, but I couldn't find you there.

Once you had said, 'Look at all these couples. As soon as they start posting how happy they are, it's divorce within six months. Like clockwork.' And some friends of mine from uni had done that – a flurry of sunset-cocktails shots with 'it'd be rude not to' and 'so it begins' and 'so grateful for this one', then *voilà*, a few short months later they announced they were splitting up. I had wanted to call you straight up and tell you, laugh with you about it. But I couldn't, of course.

Sean Sullivan consultant. Sean Sullivan surgeon. Sean Sullivan doctor. Nothing. Again, I searched for it with each hospital in the area. Nothing, nothing. My fingers were growing cold in the chilly studio.

Then, I remembered my idea. Dr Andrew Holt – the story you told me, a mix-up in the bookings. He was a colleague of yours, you'd said; some admin person at the hospital had got confused. *These temps, honestly.* A mad idea began to grow. Was it possible that you really *were* Andrew? That you'd given me a fake name once it became clear we'd see each other again? I couldn't believe it. But there was clearly no doctor called Sean Sullivan, no Dr Sullivans of any kind working in the area hospitals. I googled it so fast I spelled it wrong, but there he was. Dr Andrew Holt, Surrey General Hospital, Obs and Gynae. No photo, but it must be him. Or you, maybe? My pulse sky-rocketed. Why did you work in Surrey? I'd always had the impression you lived here in Kent, perhaps further south, Tunbridge Wells or the posh villages around it. If I went there, to the place you worked, maybe someone would know something. It was so thin, but all I had were these vague fragments of you, like a letter torn to pieces. I had to know. I was maybe going to have your child. I owed it to him, or her, to at least try.

I was kidding myself, really, if I'd ever thought I could get away with what I'd done. As the days ticked by, I knew that, really, I couldn't go back. I couldn't live for years like this, waiting to be unmasked. What I'd done was too bad. So I had to move forward. I had to find you.

I went to the front door, needing air, needing to think. Across the lane, Nora was in her front garden again, weeding. I could hardly believe there were any weeds left in that particular patch, so often had I seen her there. She waved to me, and distractedly I raised my hand. I should go out and look for Poppet again really, I knew, and I wondered if she'd come too. The ground was so wet, I was constantly afraid of falling.

It was then that I glanced into the wooden planter where my slug-ravaged seedlings were growing, and saw what was there, and screamed.

Elle

He was late again.

Things had been going so much better the last week! He'd been home by five, even, one day, and when she asked him why – still covered in flour, her hair unbrushed and make-up unrefreshed – he'd swept her into his arms and asked if he needed a reason to come home early to his beautiful wife. Her heart had soared up like a helium balloon. Maybe there'd never been a woman at all – or if there had, it must be over. She'd won. She'd told herself that if it continued for a week, she'd broach the subject of IVF. She didn't want anything to ruin this idyll. It was like the old days, drinking a bottle of wine a night, eating dessert with no fear of getting fat. Even making love, and part of her had hoped for a miracle, that a life would spark into being without the need for doctors.

But tonight he was late again. She was pacing. It was dark outside, the orange of the street light spilling into the living room. She'd left the blinds open so she could see his car. She was imagining it so hard that a few times she felt it had actually happened, that she'd heard him turn in, and the relief had settled into her like a drug. But all the cars had been the neighbours. Other husbands and wives getting home, sealing themselves in behind warm yellow windows. A few takeaway deliveries, which normally would have made her tut at how wasteful they were, how lazy and unhealthy, but tonight she didn't care. *Just please let him come home. Come back, please!*

She was haunted by images. His limbs flashing white on top of a woman. She couldn't see the woman's face but she was young, voluptuous, not thin but beautiful. Her hair colour changed from auburn to blonde to brunette. She made noises of pleasure. *Oh yes. Stay with me.* And he stayed with her, in whatever hotel they were holed up in – or maybe her flat, maybe she wasn't married – instead of coming home to his crazy pacing wife. She should try to sit down. Watch TV, like a normal person. She'd once heard one of the neighbours, Chantal, joke about how she loved it when Terry, her husband, stayed out late. *It's great, I can watch my trashy telly and binge on ice cream.* Elle could hardly comprehend how it would be to wish your husband stayed out more.

Of course he stays out. Who'd want to come home to you?

Oh shut up, Mother, shut up, I don't need you now.

Was that a noise? She ran to the window, not caring if anyone saw her. Her breaths were strung out like beads. Yes, a car. It was slowing. But it wasn't his. She knew the sound of the Jaguar's engine, its tyres. This was a smaller, cheaper car. And two strangers were getting out. The doorbell rang – the light, uplifting chime she'd chosen for this very reason, to get over her phobia of people calling to the door. Except now it was appropriate to worry. She knew that already, somehow.

She felt her way to the door, not caring that her hands were marking the expensive silk wallpaper. For a moment, she just stood there. If she didn't open this door, life would not have to change. Everything could stay as it was, a woman waiting for her husband to come home.

It rang again. She opened it, and a gust of cold air blew in. Across the street, she could see a neighbour staring through a crack in her blinds. Nosy.

The woman – dressed in a cheap trouser suit – said, 'Mrs Sullivan? Mrs Patrick Sullivan?'

And she said, 'Yes. That's me.'

Suzi

Nick sighed. 'I don't know. Are you sure you should be racing about the place, after yesterday?'

'I'm fine,' I said, with a firmness I didn't feel, pushing away thoughts of the dead animal I'd found in my planter the day before, turned inside out, red and raw to the world. 'Nora said it was a rabbit. Foxes, probably.' At the time, I hadn't thought that. I had thought it was Poppet – or a part of Poppet – eviscerated and left for me to find. By whoever was locking me out, playing music at me. Except that was all in my head, most likely. Nora probably thought I was pathetic, a city girl who couldn't cope with the reality of country life. She had taken the thing away and buried it, while I blubbered on the doorstep. It was all getting too weird inside my head, and so today there was another lie to tell Nick, to explain why I needed money. 'I heard they have a great birthing centre at Surrey General,' I told him. 'I just wanted to check it out, for comparison.'

He looked at me over his yoghurt and fruit. I didn't normally get up to have breakfast with him, and I hadn't realised how much of a health kick he was on, how little he ate these days. Fleetingly, I thought of the woman I'd imagined him on the phone to. 'But you have your hospital all arranged. Is it even possible to move? Are we not in the wrong Trust area?'

'I just want to see the place. You know, get the best for the little one.' I hated myself saying that phrase, smoothing my hands over my stomach, but he nodded, softening.

'Of course. It's a good idea to make plans. Ask about their visiting policy, and what the threshold is for using the birth centre.' He'd done so much reading up about the process, and I knew practically nothing. 'They have a big IVF unit there. I looked at it, before, when it seemed like we might struggle. We don't need it now, of course!' We'd never even discussed IVF – he'd researched it? I wondered how far he could have got me down that path without me actually agreeing to it. Just like with the house. 'Any word from the doctor about those blood tests, by the way?' he said, standing up.

'No.' I had a vague idea I was supposed to ring up.

'Well, give them a call to hurry them up. The sooner we get you sorted, the better.'

Meaning get me on to pills, I imagined. I forced a smile. 'Sure. So I can have the money?' I would have to go in to London on the train and catch another one out, since there was no public transport between the towns. Out here, not having a car was like being a prisoner.

His face creased in puzzlement. 'Of course! The money's yours too, you know that.' *Then why do I have to ask you for it?* I had access to our joint account, but there were no cashpoints anywhere near, and the taxis round us didn't take cards yet. Even if they did, he'd be sure to ask where I'd gone, why, who to meet.

'It's just – I hate having to ask for it. I miss having my own money.'

He gave me a look of bafflement. 'We're married, Suzi. What I have is yours too. Sometimes I think you don't understand what being married means.'

There it was, the tick of the bomb in the ground somewhere. I kept very still. 'OK,' I said weakly, and took the notes he doled out to me, feeling the greasy paper against my palm. I didn't know how much longer I could keep this up, begging for scraps of freedom every day.

◆　◆　◆

Once Nick had gone, I bumbled around the house getting ready. Even with things the way they were, it lifted my heart slightly to have an errand, a reason to go out. I washed my hair, even put on a little make-up. The thought was tickling the edges of my mind – what if you were there? I was going to the place you worked, if you'd told me the truth about Dr Andrew Holt. I stared at myself in the mirror, my pale winter face, the dark circles round my eyes that didn't shift no matter how late I slept. The mousy roots were showing through the red of my hair, but I wasn't allowed to get it touched up, since dye was bad for the baby, like so many things. Not to mention the pregnant belly stretching out all my clothes. Did I even want you to see me like this?

When I went downstairs, I encountered a new problem with the alarm. I couldn't get *out* the door. When I turned the handle, it didn't budge. Had Nick set the alarm wrong, put it on the 'out' setting instead of 'stay', the one for when we were home? But no, it would have gone off by now if so, I'd have triggered the motion sensors. I frowned at the control panel, a bewildering mass of buttons and lights. Was it the same code as the one outside? Oh God, my brain was like cotton wool. Tentatively, I keyed it in, and a small benign *bing* sounded, and the door opened. That was a close one. For a moment, I had almost been a prisoner in my own home, instead of merely feeling like one.

◆ ◆ ◆

The change at Waterloo was a brief glimpse of another world, a past life full of people walking fast, staring at phones, smoking in the cold breeze. The taxi driver to the hospital was chatty, to my irritation. Back in London, I'd prided myself on having good conversations with cab or Uber drivers, usually a bottle of wine in on my way home. I'd even boast about it: *Had such a great chat with my cabby, all about his family in Morocco.* So much virtue-signalling, as you'd once called it.

'Off to antenatal, is it? My missus, she had all three of ours there.'

I rubbed the bump, growing more solid by the day. He'd reminded me that life was going on, despite the quagmire I was stuck in at home. I had scans booked, midwife appointments. The baby was growing, no matter how much I tried to hold back time. 'I just want to check it out. I hear they have a good birth centre.'

'You don't want to be bothering with those paddling pools, love. Nice epidural, that'll sort you out. My missus . . .' And on he went for the whole drive, giving me the low-down not just on his missus's labours, but also on those of his two daughters and his daughter-in-law. I was trying to remember if you'd ever told me where you worked. I'd assumed Tunbridge Wells, where I thought you lived, and which I knew had a big hospital. Why would you work in Surrey if you lived in Kent? It shamed me, how little I knew about you, the man I claimed to love. I paid the driver, now one of my most intimate acquaintances, and waddled inside to the reception desk.

'Antenatal?' The woman behind the desk wore a long grey cardigan and that same look of all NHS receptionists, which I imagined was similar to that of a wartime general staring out at an invading horde. *None shall pass.* 'Third floor.'

'No, it's not that. Sorry. I'm looking for a doctor called Andrew Holt.'

'What's it in relation to?' She was already reaching for the desk phone and a thrill of shock ran through me. Was it going to be as easy as that?

'But . . .' I panicked suddenly, imagining that you might be there, working alongside this doctor. Or, if what I suspected was true, that he might *be* you. That maybe you'd lied to me.

'What?'

I said nothing. I didn't know how to explain you might not want to see me. She spoke into the receiver. 'Dr Holt's office? I have someone here wanting to speak to him. Private patient, I think. Name?' She turned to me, and I couldn't decide what to say.

'Er . . . Nora Halscombe.' The lie just popped out, and immediately I was frightened I'd be found out. But what harm could it do?

She slammed the phone down. 'You can go up. Floor two.'

'And – what's the department again?' I asked timidly.

A frown crossed her face. 'Gynaecology, of course.'

Endocrinology: the study of hormones and their effect on the body. Dopamine is a hormone, the chemical that makes us addicted, drives us to tap endlessly at our phones or scroll for ever through dating apps. Oxytocin is a hormone, the feeling of love that floods our brains when we're close to someone. The conference I met you at had been on hormones, and I knew that infertility was often caused by imbalances in progesterone, testosterone. It made sense.

I managed to get myself into the lift and find the right ward among the bewildering colour-coded maps on the walls. My heart was gasping in my chest, and I could feel the baby squirm, uneasy, no doubt drowned in a flood of adrenaline. Another hormone, the one that lets us run faster than we knew we could, lift cars off children. I waited on a bank of chairs, absorbing the peculiar calm of hospitals, the rustle of sterile paper and squeak of nursing shoes. Then an administrator in a lanyard came out and called me into a small office, and the name on its door was Dr Andrew Holt.

I got to my feet, wobbly. I was maybe going to see you. In just a few seconds. Just across a few feet of hospital flooring. Maybe your face would darken, and you'd push me out. Maybe I'd cry. I brushed at the ajar door and saw . . .

It wasn't you. The man in the room was nothing like you. He was short, around five foot seven or so, and stockily built, with a wide, smiling face, sandy hair receding on top. He wore a jumper over a shirt and tie, the sleeves pushed up. 'Mrs Halscombe. Or Ms? Please, sit, sit. I gather you wanted to speak to me, but I'm afraid we can't find your patient records. Was it a polycystic case? If so, I can see the outcome was good!'

'Um . . . no, there won't be any records.'

'Oh?'

'Um, this is going to sound very weird, but a while ago, earlier this year, I met someone who said he was Dr Andrew Holt. But – you're not him.' That wasn't exactly what had happened, but I couldn't think how to explain.

He frowned, but not in a nasty way. Like he was really trying to understand. 'Where was this?'

'At a conference. Endo – Endrocon, something like that?'

'Oh God, that shindig? I always try to duck out if I can, it's just a jolly really, and all in some awful airport hotel with mediocre food.' He looked as if he cared about food, the kind of man who'd get excited when he found a new type of dried mushroom.

'So you weren't at this year's?'

'Nope, I haven't been since, ooh, must be at least five years. Someone said they were me, you say?'

'Not exactly. He had your badge on.'

'Hmm.' He thought for a moment, drumming his hands against the desk. I noticed they were very nice, square and capable, the nails filed down. 'You know what, I think the hospital could well have signed me up. The drug companies fund it so it's no skin off their nose. There'd have been a badge for me, maybe.'

'And they don't check ID or anything, when you pick them up?'

'Lord no, why would anyone want to blag their way into that snooze-fest? Though maybe someone did, by the sounds of it.' He sat back, pleased at having solved the mystery. 'So what did he do, this identity thief? Give you some bad medical advice?'

'Oh no, nothing like that. He just – mentioned the birth centre here was very good, that's all. I wanted to look him up for some advice.' I hadn't been pregnant then, obviously, but I hoped it would go unquestioned.

'You're in medicine too? Or a rep?'

'No, I'm . . . I was at something else in the same hotel. We just got chatting.' I had to stop this conversation, before I got found out, before I laid a trail that Nick could follow all the way back. But I couldn't leave. I had to keep picking at the mystery, like a rat in a maze, scrabbling for its dopamine fix. 'Dr Holt – this might be a weird question too, but is there anyone in your department called Sean Sullivan?' Perhaps the story had been true. Dr Holt was a colleague of yours, and it really was a simple mix-up. *I'm sorry I doubted you.*

He was frowning again. 'Sean? None of the doctors, that I know of. And I don't think nursing staff. Maybe in management. I can find out, if you like? Wait a sec.' And before I could stop him he'd bounded to his feet and was opening the door to the corridor. 'Jim? Do we have a Sean Sullivan in the admin team, do you know?'

I stood. The door was half open, but I could see through the gap that he was talking to an older doctor, whose white coat was rumpled and eyes red-rimmed. Not someone I'd want treating me, I decided in a glance. When he spoke he coughed first, a smoker's rasp. And then he said, 'You mean *Patrick* Sullivan? The finance clerk?'

Dr Holt looked at me. You'd told me Sean. You'd also told me you were a doctor and that you lived in Kent. I managed to say, 'I don't know. Dark hair, glasses, very blue eyes?' Even the memory of them could send me sagging to the floor, all strength gone.

'That's him.' The other doctor fixed me with a strange look. His tone was sympathetic, but it didn't show on his face. 'Oh dear. Obviously you haven't heard what happened?'

I lurched to the door. I needed to hold on to something – the wall, anything. I knew, somehow, that whatever I was about to hear was going to knock me right off my feet.

Nora

I had just ripped out a long, satisfying frond of Japanese knotweed when I heard the taxi pull up. I'd been watching from the window as Suzi left in one earlier that day, I didn't know where to. No doubt when we spoke she would pretend she'd just needed something in the shops. Lying came so easily to her – I wondered if she even realised how rare that was. Or maybe she'd been forced into it, like an animal backed into a corner. She had been so upset the day before, finding the dead rabbit in her planter. Across the road, I had heard her scream. In the still cold air, it echoed like a gunshot.

'Suzi! What is it?' I'd hurried across the lane, this time forgetting to look for cars myself.

Suzi was shaking, pointing into the planter, a silly thing made to look like half a barrel. 'Is it him? Oh God, Nora!'

I didn't understand what she meant. In it was something dead, shining red viscera and fur and bone. Unpleasant, but nothing a country person wouldn't be used to.

Suzi was crying. 'How could he get in there? Oh God. It's my fault.'

I realised she thought it was the dog. Sternly, I said, 'Suzi, this is far too small to be Poppet. Look, it's a rabbit or something, that's all.'

'Oh.' She opened her eyes and looked properly. 'But how did it get in there?'

'Foxes, I suppose. They can do terrible damage.' I imagined Suzi was one of those sentimental types who fed predators, instead of wiping them out as was needed. 'Come on, it's not Poppet. Is there still no sign of him?'

She wiped her eyes on the sleeve of her cardigan. 'No. I'm not sure what else we can do. Nick's already put out posters with a reward.' A thousand pounds, he had offered. An insane amount for what was, after all, just an animal. I could imagine what my mother would have said about that. She'd had my favourite King Charles spaniel put down when his vet bills went over a hundred pounds.

'He's fine,' I'd reassured her. 'I know he's just fine.' But I didn't think she believed me.

Now, as I watched, she paid the taxi driver, fumbling the notes, and from my garden I could see she was shaking, breathing hard. Something had happened. Perhaps it was time.

I stood for a moment, trying to compose myself. Giving her a little space to control things, pack away the spilled-out emotions like clothes into a travel bag. Something I wished people had done for me, at the times I needed it. The etiquette around giving bad news should really be: deliver it, then go away and leave the person in a darkened room, alone. Place food outside their door, though they won't be able to eat it. Clean and tidy and step back into the shadows. But it seemed Suzi was not the kind of person who reacted that way.

She came running into my front garden, almost slipping on the damp, weed-choked flagstones. Upset again – I wondered what it was this time. 'Nora! Nora!' She was panting, and could hardly get the words out. 'Please! Help me!'

I went to her. She grabbed on to the jacket I was wearing, an old Barbour thing that had belonged to my husband. 'What's the matter?' I tried to make my voice caring, not cold, but the training was so ingrained. *Don't make a scene. Go indoors, you silly girl.* Not that there was anyone to hear us.

'He's dead! Nora, he's been killed! A car crash!'

'Who are you talking about? Suzi, what's happened?'

She choked it out: 'The man I'm in love with. The man I – had an affair with. He's dead.' And she began to clutch at her hair, almost pulling it out, so extreme was her pain.

PART TWO

Alison

FEBRUARY – Three Months Later

DC Alison Hegarty paused to kick snow from her sodden leather boots, reflecting that she should have taken her dad's advice after all and bought the walking ones in the Blacks winter sale. These flimsy high-street things were no match for the snow and ice piled up around the cottages. This was proper deep country; she'd not even had phone reception since being out here.

The first cottage was entirely dilapidated, choked with ivy and no doubt many spiders. She'd given it a wide berth as they tramped down the lane. The second at least had lights on, fighting against the gloom of a winter afternoon. The third was in darkness, shuttered up as if no one had been there in weeks.

Tom Khan looked cast down. 'I could murder a sausage roll. How far do you think it is to the nearest Greggs?'

'You should have brought lunch.'

'Yeah yeah, some of us have actual lives. I got in at four, I'm not about to get up and start spreading Flora, am I? Unless her name's Flora! Ha ha.'

Alison rolled her eyes. 'Well, aren't you the party animal. What was it this time, Tinder?'

He winked. 'It's almost too easy. Like ordering up a Domino's. Except it's her that gets the meat feast.'

Alison made a noise of disgust. 'Jesus, Tom, this is a crime scene. Someone's dead.'

'I'll be dead too if I don't get some lunch. Share with me, Hegarty? You'll hardly eat all your vegan hummus with cucumber anyway.'

'You must be joking. Come on, let's try this posh one first.'

They crunched up the paved path to what had once been an ordinary labourer's cottage, now mushroomed out with an extension out the back and a heavy sealed door, tinted windows. Kind of a cross between a rustic bolthole and a bank vault. Alison noted that the path had not been swept of snow in some time, and she concentrated on not falling over. Tom needed no more ammunition to take the piss out of her.

'Don't think they're in,' he observed needlessly. The house was in darkness, and peering through the letter box showed a heap of envelopes on the mat. What looked like Christmas cards, even – they'd been gone for a while.

'Top marks, Sherlock.' Alison pulled out her phone and checked the info they had on the occupants. A Nicholas and Suzanne Thomas. 'That's weird.'

'Huh?' Tom held up his hands, trying to peer through the windows; he was leaving smears on the glass.

'We've been out to this address twice in the last few months.'

'Which teams?'

'Traffic – there was an accident over on the slip road round September time – and then . . . Surrey Major Crimes.'

'What were they doing here?' Tom scowled; territorialism was fierce between the forces.

'You remember there was that gas fire thing over in Guildford, a death? Just an accident if you ask me, but someone was a keen bean, looked into it.'

'Lucky them to have the time. What did this lot have to do with it?' He jerked his head towards the house. You could see it had been expensive. It was a shame to gut an old place like that, but on the other hand it did look cosy inside, with red LEDs glowing from various devices and panels, and the snow had now reached Alison's socks.

'Dunno. I'll have to check.'

Tom was stamping his feet. 'How about we do the other place, then sod off back to the station? I'm freezing my balls off here.'

Alison did not want to think about Tom's balls. 'Alright then.' Likely the couple were off on some Christmas break, the Caribbean maybe, lucky bastards.

Since December though?

Maybe.

'Bit of a dump,' observed Tom, as they stepped carefully down the icy path of the other cottage. 'The one across the road is well nicer.'

'They've got the cash, I suppose.' This one was called Ivy Cottage. Slightly better than the derelict one next door, but not much. She rang the bell.

Loudly, Tom commented, 'Bloody hell, my bits feel like frozen Quorn sausage.'

'Shut up,' she hissed. 'Game face.' In response to their ring, the inhabitant of the first cottage was approaching, a dim shadow through the stained-glass surround of the door. They both put on their death-knock faces – sombre, serious. Sympathy allayed with a hint of suspicion, because nine times out of ten the murder victim had been done in by someone they knew. Awareness of this fact made dating hard for Alison, even without Tom's disgusting window into the male mind.

'Hello. I'm DC Hegarty, this is DC Khan. Can we come in? I'm afraid we have some bad news.'

Elle

'I'm so sorry for your loss.' She must have heard those same words fifty times in the weeks since it happened. The funeral director, the police, the life insurance company, explaining that no, her husband did not in fact have a policy with them, it had been cancelled the year before for some inexplicable reason. The neighbours. The morgue staff, who'd sympathetically blocked her requests to have his body back sooner. An autopsy had been necessary. Perhaps an inquest later on. Now, at least, she had been able to bury him. He was dead. It seemed – almost funny. It was stupid, because it was always him who was alive and her who was dead. She'd been dead most of her life before she met him. She breathed, she smiled, she sat in concert halls and played the piano, but she was dead all the same.

She'd been surprised how few people came to the funeral. They had no family, of course, both of them orphans and alone in the world. Or as good as, anyway. There were more ways to be an orphan than just death. Hardly anyone from the hospital, just that man James Conway, who she'd always distrusted. He had the red nose of a drinker, and she knew he'd been married three times, each time to a younger woman who left him in the end. She'd always been worried Patrick would go the same way, under Conway's bad influence. But at least he was there, and he pressed her hand with his shaky ones. The smell of him reminded her of her father, the reek coming from his room most mornings. She couldn't entirely blame him, having to live with her mother. But still. She could and did blame him for some of it.

She said, 'Thank you. I have to say, that hospital should be ashamed! No one else here! What about the theatre nurses, the consultants?'

Conway had frowned. 'Well – people are busy, Elle.'

She gritted her teeth at that, this man using her first name, the same name her husband had called her. At the realisation she was never going to hear it from him again, she staggered and almost fell, right there by the graveside – the earth sliced so straight and dark – and Conway caught her arm. She shook him off. 'It's good of you to come. Will you come to the house?'

She hadn't wanted a wake, but people expected it, and she owed it to Patrick. She had thought there'd be more people, of course, and had ordered too much food. Whole hams, plastic bowls of trifle, all of it going to waste. Only the neighbours came, eyes moving over her furniture, and some people from her adult education classes, the flower-arranging and cookery courses she'd done over the years, striving to be a better wife, forcing herself out of the safety of home – kind of them, pressing her heart in a vice – and Conway. Of course, Conway. Drinking Patrick's good whisky, lingering after she'd dispatched the catering girls, mostly locals with too much make-up, sending them away with the leftover food, unable to face waking up and seeing any of it.

No one came. What a failure you are.

'Well, thank you for coming, James,' she tried again. Why wouldn't he go? He stayed by the mantelpiece, looking at the framed pictures.

'You were a concert pianist when you met him?'

'Yes. He came to one of my recitals, got talking to me. We were together ever since.'

Him, coming up after a show in his typical cocky way. A hand on her naked back. 'Miss Vetriano? I'm sorry, I just had to say – it was utterly beautiful.' And he looked in her eyes and she saw he was saying *she* was beautiful. Of course, she found out later, he didn't come for the music; he was almost tone deaf, couldn't tell the difference between Rachmaninov and *Top of the Pops*. He'd seen the poster on his way to work and said, *Your eyes seemed to look right at me. That long black hair – I was caught*. He didn't mention the fact they'd photographed her in a low-cut red halterneck. That's how it worked in classical music. If you were pretty and young you had a chance. She was thirty when he first put his hand on her and she was running for her life – she only had a few years left to make it. And she wasn't great. Technically she worked and worked, but what the critics said was right – she had ice in her core. She played without emotion. Hardly surprising, for a dead girl.

Reviews and profiles usually dragged up all that business with Sebby and Mother and Father. They always wanted to know about that. *How did it feel, Elle? You must have been devastated. Did you feel you could only find solace at the piano?* Journalists, they wanted to parcel the world up in their neat little phrases. *I was devastated*, she parroted. *I felt my world had fallen apart, yes*. There was money and hotel rooms and applause and dresses, but there was no one. Until him. A doctor. A good man, she thought.

He'd picked up her hand that first night, at the after-show party (he hadn't been invited, she later learned; he'd talked his way in). 'We're not so different, you and me. Our hands are what matter.'

'You're a surgeon?'

'Something like that.' He held on too long. His hands were huge, they hid hers totally. 'How do you manage all those notes?'

She began to talk about reach and the difficulty of playing when you were a woman with small hands. He seemed engrossed. She laughed when she found out it was all an act; he had no idea what she was saying. She shouldn't have. Because in fact they *were* so different, her and him. She could never pretend, that was her problem. And him – he was only too good at it.

Conway was saying, 'And your own family – you were orphaned young?'

She flinched, as always when anyone brought it up. 'Sadly.'

'Only child?'

Oh, please, go away, please. She moved to pick up a stray napkin that had fallen under the coffee table. How unbearable it was, other people tramping over her carpet, their shoes still dirty from the graveside. Touching things, leaving streaks and fingerprints.

He swilled the whisky in his glass. She didn't offer more. In a minute, she was going to throw him out, and manners be damned.

You're a disgrace.

Shut up, Mother.

Conway said, 'Funny thing about that crash. They said no one else was involved, he just went into a tree?'

'He must have lost control. Maybe there was – an animal or something, or maybe a fault with the car. They don't know yet.'

'He's a good driver, though. Isn't it funny?' *Oh shut up, go away, stop talking about him in the present tense, he is gone, gone! He's dead!*

She made herself smile. 'You were a good friend to him, James. Thank you. Now if you don't mind, I'm just a little . . .'

He spoke over her. 'We were good friends, yes. The thing is, Elle, and I'm sorry to mention this right now, I really am, but Paddy, he owed me a few bob.'

'What?'

'I lent him money. You know, as a friend. And now I'm in a bit of a tight spot.'

She stared at him. Was he really in her living room, drinking her whisky, asking for money? 'It's his funeral,' she heard herself say. She hadn't even begun to think about the finances yet, his pension, the savings accounts – Patrick had dealt with all that. Their lawyer had promised to sort it out for her. He had been there earlier, offering condolences while eating his way steadily through a bowl of Kettle Chips. *So sorry. So sorry for your loss.*

'I know. Wouldn't bring it up if I wasn't tapped out.' In that moment, she wanted to kill him, with his grubby black coat and stubby fingers. Not like Patrick's, his surgeon hands. Why would Patrick borrow money from a man like this? He must be lying, trying to exploit the grieving widow.

Stiffly, she said, 'I'm seeing the lawyer tomorrow. I can't release any funds until then. I'm sure you understand.'

She held out her hand for his glass, and he must have thought she was refilling it, because he said, 'Cheers,' but instead she poured the dregs away, into the fireplace, where they hissed and spat. His face puckered into a frown of surprise.

She faced him. 'Thank you, James. I really must rest now. Goodbye.' And he went, and after the door finally shut, she wanted to scrub everything from her hand to the floor, anything touched by his puffy fingers, or his beady, sneaking eyes. It couldn't be true. Patrick would never borrow money; he had his salary and all her inheritance, her concert earnings, the life insurance from Father. In the morning, she would talk to the lawyer, and she would find out more.

Alone at last, her mind went back to that terrible night when two police officers had come to the door. *Please, let it not be true. Let me wake up and find it's all a dream.*

She hadn't even taken in what was happening until the man said: 'I'm afraid we have some bad news.' The woman was in the kitchen, trying to make tea. She'd never be able to operate the coffee machine . . .

'I don't understand,' Elle had said for what she thought was maybe the third or fourth time. Time seemed to have frozen.

'There was a crash. Your husband's car went into a tree. The ambulance came – he was alright then – but later he had a haemorrhage. I'm so sorry, Mrs Sullivan – he's dead.'

'But he works at the hospital.' She was in disbelief. You couldn't die in a place that you worked.

She didn't know how long they were there for, repeating to her that he was dead and her insisting he couldn't be, because he worked at the hospital, before it sank in. How stupid she was! Anyone could die at any time – she'd known this since she was sixteen.

Suzi

You were dead. I couldn't bring myself to believe it, so I kept talking to you, inside my head, where no one would ever hear it or see it, where I couldn't forget to log out. The thing that had crossed my mind in my maddest moments, as an explanation for where you'd gone, but even then I'd known I was just kidding myself. But it was true. On the way from our last meeting – when you dropped me off at the side of the road, promising to tell her that night, and I ran home, terrified and excited at the same time – you had driven towards the slip road for the M25, but before you could reach it you had, on the deserted country lane, wrapped your car around a tree. Later that day, in hospital, you had been pronounced dead. I had looked it up and finally found the news reports I'd dreaded all this time, under the correct name. Patrick, that was your name. Not Sean.

It said in the reports police didn't understand why – it was a mild day, nothing in the weather that would have made you crash, no other cars nearby. I thought you must have swerved to avoid an animal. A dog maybe, or a wild thing like a rabbit or fox. An innocent killer. I couldn't stop replaying what they'd told me at the hospital. The worst ten minutes of my life, even worse than what happened with Damian and after. I didn't know if I'd ever get over it. And below the huge, horrific fact of your death, which had punched a crater right through me like a meteorite, there was another – you had lied to me. Your name wasn't Sean. And you were not a doctor at all.

'I don't understand.' I'd said this at least five times in as many minutes. I was sitting on the chair in the office of Andrew Holt – the real Andrew Holt – an untouched plastic cup of machine tea in front of me. He was hovering kindly above me, while the other man – a Dr Conway, who I had gathered was an anaesthetist of some kind, the man who gave the epidurals, perhaps – stood shiftily in the doorway. 'He's not a doctor? He wasn't?' The shock had messed up my tenses.

'A doctor, no, nothing like.' Conway sounded scornful. 'He worked in admin.' He spoke to Dr Holt. 'You remember him, the pen-pusher who came around with the expense forms. He went by Patrick here. I think Sean was a middle name.' Was nothing you'd told me real? Patrick Sullivan, not Sean Sullivan.

'Oh, right. I didn't realise he died, how awful.' Dr Holt sounded merely surprised, whereas for me it was the worst news of my life.

'There was an email. We sent flowers.'

'I guess I should really start checking them.'

I was replaying every conversation we'd had in my head. Had you actually said you were a doctor, or just that you worked at the hospital? Had I assumed, seeing you in your borrowed lanyard, at the conference you'd blagged your way into? I wondered why anyone would do that. Just to stay at a hotel for the weekend? Maybe looking to pick someone up, and there I was, ripe and ready and drunk? 'I'm sorry,' I said, trying to pull myself together. 'You must have patients to see. I'm just – I really thought he was a doctor.'

'Let me get this straight.' Dr Holt was looking as confused as me. 'You met a man wearing my name badge, but he was really Patrick from our admin department? And he said his name was Sean, but you thought he was a doctor?'

'Yes. No. I thought – he said there'd been a mix-up. That you were a colleague.' And that was true, he was your colleague. I felt like I was losing it. Had you lied? Or had you been true to me? The name Sean, that was a lie too, unless you used it sometimes; I knew some men went by their middle names.

'I need to be in surgery in five minutes.' Dr Conway turned, and I could smell his breath across the room, the unmistakable tang of booze. Had he been drinking, when he was about to put someone under? His dark eyes, red-rimmed and baggy, fell on me, and I saw it – *he knew who I was*. He knew all about us. You must have told him, though you'd insisted you never would, that I should tell no one either.

'Of course, off you go. Thanks, Jim.' Conway left the room, and Dr Holt turned back to me. 'Are you sure you're alright? I could get the nurse. You can lie down in the exam room if you—'

A sharp stab of panic went through me. If I let them treat me here, there would be records. A way to trace me to this place, to my stunned reaction at finding out you were dead. *Dead!* 'I'm fine. Thank you for your help. Sorry. I have to . . .' And I got up and ran down the corridor after Conway, as fast as I could. He was almost around the corner.

'Wait! Dr Conway.' I was out of breath already, winded and weakened by shock. I leaned against the monochrome wall of the ward.

'What do you want?' His tone was cold.

'Please – I need to know what happened to him. To Sean. Patrick, I mean. I'm Suzi.'

I waited for a reaction, and after a few moments he nodded. 'I thought so. What are you doing here?'

'I needed some answers! He just disappeared. I had to try and find him, but now I learn he wasn't even a doctor?'

'No. He wanted to be, but he failed the course. So sometimes he – liked to pretend. I imagine that's why he went to the conference.' The sneer was still there. 'You didn't know what happened to him?'

'No, I had no idea. I didn't see anything on the news.' How would I, when I'd been looking for the wrong name? When you hadn't even lived in the county I thought you lived in? I'd been scrolling through the wrong local news.

'Well, yes. It was sad, but there you go.' No sympathy in his tone.

'Why did it happen? How?'

He shrugged. 'We don't know. The car went into a tree, but we couldn't find any evidence of a brain aneurysm or stroke, nothing to explain why he did it.'

Why he did it. A new thought mushroomed in my mind, one I hadn't even considered before. 'You don't mean he – you mean he could have done this to himself?' I'd just told you about the baby, that I needed you to leave your wife and be with me. I'd said I was almost sure the baby was yours, based on dates, on how hard I'd tried to avoid Nick knowing my fertile time. Maybe that was why you did this. 'Oh my God.' I began to breathe hard, the walls seeming to tilt. 'I don't – please, it can't be true.'

'I doubt we'll ever know. Coroner said accidental death.' He gave me another head-to-toe look, and I felt my flesh creep. 'You should go home. Rest.' His eyes travelled down to my bump, and I wondered how many more of my secrets he knew, this man I had never even heard of before.

◆ ◆ ◆

It was only after the first few hours I even thought of her. Your wife. I don't know how I got through that journey home. I was shaking, hot and cold all over, delirious almost. *But how could you . . . I really can't bear . . . Oh my God. Oh my God.* Funny how when the words run out, in lust or in shock or in grief, we call to a God we don't believe in any more.

There was too much to even unpick it, the crushing disbelief – you couldn't be dead. I'd have heard. Someone would have come to tell me. And then the loss, bone-scraping. And the fear – I was still pregnant. It hardly seemed credible I could go through all this and still be pregnant.

Oh darling. I couldn't believe it. In my head you were somewhere on a sandy beach, watching the surf, and your feet were bare and strong on the wet sand. You hadn't gone. I would see you again. When the cab drew up at home, and I somehow managed to pay the driver, my only thought was to run to Nora. Nora would help.

I had still not found any trace of your wife's name, not even in news reports, of which there weren't many. I'd spent the journey home crying or looking it up on my phone, heedless of the danger. *Mrs Sullivan. Patrick Sullivan wife. Crash death widow.* But there was nothing. She may as well have been a ghost.

Nora

Suzi poured the whole thing out to me, sitting at my table, weeping into her hands. The noise she made was halfway between a scream and a bellow, anger and loss and shock all boiling up in her. I patted her shoulders, offered tea that grew cold without her touching it. 'I'm so sorry.'

'Oh Nora. I just – I can't believe it. I thought he'd gone. He'd dumped me.' I almost asked if you could call it dumped when you were having an affair, but I didn't. She didn't need any judgement right now, and since I had seen her and Nick together, the way he spoke to her, I wasn't surprised that she would look elsewhere.

She told me everything – how they'd met at a conference, well, different conferences in the same hotel, how he'd emailed her the following week and asked her to lunch, the various lies she'd told herself in order to go forward step by step, like advancing into the sea until the water is around your neck. Then today – learning he'd told her the wrong name, that he wasn't even a doctor. I could almost have sympathised, under different circumstances. I knew how it was to be lied to.

'I never meant for it to happen,' she said dully. She was clutching a mass of tissues in her fist, staring at the floor. Every so often her shoulders would heave. 'I just – I'm so lonely down here. And then he was so – and it just happened.'

It just happened.

I never meant for it to happen.

The same things everyone says at these moments. As if an affair was a lightning strike, a burst tyre, a heart attack. Something that could not be predicted or avoided, rather than two people making a choice to do it, act on it. Maybe she was right. I didn't know.

'I was so drunk. And Nick – well, you see how we are.' Fresh tears rose in her eyes. 'Nora, I just – I don't know what happened to us. He never touches me, only my belly. Only the baby matters to him. Sometimes when I think about him, about my life, I can't believe it's happening to me. Like if it was someone else I knew, I'd tell them to run. I'd be googling divorce lawyers.'

My mind was whirring, calculating how this changed my plans, now Suzi knew he was dead. What I should do next. 'Is that what I should tell you?'

A pause. She bit her lip, and even though she was devastated, she looked so pretty, flushed and tearful, her red hair falling down around her face. 'Where would I go?'

'If it's that bad, you should leave.'

She shredded the tissue in her hands. 'I know he loves me. He just – he doesn't trust me any more.'

I didn't say that I could see his point. It wouldn't have been helpful. 'Oh?' I waited. I'd learned, over the years, to use silence as a tool. Another skill gained at Uplands.

She took a big shuddering sigh. 'It isn't the first time I've done – this.'

And there it was. She told me a story about another man, another affair earlier in the year. 'Not an affair' was how she described it, but it was, all the same. 'We worked together. I thought we were friends. We used to go for drinks, lunch. Chat over the messaging system. Then one night . . .'

She told me the story of the pub, his hand on her leg. The alley-way. Kissing. Then more. Her bag dropped into a puddle of urine, and this was a detail that seemed to obsess her, for some reason, a sign of her degradation and shame. 'I never meant for it to happen.' There was that same phrase. Did she even realise? How many things happened to this woman that she didn't intend?

'Oh Suzi. You have been through a lot.' And I took her in my arms, and she cried against my shoulder, leaving it damp and salty. I actually meant it. It was hard to look at her distress and stay unmoved, even when she spoke of her affairs. And this other man – was there a way to use that, to get what I wanted?

'I'm a bad person,' she said, when she came up for air. 'Twice! I can't believe it. I never meant – I never thought. God, what a mess. What can I do, Nora?'

'The baby – is it Nick's?'

I had learned to read her eye movements. 'I – I don't know.' Maybe she couldn't say it out loud, this extra shame. Probably she really wasn't sure, but she must have an inkling. I wondered what she had told him. Sean, as he called himself. If he'd known about the baby, before the accident. She wiped her face. 'I haven't any money of my own. I don't know where I'd go – I can't be in a flat-share if I'm pregnant. I'm just so confused.'

'It's OK. I'll help you.'

She looked up, eyes shining through tears. 'Oh Nora. Will you really? You see, I'm just so alone. I can't tell anyone else about this, they'd hate me.'

'Of course I will.' I patted her hand. 'Suzi, this is important. Have you thought about what you'll tell the police?'

'What?' She looked puzzled.

'This man. You were with him in his car before the crash, yes? So what if they find traces of you? Who knows, they might be look-ing for you even now.'

After she left, I went over everything she'd told me. Despite her distress, I thought she would feel better in a while, knowing he was dead. She'd rather be bereaved than dumped, to believe he would have come for her, they would have lived together. Perhaps now she would come to the point of leaving Nick. It was crazy, the prisons that people made in their minds. Suzi was an educated middle-class woman, with a living, affluent mother, who perhaps was not the most supportive, but would hardly turn her daughter out on to the street. The law was there to protect her, make sure she wouldn't get kicked out of the marriage with nothing.

So what was she so scared of? The loss of social standing, the failure of a divorce, perhaps the loneliness, raising her child alone? I wished I could tell her how insignificant these things were, compared to what other pain life had up its sleeve. If she left Nick, I guaranteed she would barely give him a backwards glance. I had weighed up the different possibilities. On the one hand, if she left him, she might go far away from me, where I couldn't follow. That was not an option. On the other, it would only serve my purposes if Nick was out of the picture. If she had the child, it was likely she would keep the house too (not that she'd want it, I imagined). So maybe it was down to me to give her a helping hand.

Since I moved out here and everything changed, I had found myself thinking more and more about Nick. Nicholas Thomas. I had been worried for some time now that he would upset my plans, so tight was the control he had over Suzi. I'd friended him on Facebook after our dinner, in the account I'd set up under Nora Halscombe. I doubted they would think to google me, and if they did, they'd find nothing under that name. I had friended a few other random people to make it seem like I had an established profile, and he'd accepted the request after a few hours, doubtless not even thinking about it, and so I had access to his whole life, and could run my fingers over it looking for the cracks.

As soon as it got dark, I went out for my evening walk, the one I never invited Suzi on. I crept past their windows, glad they had shut their electronic blinds. It had snowed, which made things more difficult than usual, but luckily I had good boots and didn't need to go far. When I got back in I washed my hands as usual and sat down at the laptop, ready to make a new plan.

My husband had never wanted me to go online. He'd persuaded me it was bad for me, would only make my head worse. Probably, he was right, but I needed it now, for my plans. How much easier it was to do research, in this era of social media! People were falling over themselves to tell you their birthdays, maiden names, middle names, first primary schools, all the things you might use as security questions. Nick was the kind of man who would never have changed his name. If he'd done things to women, and I was sure that he had, sure as the frozen ground beneath my boots, they would always have been under the guise of romance, or protectiveness, or love. So that the woman – and I was sure there would be several – would never tell anyone, certain that the problem was with her. Sure that she was somehow defective, as he kept on telling her. Believing she was going crazy when he denied the truth of her eyes and ears. Now that I had the internet, I had learned there was a term for this – gaslighting. And Nick, I was sure, was the gaslighting type.

I scrolled back through Nick's old photos, and quickly identified two women he'd been in relationships with before Suzi. They both had a similar look to her, pale and a little quirky, a flower beside Nick's dull, neutral-coloured stem. One, a Catriona Murray, seemed to live in Canada now – her profile picture showed a woman in ski gear, on top of a mountain. I clicked through pictures of the other, Lisa Ragozzi, with Nick at the Taj Mahal, on the Trans-Siberian, toting backpacks and wearing tie-dyed trousers. A university relationship, I deduced, which had carried on for a while in the real world, then floundered.

I clicked on her profile, which of course I couldn't see most of. She looked to still have the same name, so maybe not married. I could see a few of her profile pictures, arty landscape shots, and the odd public post like charity fundraising, or political causes. Lisa seemed like an earnest, do-gooding person. I sent her a message, explaining that I knew it was strange, but a friend of mine was in a relationship with Nick Thomas, and I was worried about her. Did she have a minute to chat to me about him? They were no longer Facebook friends, Lisa and Nick, so it was possible she didn't know he was married. It was also possible she'd contact him and tell him everything. But I had to try.

Suzi

It snowed overnight. Nick was excited, wiping at the steamed-up window like a child. 'You never get this in London, not thick like this! Isn't it pretty?' He sighed. 'Poppet would have loved this. Poor boy.'

I couldn't share his excitement. 'I hope Nora's alright. It's freezing in Ivy Cottage.'

He frowned. 'Must you always think of other people? Can't you just, I don't know, be with me for once, in the moment?'

It was beautiful, the white overlaying the fields and trees, the still breath of it all. But all I could feel was terror, thinking of what Nora had said about the police. It wasn't a crime, what we'd been doing, but they didn't know I'd got out of your car before you crashed. Even if I was innocent, they might still come, and how would I explain it to Nick? My heart failed at the thought. There'd be my fingerprints all over the car, my hair even – you were always complaining you had to check it every time for those distinctive red strands.

If the police did come, I had decided I'd say you'd given me a lift – you were a total stranger, you'd just seen me walking along the road on such a warm day. There were holes in the story, of course. There was your phone somewhere, presumably, and if you hadn't got around to deleting everything, they might find me. You had called me briefly before picking me up, to see where I was. And Nick would want to know why I'd been anywhere near that place, walking along a bare stretch of country road with no pavement. But it could be denied. That was the thing. The tissue of lies was just strong enough to hold up.

'What if we get snowed in?' I said, remembering the estate agent's words in spring.

'That's why I bought the four-wheel drive, so I can get to work,' Nick said. 'Anyway, I ordered plenty of supplies when we moved, water and cans and that.'

'You did?' *But what about me?* I wanted to say. *What about me?* 'What if – something happens with the baby, and I need to get to hospital?'

He gave me an irritated look, letting the curtain fall back down. 'Suzi. Can't you just enjoy it?'

I'd learned since being here that many things are only enjoyable if you do them with someone else. If you'd been around, if we were together like I had briefly, foolishly thought we could be, we could have gone tramping over the fields in wellies, perhaps sliding down hills (very gentle hills for me), making a snowman, stopping off at some pub for hot chocolate laced with Baileys (again, not for me. Pregnancy ruined so many things). I felt briefly nostalgic for something that had never happened, a fantasy from the past. It would never happen now. You were *dead*. Once again, it struck me like a punch to the stomach. I couldn't believe it.

I went downstairs while Nick was in the shower, put the kettle on the Aga. The room was freezing, despite the fancy new underfloor heating, so I turned up the dial, and was glad to feel it start on my icy feet. I scrubbed a space in the window and stared out, pleased that I at least wouldn't be expected to garden today. Even Nick must understand the concept of a snow day. And I was grieving, though he didn't know it. What difference did it make, to know you were dead, if I was never going to see you again anyway? It meant you didn't dump me. Maybe you were on your way right then to tell your wife. Maybe we could have been together. A spasm of what might have been hit my solar plexus. I couldn't think that way. Had to keep going for the baby.

Was there something in the snow out there? Tracks – an animal of some kind? Maybe Poppet had come back. Thinking how happy Nick would be, I wiped aside more condensation, my hand dripping and chilled. Then I went cold all over, a cold that came from the inside this time.

In the snow was written one word, in deep angular letters. SLUT.

◆　◆　◆

Nick thought I was crazy. 'You can't go out in it, it's freezing.' I was doing my best to stop him looking out of the window.

'It's just so pretty!' I sounded vaguely insane. 'I'll run out and take a picture.' That was plausible, at least. I put on boots and seized my phone and then I was out, turning off the alarm and scuffing my foot through the words in the snow, heart hammering. Who had done this? No one ever came here, except me and Nick or Nora. She'd been so supportive, why would she do something like this? Someone must have come in the night.

My first thought was Damian. I could still hardly think of it without getting red all over, hot and agonised with shame, a sluice of sheer fear in my veins.

You had asked me straight up. Or rather you told me – 'You've done this before.'

'Um. Not really.' I couldn't lie to you. I loved it, the scrutiny. Nick was so easy to lie to I didn't know how I'd ever stop. 'I slept with someone,' I said. 'Not like this. A one-off.'

'Someone you know,' you said. Merciless.

'Um—'

'Don't lie to me, Suzi. Don't ever lie to me, OK? Promise me just that one thing.' And that was potent, wasn't it? When we were lying to everyone else.

'A colleague,' I said. The pause widened. 'Damian.'

Damian. But the idea was insane – he lived miles away, in East London, and I hadn't heard from him in months.

Back inside the house, I shivered, my feet wet from my inadequate boots. Nick was upstairs getting dressed, and I leaned against the Aga, trying to get warm. Piecing it all together. The feeling of being watched. The dropped calls, strange music, dead thing in my planter. And now this. At first I had thought, crazily, maybe it was you, but you were dead. If not Damian, the only other person I could think of was her.

Your wife.

Elle

She cleaned the room three times before the crawling on her skin subsided. That disgusting man, coming to her home and telling such lies. Patrick would never borrow money, he was the senior consultant in the obstetrics department. He earned a fortune! She wasn't sure exactly how much, it was vulgar to ask, but enough for this luxurious house and four holidays a year, business class.

But yet. Scattered moments were coming back to her. Patrick coming in, seeing the post she'd left in a neat pile. *You didn't open this, did you?* Tension dissolving when she swore she never would. *Can you sign this, darling? Just moving some cash around, taking advantage of better interest rates.*

Checking into a hotel, a card being declined. Rolled eyes, *that bloody bank*, another credit card given instead.

A holiday cancelled at the last minute – *I don't have time, darling. Too many patients. Can you ask for the money back?*

She had thought nothing of any of these moments. But now, on her knees in the living room, a bucket of soapy water beside her, hands in yellow gloves, she began to.

Once she started, she couldn't stop. She tore through all the papers in his office, a bewildering mass of letters and statements, numbers, codes. She had no idea any of these accounts existed. Nothing jumped out at her – some of the numbers seemed lower than she might have thought, but if it was divided over lots of different holdings, that would explain it. Likewise, she found some payslips from Surrey General Hospital, but the amount he'd been earning seemed very low. She struggled, trying to do the sums in her head, understand the deductions. Maybe it was a tax or pension thing. He was clever about things like that.

Had been.

Then it occurred to her. The box. The contents of his car, which the police had given back to her. There had been so little damage to the Jaguar, just a crumpled bonnet, just his head thrown against the side window. He was wearing a seat belt, of course, but all the same he'd hit his head in some small, catastrophic way. She hadn't been able to bear the idea of the box before now, so it was still in the garage, lurking. Too heart-breaking, to put her hands on it and know these things had been with him when he died. Maybe there would even be spots of blood, though she was sure the police would not be so cruel as that. Would they? She didn't know.

She found the key to the garage, inside a mug in a kitchen cupboard, and unlocked the connecting door, switched on the light. It looked so empty without the black Jaguar there, polished to a shine once a week. So many evenings watching him climb out, waving at her, often on his phone, and the burst of pleasure under her ribs to know he was home.

The box, stored on some metal shelves, was the kind that office supplies came in, printer paper. She imagined some police officer hunting around the office for it, finding it, scooping up all the things that had been in the car. They'd have meant nothing to him or her, but Elle's fingers were already trembling as she lifted up the cardboard flap. There was a leather-bound book containing details about the car, a rich expensive smell. A clicker for the garage door. His gloves, also leather, a Christmas present from her, soft as a baby's skin. An air freshener, a phone case. The actual phone had been returned to her from the hospital, but she couldn't get into the locked screen. A glass water bottle, still half full. She imagined the pressure of his mouth on its lip, and for an insane moment thought about pressing her own over it. There was nothing out of the ordinary, nothing that suggested her husband had been broke. She didn't know what she'd expected to find – bank statements, final demand letters. Of course not. Conway was lying about the money, that was the most likely thing.

She had lifted the empty box to put away when she heard something. At the bottom, something was rattling around. She fished it out – a small pink tube. Lip balm, tinted. Elle stared at it for a long time, puzzled. He would never have bought something like that. Nor would she – it was a cheap supermarket thing. A woman's thing. Her mind revolved slowly through the possibilities. He'd given a lift to a colleague. He'd picked up a hitch-hiker. But no, the car got cleaned on Thursdays without fail, so it was unlikely he'd given anyone a lift in the twenty-four hours between that and the accident.

She held the small tube between her fingers, light and cool. It was slightly sticky, and a fur of small fibres matted its neck. The police would be able to do tests on that, maybe, find out who it belonged to. If someone had been in the car with her husband when he crashed, on a quiet road on a perfect still day.

Suzi

When we first moved down, I had raised the issue of a second car a few times. 'A little runaround' was how I put it, though I had no idea where I'd picked up a phrase like that.

Nick had frowned. 'It's so wasteful having two cars. Think of the environment.' And I had subsided, chastened.

That night, galvanised by fear, I resurrected the battle, which he must have thought long won. The word in the snow had rattled me enough to do what I'd always sworn I wouldn't. This wasn't just a mix-up with the home-control console, or my imagination – someone was doing this. Whoever it was had found me, all the way out here in my isolated cottage, and wanted to hurt me. I had to tell someone what was going on.

'I want to go to London tomorrow,' I announced, when I'd placed his dinner – pheasant breasts with celeriac mash – in front of him. I stayed standing, without serving any for myself.

'What?' He reached for the salt without even tasting the food. 'Why?'

'I'm just so stuck here, Nick.' It was five miles to the nearest station, too far to walk. I fantasised about the station a lot. Only a tiny branch line with a freezing waiting room, not even a coffee stall, it represented escape. My lifeline to London, and my old self. Except I couldn't get there.

He turned that same face to me, the baffled one, that said – *I give you all this and still you're not happy.* 'Stuck in your lovely house, with all the time you wanted to paint?'

'No, I know, it's just – I miss my friends. I want to see Claudia.'

'I got you the dog for company.' The unspoken accusation. *And you lost him. You didn't care.* Scrape scrape scrape went his fork against the plate. Forming the food into neat piles, squares of meat and vegetable. 'Honestly, I think you're better off without those people. You know how bitchy Claudia is. And she hates kids, she's not supportive of our choices. She's only visited once in all this time.'

I stared down at the table, the grain of the reclaimed wood. Was he right? Was Claudia, who I thought of as my best friend, not even that bothered about me?

'I just – she invited me for lunch.' Not true, as it happened; I would have to invite myself.

'A boozy lunch?' He raised his eyebrows. 'Is that really appropriate?'

'I never mentioned booze. Anyway, I need to do some shopping for the baby.'

'I'll get you anything you need.' He picked up the salt again. I watched the flakes fall on to the food like the snow outside, holding fast still. A flare of panic – would the trains be running? Would a cab come out here?

'I need maternity clothes. You can hardly try them on for me, can you?' I put in a little laugh to soften it. 'Anyway, I'm going.'

What could he say to that? He couldn't actually stop me. That would be a new line to cross. He said, 'It'll be expensive, with the train and taxi. Aren't you going to sit down?'

'Oh, I'm not hungry. It's too early for me to eat, I told you. Anyway, pregnant women aren't supposed to have game.' He'd never stipulated we had to eat together, just that his food should be ready when he came in. I moved behind him, wiping the counter, and could see he was irritated, having to turn his head to talk to me. 'If we had a second car, I wouldn't need to spend on cabs.' How easy that would have made things with us. I could have gone anywhere to meet you, though I suppose he would have checked the mileage.

Nick sighed. 'Not this again. Don't you care about the planet?'

'One car won't make a difference.'

'Tell that to our baby,' he said, banging down the salt cellar. 'What if everyone had that attitude? He'll grow up in a world flooded by climate change.' We didn't know the baby's gender yet, but I'd noticed Nick use this pronoun a few times.

'And yet you drive *your* car,' I said airily. The counter was clean, but I went on wiping.

'There's no other way to get to work! Suzi, what's the matter with you tonight?'

'Oh, nothing's the matter, darling. Just having a logical conversation. You know, if you don't like driving, we could always think about moving back to London. Keep this place as a weekend bolthole.' Bolthole, another term I could not remember ever saying before.

I'd pushed things far enough for one night. Nick gave me the same hurt, confused look, then went back to eating his mash in silence. The next day, I found fifty pounds in notes left on my bedside table, enough for the taxi and train but not a lot else (he was right, it was expensive to go to London). As I counted it, I thought about the other women who wake up to find cash on the nightstand. There wasn't much difference between us.

I almost didn't make it to town – the taxi was twenty minutes late, grousing about ice on the road, and then the train was delayed by snow on the rails. But I did make it. Claudia worked in the centre of London, near Old Street. As I lumbered out of the Tube, I was assaulted by the city – the noise, the blare of traffic, the smells of petrol and food and the homeless man camped out near the station. I dropped a pound into his cup, mumbling some kind of apology. Here, among the rush of life, my fears seemed absurd. Complaining that I didn't know how to use my expensive speaker system? That I was alone, in a beautiful house, with no work to do? That my dog had gone missing, through my own carelessness? But the word in the snow. That was real. As I wearily crossed the city, I was shocked to find Christmas decorations up already, reminding me that time was marching on. Nick and I had barely discussed what to do this year. I had a horrible feeling he wanted his mother to come.

When I met Nick five years ago, a punt on an unpromising online date, I had felt smug, home free, panting on first base. I didn't look at anyone else. We sailed through cohabiting, in our private world of two. My career flourished. I put on two stone. I stopped painting. So we got married, because that was what you did when you were this happy and you already joint-owned a blue retro toaster. On my wedding day, as Claudia helped me into my dress, so tightly boned I couldn't breathe, she had whispered a question in my ear. *Are you sure, babe?* Petulant, I'd insisted I was. And now I had to find a way to tell her – I had been wrong.

Claudia hadn't wanted to meet, I could tell. She'd said: *I don't know, babe, weekdays can be tricky. We don't really take lunch.* But I insisted, too far gone for pride. I had to talk to someone who wasn't out there, marooned in the countryside. Someone who knew the old Suzi, not this new, housebound, whale-like version of myself. So we were meeting in a restaurant near her office – she'd more or less forced me to pick the place, with her vagueness and slow replies. When I got there I saw it was all wrong: too shiny, too much glass and steel, and noisy, the kind of place voices roll off the walls and back again.

Claudia was eight minutes late, pushing open the door with her elbow, tapping at her phone. I waved when I saw her, too hard. She threw me a distracted smile and kept typing as she sat. 'Hello, darling. Sorry. Manic day.'

'We should order.' I slid the menu, a sheet of heavy crinkled paper, across to her. I'd looked it up online and chosen my food already.

Minutes ticked by as she cast her eyes over it and back to her phone, menu then phone. I signalled for the waitress but her eyes slid off me. Claudia looked at her watch. 'I don't have long.' I remembered us at university, the hours we used to waste in cafés, jawing over the boys in our lives, making a pot of tea last for hours. How had we ended up like this? My closest friend – the work ones had all ditched me after Damian – and she didn't have an hour spare for me.

I was torn between getting the waitress and needing to start talking in the limited time I had. Eventually, I pushed a loud 'excuse me, can we order' in her direction, catching curious glances. She took our orders without writing them down, causing me an irrational spike of anxiety.

'Thank you. Sorry.' Claudia smiled at the waitress. I felt she was trying to make up for my rudeness, and I wanted to cry. 'So!' Claudia's voice was bright when the sullen waitress left, her long dark ponytail swinging. 'How's the country life? Can't believe how big you are.'

'Oh, it's – you know. Quiet. I feel like I'm dead and buried sometimes.' I forced that same laugh again.

She looked at me quizzically. She was wearing wide navy trousers, seventies-style, and a cream silk blouse. Her nails were done in dark red gel – I couldn't remember the last time I'd had my nails painted; another thing that was supposedly toxic for the baby. One was still torn and black from shutting the garden gate on it. I hid my hands under my napkin. Claudia said, 'Everything's OK, right?'

It wasn't. I'd had an affair, and my lover was dead. I was pregnant, probably with his baby. I opened my mouth to say something – I didn't know what – then caught a glimpse of her kind, worried look, a moment of focus amid her distraction, and was horrified to feel my nose start to sting.

'Oh babe! What is it?'

'Nothing! God, so stupid. Pregnancy hormones.' People were looking. I dabbed my eyes on the napkin. 'It's just hard. Leaving everything behind.'

'Well, I'm sure. But I thought that's what you wanted? A fresh start?'

'I . . .' It was what Nick wanted. What I'd maybe sometimes said in passing might be nice, but I didn't mean it. How terrible it was when someone took you at your word. 'It's not what I thought. It's so isolated. I can't even get to the station unless I ring a cab – no Uber, nothing like that.'

'God,' murmured Claudia, the thought of no Uber clearly horrifying her.

'Nick's out at work all day, and I'm alone in the cottage. It's just so quiet. I suppose you get used to the traffic and foxes and drunks shouting outside your window.'

'You want that, you come to mine any night of the week,' she said, rolling her eyes, though I knew she loved her tiny flat in Angel, so small she'd had to have the sofa custom-made.

'God, they're slow here,' I said, as she checked her phone again. 'Sorry. I should have picked somewhere else.'

'It's fine. But tell me, are things alright with Nick?'

I shrugged. 'He works a lot. I have to ask him for money, and he expects me to cook and clean and all that, for when he comes home.'

Her brow furrowed. 'God, really? That's a bit retro, isn't it?'

'I suppose when I'm at home all day . . . He used to cook a lot, in London.' Sometimes I felt like we'd been totally different people here. Like the Nick and Suzi who lived in the countryside were clones of us, with other personalities. Which was the real version?

The food came, Claudia's tiny, artful salad, my steaming bowl of pasta. She ate three bites then picked up her phone again. 'God, things are just mad. The pre-Christmas rush, you know. I'm sorry, darling. Why don't you ring me one night, we'll chat properly?'

With Nick listening to my every word.

'Sure. I'm sorry, I'm fine really. Just hormonal, like I said. And kind of lonely.'

'That's to be expected, with such a big move. Your life has changed, Suze! That always feels weird.'

'Yes. You're right.'

For the rest of our brief lunch, I asked questions about her love life – hot and heavy with some guy from Tinder who didn't even have a bedroom, but slept under the stairs in a shared house; her job – 'Salma's breathing down my neck about the hot spring skirt length, and I am so bricking it I called A line instead of mini'; and her social life – Zumba, circus skills, gin tasting. I felt about a hundred years old. She left not long after, dropping a kiss that barely grazed my skin. I'd offered to pay, since she was in a hurry. 'Thanks, babe. I'll get the next one, yeah?'

I didn't think there would be a next one. And Nick would see the charge on the debit card and ask why it was so high, why I was treating Claudia when she had a job and I didn't. He'd ask what we ate. If we ordered wine. I was exhausted just thinking about it.

When I'd paid – an eye-watering amount for what we had – I lumbered back out. I didn't need to leave for another two hours to be home for Nick. The thought of rushing back to the quiet, insulated cottage made me gasp for breath.

We weren't far from my old office here, near Liverpool Street. Claudia and I used to grab drinks after work, back in the old days (less than a year ago!). Before I'd fully formulated a plan, I found that my puffy, flattened feet were already carrying me there.

I was spooked, being in London. It was too easy to imagine my former self loping round a corner, late, in high heels, on my phone, my trademark silver rings flashing. I hadn't been able to get them on in months, my fingers were so swollen. The office looked the same, the place I'd come to every day for three years, even on weekends sometimes. My hand flexed with the muscle memory of keying in the entrance code. Was it the same?

I looked at my watch – it was just 1.30 p.m., since Claudia and I had rushed our lunch. I remembered that Damian ate late, a continental affectation, and that he liked a smoke break outside. Maybe if I waited, he would come out.

I felt like a private detective on a stake-out, except I was so frumpy and pregnant I wouldn't have been able to pursue anyone at speed. I was surprised, then pleased, that the owner of the Italian café across the road still recognised me. 'Miss! Where you been all this time?'

'Oh, I moved to the country,' I said awkwardly.

His bushy eyebrows went up. 'Why you wanna leave London?'

Well, I didn't, Mr Café Man.

The aroma of coffee was like a drug, but I made myself order green tea. Nick was always nagging me to drink it for the health benefits, but the grass-clippings smell made me gag. I warmed my hands on the cup, staring at the door of the office across the road, the trendy lower-case letters spelling *graphix box* (stupid name), afraid I would miss him. I was also worried I might see someone else from the office, after I'd left under such a cloud. I could still remember the glances when I walked in the day after the alley incident, the way conversations would fall silent when I passed the break room. People knew what I'd done. It was possible someone had even told Nick. I'd driven myself insane trying to work out who – easier to walk away and leave the whole mess behind me.

Damian came out after about twenty minutes, already lighting up a fag before the door swung shut. His lanyard looped about his neck, bare arms in rolled-up shirt sleeves. My heart leaped up as my stomach lurched, and in the café I gathered my things and my bulk, trying not to rush but also not wanting to miss him. The lights at the pedestrian crossing took ages. I hoped he wouldn't see me before then, so I'd have to do that awkward wave-and-walk-towards thing. Maybe he'd go back inside. We hadn't left things on good terms.

As it happened, I was close enough to tap his shoulder before he saw me – because he didn't recognise me at all. I saw it bloom in his eyes.

'Jesus! Suzi?'

In other circumstances, I might have enjoyed his shock. He looked like he'd seen a ghost.

Nora

I waited outside the council buildings for almost an hour. I had never been to Sevenoaks before and found it a small, pretty town, full of expensive shops and red-brick cottages. It was freezing, an icy wind nipping at my fingers and face, but I didn't care. I had a purpose again, a new plan. None of this confusion, this backing out of what I'd steeled myself to do.

Eventually, on the dot of 1 p.m., Nick came out. He was bundled in a long black coat, with a scarf I could tell was expensive tucked around his neck. Leather gloves, the kind stranglers wore. He didn't see me. No one notices frumpy middle-aged women, which was what I'd let myself become. Grief had etched lines into my face, and I'd allowed my hair to go grey. I'd put on weight, letting sugar and fat fill up the emptiness inside me.

I followed Nick all the way from his office down the high street. My heart raced, afraid that he might turn and realise he knew me, but I had a bobble hat pulled low over my face and had put on several extra jumpers to change my shape. With this rudimentary disguise, I was able to position myself just one person behind Nick in the queue for the café he turned into. It was a fancy place, serving mixed salads and falafels in waxed cardboard boxes, ethically sourced coffees and teas and matcha, whatever that was. I used to think I was sophisticated, travelling the world as I did for concerts.

But I rarely saw more than auditoriums and airport hotels, and in the years I'd stayed obediently at home, the world had moved on.

Nick ordered a chicken box, with three types of salad, and a juice made with carrot and apples. That was strange, because I knew he made Suzi pack him a lunch every day. Often she forgot, and had to race from bed while he was in the shower, going down to the cold kitchen with her bare feet and heavy belly. He must have been throwing the lunches away. His bill was twelve pounds, and then the woman in front of me was served (skinny cold-brew coffee), and suddenly the boy behind the counter was staring at me.

'Can I help you?'

Nick was right nearby, looking at his phone as he waited for his order. I couldn't speak. I waved a hand to indicate I hadn't decided yet, and stepped back, behind him. Nick didn't glance up, and from this angle I was able to see his phone. Camera footage – it looked like a home security feed.

With a shock so great I almost knocked the cold-brew woman flying, I saw that he was looking at video of his house. Suzi's office. A little box in the corner said 'live'.

'Order for Nick?' said the girl behind the counter, heart-breakingly young, with clear brown skin and dark curls.

Nick stepped forward, leaving his phone for a second on the high table he'd been standing by. He exchanged a few words with the girl – flirty, I thought, in passing – then moved over to the cutlery and napkin counter. I had seconds.

'There you are!' A woman had come into the café and greeted Nick. My first distracted thought was that she looked like Suzi, pale red hair and white skin, wearing a trench coat. 'You ran off without me.'

'Thought you were still in the budget meeting. How was it?'

'Oh God, hellish . . .'

As they chatted, and his gaze was fixed on her, my fingers grazed the metal edge of his phone. Such a small rectangle, but it would tell me everything I needed to know about him. I glanced up – Nick was nodding at something the woman had said, holding wooden cutlery in one hand.

Heart hammering, I slipped the phone into the deep pocket of my coat, and exited the café, sucking in cold air. They'd have cameras, probably. I might get caught, arrested even. Though of course it wouldn't be the first time.

I couldn't resist it. Luckily – and luck was something that had deserted me a long time ago – the phone screen had not yet locked itself. As I trotted along the street, trying to put distance between me and the café, I clicked the back key, and saw a whole host of feeds. It looked like a bank of security cameras, but all trained on rooms in Nick and Suzi's house. Suzi wasn't there – I'd seen her leave in a taxi earlier that day, on another mysterious errand. I clicked back again. I was in an app called Home, and it controlled temperature, music, lights, door locks.

I had one more thing to check. Under 'Find My Friends', an app I had discovered on my husband's phone and realised could be very useful, there was Suzi, clearly marked. She was in London, somewhere in the City. He could follow her every move. Had she any idea? She couldn't have. Suddenly I was afraid for her. She knew she had to be careful, but did she know just how careful? Did she know how much he could see?

Suzi

Damian and I went to the small public garden around the corner, which even in the freezing weather wasn't empty. Awkwardness kept us several feet apart, and all I could think about was the last time I spoke to him, that day in the office kitchen. *I didn't want it*, I'd said. Had it been an assault, as you had insisted when I told you? I didn't know. I felt too ashamed to ally myself with real victims, women pulled into bushes on their way home, hands pressed over their mouths. I had brought this on myself.

We walked around, hands jammed in our pockets to stay warm. Damian said, 'So what are you doing here? Are you coming back to work?'

'No – I can't really right now.' I laid my hands on my belly. Trying to use it as armour, shield myself from the flood of memories he brought back. My stomach was queasy, roiling with undigested pasta and green tea. The smell of that alley. The wetness of his mouth against my neck. *Oh God, Suzi.* 'I just – I needed to talk to you. Do you remember when someone smashed your car up a while back?'

'Yeah, but . . .' He frowned. 'Hadn't you left by then? That was like, in the summer?'

'I just – I saw it on Facebook. Well anyway, the same kind of thing's been happening to me.' I told him about the issues with the alarm and speaker, the dead thing in my garden, the writing in the snow (glossing over what it said). His frown deepened. We'd stopped walking now, and he was bouncing on the balls of his feet, his breath like smoke in the cold air.

'That's fucking weird.' The twang of his South London accent took me back, all the times we'd smoked together, gone for drinks, lingered in the kitchen to talk. More than once we'd sat on that bench over there eating lunch. I could almost see our past selves if I blinked.

'You didn't – you don't think the same person could be doing it?' I said.

I didn't even ask if it was him, though that had been my initial thought. I could tell from his reaction on seeing me that I'd barely crossed his mind in all these months.

'Who?'

'I don't know.' *My ex-lover's wife? That is, my other lover?* But how would she even know about Damian, or care? I couldn't put the pieces together. I'd been sure it was you who smashed up the car, but you couldn't be doing these things to me.

'The thing is, Suze . . .' His old nickname for me, in the circumstances, felt cruel. 'I always thought maybe that was you.'

'What? You thought I busted up your car?'

'You know, a woman scorned and all that.'

I gaped at him. This man had been my friend for two years. Had been more than that. 'I wasn't – you didn't *scorn* me. Jesus, Damian, that's not what happened at all. We crossed a line, and I felt terrible about it. I'm married, so I ended it.'

He shrugged. I could see him thinking, *you tell yourself that, if it helps.* 'Water under the bridge. If anything else weird happens, I'll let you know. Get you on Facebook?'

I could hardly say, *don't contact me publicly, because Nick will see it, and if he knows I've spoken to you I'll be in a whole world of pain.*

I couldn't admit this, not to him, a man I'd thought cared about me, who it turned out was only after five minutes inside my knickers. 'Maybe just email. I have a new one. Here.' I typed my secret one into his phone, feeling the awkward intimacy of the gesture. It seemed disloyal, giving him our private email account. But you were gone, and I'd never hear from you again.

'Listen, Suze . . .' He scratched his head. 'What you said that time . . .'

Fear ran through me. I couldn't have this conversation, not with everything that was going on.

'I'm sorry if you . . . if it wasn't what you wanted. I thought it was.' Was that an admission?

What could I say? 'I . . . felt so terrible afterwards.'

'I know. Me too. You think it's going to be so sexy, but instead it's just – you feel like crap. Seedy.'

'Yeah.' I risked looking at him, his dark eyes, the dimple by his mouth that I had once spent hours thinking about, day-dreaming at my computer. We had been good friends once – would perhaps still be, if it wasn't for the alley. For what happened. What I'd made happen.

He nodded his head to my belly. 'Congrats, by the way. Hope it all goes OK.' Was there any more awkward conversation to have than that about a pregnancy, with a man you'd once slept with? Was *slept with* the right phrase? My mind shied away. At least I was in no danger. He would never fancy me like this, huge, in country casuals. But as we said our awkward goodbyes, and I waddled to the Tube, I found I had tears in my eyes for the loss of something. The way he'd seen me once, maybe. The person I used to be.

Luck was against me that day. When I got to Victoria, I could see at once it was more crowded than usual. People stood around tutting, staring at the large display screens as if they were oracles. A sense of panic and anger in the air. All the trains to Kent read 'DELAYED' – of course, the snow had predictably messed up the lines. I checked my watch – if I was lucky, I'd just make it home before Nick. Was there anything to cook in the house? Maybe if I dashed to M&S now, I could get something, bash it up a bit to look home-made. I was sure he'd know. He seemed to know everything I did.

I was not lucky. A platform number appeared on the sign after I'd spent half an hour standing, afraid to go into a café and sit down in case a magical train appeared and I missed it. I lumbered towards the platform, exhausted, and watched people on the train avert their eyes from me in case they'd have to offer me a seat. In the end, some kind young woman gave me hers – it was always women – and I almost cried. I rested my head against the cold glass, as the train inched south. It stopped so many times en route, waiting outside Otford for what felt like twenty minutes. I played with my phone, the battery close to dead again – I should really have texted Nick, but there was still a chance he'd be late and I'd beat him there. I saw I had a message from Claudia, who was perhaps feeling guilty: *Call me anytime you need babe. Stay strong xx.* I deleted it – I didn't want Nick to see.

Inevitably, I found myself reliving it all, everything with Damian. Ruminating again. I'd told you all about him when you asked. The new guy starting at work, catching his eye and an overly long smile when he was brought over to say hello, the chats in the office kitchen long after the kettle had boiled, flirting by email, the drunken nights in the pub when we'd inch closer and closer together, shouting out jokes to each other, the cold drips creeping down my glass of gin and tonic, then the final night, feeling his hand on my leg under the table, the thrill of it, everyone melting away, and it was so late I'd forgotten about my last Tube, and then suddenly the alley and the cold stone under my back. His tongue was in my mouth. His hand was between my legs. My knickers were gone. The whole alley stank, and behind us, over his pumping shoulder, I could see people walking on the main road. I didn't want this – no, I hadn't wanted it – but it was too late to stop him and he was in me. There was pain – then it was over. I'd been breathing tight against his shoulder, wet on his Paul Smith shirt.

'Oh God,' he'd gasped. Then he slipped out and I was hunting for my underwear, my hands shaking with what had happened. Out on the main road he was distracted, checking his phone. 'I better shoot. Last Tube's almost gone.' And he'd left me and I had to find a cab, and I'd no money, and I had to make it stop for cash, and I saw six missed calls from Nick on my mobile, and it took me three goes to text him: *Missed train on my way.* When I got home, I tiptoed to the bathroom. I washed between my legs, which made me wince. A shower would have been too suspicious. When I crawled into bed, holding my breath, Nick said in the dark, 'Good night then?'

'Mm . . . sorry. I just missed the train.'

A pause. 'You stink of booze.' He rolled over.

I waited for morning, and my punishment. The next day when I picked up my handbag from the stairs, I could smell piss had sunk into the leather from where it had rested on the ground, and I couldn't get it out, no matter how much I scrubbed.

When I told you this story, you went very still. 'If he comes near you again, I'll kill him.'

How I loved you for this. Your anger. I linked my arms around your neck – we were in the Travelodge, where we used to meet. A bland, even unpleasant room, somehow made perfect by your presence. 'How would you kill him?'

'It's easy for a doctor.' You rolled me over, and then you were on top of me and then inside me. I groaned. I wanted you to fuck it all out of me: Damian, the alley and even Nick. 'We have power over death. We can make it look like an accident, a heart attack or a stroke – anything.'

A few days later, I went upstairs to the bathroom. I had my phone – I'd got into the habit of always taking it with me, safer that way. I put the phone on the floor while I peed, and idly glanced at Facebook.

I had to stay friends with Damian on there, of course. If I'd blocked him, he might have hit back. I knew every one of his wake-boarding festival-going beer-drinking photos. He'd done a status update. It said: *Car windscreen smashed up. Paintwork wrecked. WTF! Supposed to be a 'low crime area'.*

I had clicked out of FB and wiped the history, hands shaking. It seemed a huge coincidence, after our conversation in the Travelodge. Had you? Taken a brick or something and attacked his car? How would you even know where he lived? I hardly dared believe it. I clicked into our secret email. You never emailed in the evening – too risky. I messaged. *Damian's car. You didn't?*

I hadn't expected a reply, but suddenly one winked in, making me start. *Don't know what you mean ;). Goodnight, darling.*

'Suzi?' Nick's voice. Right up against the door. 'What are you doing?'

The tap was still running. 'Just cleansing.'

'That wastes water, you know.' Pause. 'Five minutes and I'm putting the light off.'

I closed my eyes. 'OK. I'll be there. Promise.'

I already knew I wouldn't.

When my taxi pulled into our drive, Nick's car was there. I dragged my shopping in.

'Sorry. I'm sorry. The trains – I left hours ago.' Tears welled up in me. 'I've just – I've had a horrible journey, OK, so please don't have a go.'

To my surprise, he spoke mildly. 'I wasn't going to. Are you alright? Sit down.' He took the bag of food, only one raised eyebrow commenting on the fact I'd been planning to feed him a ready-made dinner. 'This is why I didn't want you going, see. There's so many delays just now, it's not good for the baby.'

'Or for me,' I muttered.

'No. Not for you either. I did say.' He bustled about, putting things away, turning on the oven. Somehow, the kindness made things worse, and that, combined with my exhaustion, with seeing Claudia and Damian and all those memories stirred up again, broke me. He said, 'Did you text? I've lost my phone, or it's been nicked maybe. So annoying. I'll get a new one tomorrow, but in the meantime . . . What's wrong?'

'Oh *Nick*.' A sob tore out of me, and I put a hand over my mouth. 'I . . . I can't go on like this. Things are so bad, we never talk, you're always mad at me . . . I'm sorry! I'm trying! I really am trying!' The rest was lost in a garble of tears.

Nick hunkered down in front of me. 'Hey, hey, it's alright.'

'It's not alright! Things between us are so bad . . . I mean, aren't they?' Oh God, was it possible he hadn't realised? That he thought we were happy?

He said nothing for a while, just peering into my face, concerned. 'I know the move's been hard on you.'

'I'm so lonely, Nick. I feel so – having no job, no money, it really sucks.' He opened his mouth, doubtless to say I did have money. 'I know what's yours is mine. But I have to ask you for it, don't I? I can't just pop out and get cash, and the car situation . . .'

More tears welled up, as I realised we were going over and over the same rows. Was that what the end of a marriage was like, being stuck in some Groundhog Day of misery?

'I thought you'd be happy here,' he said, standing up. 'In London . . . I felt like I was losing you. You were always working, or out.' Between us, the truth lay just beneath the surface, a treacherous river under a thin layer of ice. I could tell him. *Nick, I had sex with Damian. I didn't want to but – it happened. I'm sorry. Please, I'm so sorry.*

But then how to explain the rest? Oh, and I had a second affair, and now the man was dead? He could count. He'd work out the baby likely wasn't his. I couldn't do it. I wiped a hand across my face. 'I'm sorry I went out so much. I know it wasn't fair on you. I – I want to be different. But please, Nick. You never touch me any more. You never look at me.'

He was nodding, slowly. 'You seem so far away.'

'I'm not, I'm right here.'

'Are you saying you're willing to try – you want things to be better between us?'

'Of course I do.'

'You know these things I do – worrying about where you go, what you eat – it's just because I love you. You and the baby.'

I stood up too, and walked the few steps between us. Tentatively, I put my arms around him, feeling his solidity, the warmth radiating out from under his woolly jumper. Perhaps I had not touched him either in months. 'I know. But please – don't criticise me all the time. I will try harder, I promise.'

'Alright.' He went slack in my arms, then hugged me tight, his arms almost crushing the air from me. 'I love you, Suzi.'

I made myself say, 'I love you too.'

I had, once. Perhaps I could again.

Later, as we cleaned up together for a change, him washing the dishes and me wiping the counters, Nick asked, 'How was it anyway? Lunch?'

'Oh . . . a bit rushed. Claudia didn't have much time. An eat and run situation.'

'Hmm, yes.' He ran the tap, and said innocently, 'See anyone from work?'

Suddenly I wanted to be sick. My hands began to shake. 'My work? No, why?'

His voice was as reasonable as could be. 'No reason. I just thought you might have stopped by. It's near Claudia's office, isn't it?'

He couldn't know. It wasn't possible. 'Not really.'

Then he said, casual-like, 'By the way, I almost forgot: when I called the police about my phone – not that they were at all helpful – they mentioned they'd been planning to talk to us.'

Blood buzzed in my ears. 'What? Do you know what about?' Hadn't I worried about this for days now, a phone call, a car drawing up the narrow lane, stopping by our door? What did they know? What had they told Nick? In all my imaginings, I had never thought he would be here when they came and not me.

'I think it's just routine enquiries. Some accident over on the slip road. Did you hear about that?'

I turned away, putting the plates in the cupboard. 'I don't think so. Recent?'

'A few months back. A man died.'

Oh God. Oh God oh God oh God. Liquid fear sloshed through my veins. 'Oh, that's sad. What did they want with us?'

'Just checking if we heard anything. Maybe you could call them back, they left a number.'

'Sure. I don't know how I can help, though.'

Nick looked at me, and I wanted to cry again. I had failed at being a friend, being an employee. There was nothing left of me but this house and marriage, and even that I couldn't get right. 'Hey, you look tired,' he said, concerned.

I rubbed my eyes, tears just under the surface. 'I am. I forgot how awful it is, the commute.'

'No more trips to London for a while, I think,' he said, and I found myself agreeing with him, the suggestion that I should no longer go anywhere by myself. This was how easy it was to lock your own jail cell, from the inside.

When we first moved to the country, I'd asked Nick what the road signs meant that said Passing Places. He showed me when we passed a car on the road and he reversed back to let it by, and the driver waved thanks to us. I thought it was nice. Later, I thought that was what Nick and I had lost – neither of us was prepared to move back and let the other one through, and so we were stuck there, beeping our horns and flashing our lights, all for nothing.

Elle

A woman. There'd been a woman in his car with him. Did that mean she'd been right, all those times? Every time he said, *Darling, are you getting funny again? Are you taking the pills? You're not going, you know, like your mother?* Every time he'd denied it, made her think she was crazy – there really had been another woman?

She tried to keep busy after the funeral. Scrubbing the house from top to bottom, calling the bank and electricity company and graveyard, all the bewildering bits of admin you were supposed to somehow handle while going through the worst pain of your life. The meeting with the lawyer was scheduled for later that day, that gave her something to focus on. He would confirm that they had plenty of money. That her husband hadn't been broke, or borrowed cash from unsavoury types. That everything she'd thought was true still was. But all the same a tiny hummingbird of panic was trapped in her chest, making it impossible to eat, or sleep, or sit still for more than two minutes in a row.

A woman in the car with him. Perhaps she would know what had happened to him. Perhaps she had even caused it, grabbing the wheel, making a scene of some kind. Maybe he was trying to end it with her, and she did this rather than lose him. Or maybe she told him something that shocked him, made him drive off the road. This woman, whoever she was, had perhaps caused his death.

Left him there to die instead of getting help – Elle knew the ambulance had been called by an elderly couple, passing the accident spot some time afterwards. This woman, this faceless woman, had not only led Patrick astray, caused him to cheat – she was maybe responsible for Elle being a widow.

Elle stood in her living room, in which not a speck of dust remained, gripping the marble mantelpiece. Staring at the wedding photo, herself so young and slim, red lips, black hair. Him so handsome. Laughing. Had they been happy then, or was it all in her head? Had he ever been happy? Was it possible to love someone and still cheat on them? How could he do this to her?

As if anyone could ever love you.

She was aware of a new sensation, dripping into her veins like coffee into a pot. Anger. Rage, travelling through her veins and into her heart. Galvanising her, like a jolt of electricity through dead flesh. Where she had been so lost, hovering near to the grave herself, unable to see a way forward, she now had a purpose. Find this woman, and destroy her life just as surely as her own had been destroyed.

The doorbell went, and through the glass she saw the small round shape of the lawyer, heard him coughing in the cold air. Of course, the money. It almost seemed insignificant now that this new plan had come to her. She would hear what he had to say, instruct him to do whatever had to be done paperwork-wise, and then she would take action.

She opened it, smiling properly for the first time in weeks. 'Hello, do come in.'

He looked stricken. 'Elle, dear, I'm afraid I have some bad news.'

Suzi

'It's going to be OK,' said Nora placidly. Nothing seemed to alarm her about my situation – not my affair, not my baby who likely wasn't Nick's, not the fact the police wanted to talk to me. 'It's not a crime to have an affair, even if the police did work out you were there.' We were in my living room, and outside more snow was falling, silent, all sounds cut off by our thick windows and insulated walls. I was glad Nora was there. If it was just me all the way out here, I wasn't sure I could have stood it.

'But they won't know I got out before it happened. They might think, I don't know, I left the scene of the accident. Or that I was driving, even! I mean, it doesn't look right, does it? How do you hit a tree on a clear road, on a sunny day?'

'It is strange.' Nora's lovely hands traced patterns on the expensive reclaimed-wood coffee table Nick had bought. 'Did the hospital have any insights as to why?'

'They didn't say anything. I guess maybe a brain thing, or a heart attack, or, I don't know – something startled him.'

She fixed me with her grey eyes, shaded with the purple of sleepless nights, lines fanning out from them like the contours of a map. She had been very beautiful once, I could tell. I wondered what had aged her so – was it grief and being outdoors so much, or did this just happen after forty? Would this be me in a few years? 'You got out before anything happened.'

'Yes! God, of course. I'd have called for help otherwise. He seemed fine. Well, I mean, a bit confused and agitated, I'd just told him I was pregnant, but he was happy.'

'Are you sure he was happy?'

I stared at her, hurt.

'I'm sorry to ask. It's just – he might have panicked, done something stupid. It's a lot to take in. You say he was planning to leave the wife?'

'He promised. He was looking at places to rent, even. He was going to go home and tell her right then, and I'd tell Nick. God! Thank Christ I didn't.'

'If you had, you might be already settled, you know. Free of him.'

I frowned. Nora was so strange today, offering these odd bits of advice that I'd never heard from her before. 'But where would I live? I don't have a job. Plus, Nick's good at all that legal stuff. I bet he'd find a way to get the baby.'

Nora made a noise of frustration. 'Suzi, it's the twenty-first century. They don't take babies from their mothers.' She hesitated. 'Unless they're in prison, of course.'

I stood up, almost knocking over my tea. Nora righted it. 'Oh God. I can't go to prison, can I? I didn't do anything! I just got dropped off on the verge!'

'They don't know that, of course.'

'Alright, so what do I do? Please, Nora. You're so clear-minded and I'm so – my brain's like tangled-up wool. What do I do?'

'Do you really want my advice?'

I leaned forward, thinking how strange it was that this woman I barely knew was now my lifeline, the only person I could confide in, who could help me out of this mess I'd made for myself. 'Please, Nora. Tell me what I should do.'

I waited all through the day, my panic gradually subsiding to a dull pain. I jumped at every car that came down the lane, every ring of the phone – Nick's mother again, PPI. The police didn't call. They would have come before, surely, anyway, if they knew about me. You had died months ago. I must have left no trace on your life after all. It could be like I never existed. It could be like it never happened – except for that line on the pregnancy test.

The weather was still bone-cold, and I spent hours trudging round the countryside, looking for Poppet again, finding no trace. My ankle throbbed with every step, and my bump weighed me down, but I made myself go on, trying to atone. Not just for losing the dog. For everything. It was chilling how little there was near us. Apart from Nora, we'd have to walk for an hour to reach the nearest house. The landscape was nothing but fields and scrubby woodland, and the sense of loneliness intensified with each step. I hadn't realised what good company a dog was, as annoying as I found him. Now there was nothing. Not a single living breath except my own.

Nora thought I should leave Nick. Or rather, make him leave me. Tell him to move out, give me the house. Be even more alone out here. Madness. I'd just stared at her, then mumbled my excuses. What I had to do was find out who knew about us, who could have left that message in the snow. If it was your wife, what was to stop her going to the police? Did she know somehow I'd been in the car with you – was that why the police were asking questions now? My life could come crashing about my ears at any moment. I couldn't rock the boat by overturning my marriage, that was a terrible idea. No, I had to find her. Your wife.

152

How did I find a woman I knew nothing about? Only the barest of details. You had told me, reluctantly, and only I think because you couldn't avoid it without a scene, that she was older than you.

'How progressive,' I'd said, made snide by jealousy.

'Mmm.' You didn't want to talk about her.

We were in the Travelodge. My blouse was half off my shoulder, revealing the lacy black bra I wore for you. After that I became obsessed with her, as you do with your lover's wife. Was there anyone more hated, even though I was the one stealing from her? Even though she likely had no idea I existed? I remembered asking: 'What colour hair does she have? Your wife?'

You didn't want to answer that. After a while: 'Dark. Black.'

Increasingly, throughout the few months that we saw each other, I thought it might be OK if she knew about us. Then we could leave all this, stop pretending. I wouldn't be telling you this, obviously, if things weren't the way they were, but there you go. I used to think shameful things. Accidentally on purpose texting when I knew you were at home. Emailing her, even. But how would I get in touch with her? All I knew was her surname, assuming she'd taken yours, and that she had black hair. You wouldn't tell me her first name.

When we were together – such a brief handful of times, really! – I would sometimes ask you questions about your life. Innocent-sounding ones, like *do you have stairs in your house?* You would go quiet, give me a look as if I was laying a trap. And maybe I was. You were very good at not telling me things, but even with that I picked a few bits up. I knew you had a tree in your garden with red leaves – you had even sent me a picture once, romantically comparing it to my hair. I knew you had paving stones on your drive, because once you'd had to ring a man to come and clean them. They were mossy, and your wife was afraid of slipping, which made me think of her as weak, fragile. The online article I found about your death had mentioned you lived in Guildford (not where you'd told me, of course), on Carnation Drive. I was fairly confident that if I went there, I would be able to find your house.

It was getting too cold to be out, and my body ached. Swollen ankles, swollen belly, a feeling that the air couldn't fill my lungs. Ivy Cottage was in darkness, and I wondered where Nora was, why she hadn't mentioned she was going out. Obscurely, I felt a stab of resentment, at being left out here alone. Ridiculous. As I approached my own cottage, I saw to my surprise that the windows were lit up, the blinds drawn. Had I done that before I left? Was Nick home? It was far too early for that, only three o'clock, though the light was already weakening, dying. But the alarm box glowed red, not on 'stay' mode, so he couldn't be back. Puzzled, I carefully keyed in the code – no squawking of a wrong key today – and went inside. The house was warm, welcoming, all the lights on, soft music playing. Had I set this before I went out? I went over my movements in my head: putting my coat on, finding my scarf, setting the alarm. I couldn't remember. Hurriedly, I turned it off, wanting the music gone.

'*Suzi. Suzi.*' In the silence of the kitchen, my own name echoed. Tinny, electronic, impossible to tell if it was a man or woman's voice, a machine or a person. Oh God. I hated this thing.

Of course, it wasn't so simple, going to Guildford. I didn't have a car and I had to explain each trip out I made. Again, I used the baby as an excuse. I wanted to go and look at cots, bouncy seats, that kind of thing. I pretended I was going to London, since he'd think it strange to go to a town so far away.

Nick wiped a dish with a tea towel. He'd started taking ages to reply to my statements about where I might go (I wasn't asking for permission. And yet I was). 'London. Again?'

'Just getting organised. We'll need things for the baby! Lots of things.'

'But I'd like to go with you for that. Choose them together.' I'd thought he might say that.

'I know, but I just want to get a head start. Don't deny me the chance to coo! And you know me, I take years to choose anything.' Silly Suzi. What an airhead. 'Remember all those weekends in Spitalfields Market?'

He smiled, recalling the people we used to be, our golden London Sundays buying old-age junk for our tiny flat, paying fifteen pounds for avocado toast and coffee. 'Yeah. Well, alright. Just don't get tired out.'

As I picked up the plate he'd dried, I almost wanted to punch the air in triumph. I'd trapped him this time. In the morning he left me an even bigger pile of cash. I got dressed with more care than usual – not hard. I brushed my hair, selected a new maternity jumper and jeans. I even did my eye make-up. I wasn't sure why, but my heart was racing in my chest. I had to remind myself you wouldn't be there, not ever. You were gone.

The crowds in Guildford were terrible, Christmas shoppers already out in force, tramping the remnants of snow into grey slush. The night before, as part of our reconciliation, Nick had brought up the holidays for the first time, and, as I'd predicted, suggested inviting his mother (mine was going on a cruise, thankfully). I thought about another week with Joan creeping about at 5 a.m. to listen to Radio 4, rewashing all my dishes, constantly wiping the counters;

having to find National Trust properties to take her to, not being able to watch any TV I wanted because she'd tut at any violence or sex or swearing. I'd have to think about Nick's present, when there wasn't a single thing I could imagine him wanting. It was exhausting. I thought about getting a cab or an Uber to your house, but I felt an obscure paranoia that Nick might check, that he could look it up online and see I'd been somewhere I had no good reason to go. It wasn't so far-fetched. In town, I bought a few things without thinking – some babygros, a scarf for Nick – in case I was too upset afterwards to do any shopping. I'd have to hide the receipts with the shop addresses on. The woman in the baby shop smiled at my bump. 'When are you due?'

'Oh!' I somehow hadn't made the connection that the babygros were for my baby, that I'd dress small, wriggling limbs in this soft brushed cotton. It was still abstract, my life stuck in limbo. 'February.' God, it was so soon. Why had I let this go on so long?

'Lovely. Spring baby.'

Spring seemed impossible to imagine. Would I still be here then, living like this? I threw her a smile that was more of a rictus and left. The paper bags bashed against my leg as I walked out of town, towards Carnation Drive. It was all so suburban, so boring. The mock-Tudor fronts, the two cars in the driveways, snow swept neatly up into piles. The boxy hedges, the paved drives. I was beginning to feel very tired, and also aware of a strong need to pee. *Not now!* I asked myself why I was doing this, what on earth could be gained by going to look at your house. I didn't know. Just that something didn't feel right, that I couldn't accept you were dead and out of my life, not when I in all likelihood carried your child inside me, pressing on my bladder.

I didn't know the house number so I looked for one with a red-leafed tree and paving. I found it, halfway down, a few leaves still clinging. Was this your house? It was so normal, so neat, the hedge trimmed, the paintwork fresh. Would you, so passionate and alive, live in a place like this? The door was black. The letter box and handle chrome. And there was a For Sale sign outside. No car.

For some reason, this had not occurred to me. Your wife – your widow – had obviously decided to move away. Too painful. Or maybe she was short of money, since you'd mentioned a few times she didn't work.

The front door was opening! I almost keeled over. What if it was her, what if she guessed who I was? I pressed a hand to my chest, but it was an estate agent, of course. A woman in a trouser suit, with shiny bleached-blonde hair. I could see her little branded car now, parked in the street. A young couple were being shown out – the man had a baby strapped to his front. As I stood there, they walked past, casting me a curious look, and unlocked a people carrier parked nearby. The woman said to her husband, 'Shame, it looked brighter in the pictures. What about that three-bed I sent you this morning?'

So they weren't going to buy it. The estate agent had a large bunch of keys, she was searching for the right one. This was my chance. I was walking towards her before I could think about what I was doing. 'Hello!' I made my voice bright. 'I don't suppose I could take a peek, could I? I was just passing, I've been looking for something in this area.'

She frowned. 'Normally we'd ask people to make an appointment at the office.'

'Oh, I know, but since I'm here and you're here – just a quick little look.' I rubbed my stomach. 'Moving's become a bit more urgent, if you get me.' Being pregnant entitled you to all kinds of special treatment. She glanced at her watch and nodded reluctantly, and then she was taking the key and letting me in, and it was only then I thought to wonder if your wife might still be there.

Elle

The money was gone.

She hadn't taken it in at first. The lawyer was saying phrases, and she could see his large frog-like mouth moving, but nothing made sense. '. . . not as expected . . . significant withdrawals . . .'

She interrupted him. It was rude, and she imagined Mother scolding her, but she just didn't understand. 'I'm sorry, I don't . . . What do you mean?'

He had looked at her with kind, dark eyes. 'I'm so sorry, Elle. There's no money left. I'll keep checking for any hidden accounts or savings, but – so far, there's nothing.'

Seconds ticked by. 'But . . . there's all the savings accounts. The trust documents.' He had worked on her family business for years, he knew all this. He knew about the vast sums her father had left to her, the only surviving child, her parents' life insurance, the insurance on the house too. The company had dithered over paying it, after all the rumours, but in the end it had come. 'They can't be empty.'

'Elle . . . as you know, we maintain your funds. But they are yours, to do what you want with. We don't interfere with withdrawals, so long as all the security checks are in line.'

He didn't mean *all* the money. He must be misunderstanding. What about all her earnings, the thousands she had made from concerts, so much she simply stopped looking at her accounts, knowing she could buy whatever she wanted? 'Yes, but . . .'

'There were a lot of big withdrawals over the last ten years. Always just at the limit where we'd have to call you to double-check – which is, as you may recall, twenty thousand pounds. There was a lot in the accounts . . . but this is quickly used up by heavy spending.'

'But . . . I didn't take it.' She was still clutching at hope. 'Some mistake? Fraud, maybe?' Didn't the government protect you against that? 'Identity theft?'

He looked wretched. 'Elle, dear . . . your husband had full control over all the accounts too.' Then, she finally understood.

Carefully, she said, 'What was it spent on?'

He fumbled pages out in front of her, seeming grateful for the support of something concrete. She glanced over the tiny figures, crawling like ants. Holidays. The Jaguar, replaced every two years. Haircuts, clothes, massages. Meals out that she knew nothing about, bars, even hotel stays. He'd been spending money on *her*, perhaps. The woman. Elle's money. 'But . . . I don't understand. He was a doctor, he earned a lot.' That was her last straw to cling to. Even though he clearly spent more than she knew, much much more, he must have had his own money coming in too. She'd seen his payslips, though it had been for less than she thought. Maybe he got paid in different instalments, or it was weekly instead of monthly?

The lawyer hesitated. 'I contacted his workplace, to ask about final pensions and so on. Elle – he did work at Surrey General, yes, but he wasn't a doctor. I'm afraid, my dear, you have been rather . . . misled.'

Suzi

'No one's here then?' Of course not, the agent would have knocked otherwise. The house was empty, walls trailing TV and internet cables. My voice echoed in the void.

'It's been vacated already, yes. Ready to move in, and there's no chain obviously.'

'Great, great.' Pretending to care about the boiler and car parking, I moved around your house. I was inside your house. Of course, you weren't here any more, but you had been. You had maybe stood by the patio doors on the phone, looking out on the garden. That was painfully neat, trees and grass clipped into right angles, so your wife must have left quite recently. I moved into the kitchen, which was large, with a marbled island. The same floor tiles Nick and I had looked at, from Baked Earth. I opened a cupboard, spotted a stray grain of dry rice in the corner. I wanted to take it with me, if I could have done it without looking crazy. Upstairs, three bedrooms with cream carpet, streaming with light. 'Did they have any kids, the owners?' I asked innocently. 'Just wondering about those stairs.' You could have lied to me about that too. Perhaps you had several children, half-siblings to my baby. I would have believed anything at this point.

'No, they didn't. Just a couple on their own.' She didn't mention the accident, or your death. Perhaps she thought it would put me off.

I probed a little. 'Any reason for the sale? You know, just wondering about neighbours, or any issues.'

'As far as I know they were downsizing. It's a big place when there's no little ones.' She smiled at me as she lied, her lips moving and leaving her eyes untouched. 'This is your first?' Nodding to my bump.

'Third!' I said, inventing some random children. 'That's why we need a bigger place. This is lovely.'

'Yes – a wonderful property. The owners were very house-proud, maintained it all beautifully, as you can see.'

'Cream carpets, though. My lot would have this trashed in seconds!' I was quite enjoying my alternate persona, a cheerful mother of almost-three. Probably she baked and rolled her eyes, laughing, when the kids drew on the walls.

I moved into what I could tell had been your bedroom. Built-in wardrobes slid aside to reveal nothing. I didn't know what I was expecting, suits or shoes or something.

'Lovely.'

She burbled on about storage and hot water pressure while I breathed in. You had been here. Your essence was still in the air. In the bathroom, she turned her back to check her phone, and that was when I spotted it. Something had been left behind in the mirrored wall cabinet. It was built around a corner, so that the inner space was hidden unless you put your hand in. Probably your wife had had cleaners in, and they hadn't been too thorough.

I pretended to check the light fitting; the agent wasn't looking. In a flash I stuck my fingers into the cabinet and pulled out the thing, shoved it into my bag. She looked at me. I moved the mirrored door between us, hiding my face.

'Well, it's certainly something to think about. Maybe I'll come back with my husband.' I wondered what his name was. Gary, perhaps.

'Let me take your details, so we can keep in touch. I didn't catch your name.'

'Oh, it's Lydia,' I said, thinking of a girl I'd been to school with, a fearless chancer who once broke into the teachers' lounge and stole a tin of biscuits. 'Lydia Hutton.'

She asked for my email but I said I didn't really have one, 'Bit of a Luddite, ha ha', and I reeled off a fake mobile number. Whoever it belonged to would be getting all those spam texts estate agents send you. Houses that cost four times what you said your budget was, totally different to what you'd asked for.

'I'd make an offer soon, the couple who were just here are very interested,' she said. I wondered how they were able to lie so convincingly, estate agents, if they trained them or recruited people who were already good at it. But then, I was learning that lying was not so very difficult after all, if you had a lot to lose by telling the truth.

When I stepped outside I felt hot and flushed, as if I'd just gotten away with something. As soon as the agent – I'd already forgotten her name – drove off, I stopped on the pavement and rooted in my bag for the thing from the cabinet. I saw it was an empty box of pills, in the name of Mrs Eleanor Sullivan.

I felt like I was going mad. You weren't a doctor, you weren't even called what you said you were called, you didn't live where you said. Your wife was named Eleanor. I had her pill prescription in my bag.

When I arrived home in yet another taxi, the money Nick had left all but gone, I was relieved to see the house in darkness.

Before leaving, I'd made sure to check I hadn't turned anything on, no longer trusting myself. Nora's house was also in darkness, and I didn't see her familiar shape at the window, eyes shaded. Perhaps she was in the garden, though it was late. No strange music played this time, and I got the alarm code right. But the house was boiling, so much that I gasped for air. I went to the control dial, but it read nineteen. Nineteen! It should have felt cold. Maybe it was pregnancy, affecting my hormones. I stripped off my coat and jumper and T-shirt, leaving just a vest top that strained over my bump. I went to the studio and turned on the big Mac. The screen was so bright I had to shield my eyes. Then I started googling the name of the drugs your wife was taking. Quickly, I found what it was. A high-dose therapy for forms of psychosis. When I read that, I started to shake, although it was so hot. Oh God. Oh my God.

I needed to talk to someone, to say out loud what I had found, what I feared. Without really thinking it through, I was grabbing my jumper and moving to the front door. Ignoring Nick's rules for once, I didn't put my coat on or set the alarm – it was so close – but as soon as I stepped out, just the key jammed in my pocket, I felt the cold air bite into me. I dashed across the narrow road, looking left and right like Nick always nagged me to do, and for a split second I teetered on an icy patch, righting myself. I could just imagine what Nick would say if I had another fall.

As I put my hand up to Nora's door, I heard a noise nearby, further down the lane near the ruins of Holly Cottage. A growl or a howl, some kind of animal maybe. Very conscious of the darkness closing around me, I knocked. Nothing. A shiver ran through me, and I felt madness rise inside me. This was crazy. I had to speak to another human, and it couldn't be Nick. Where was she? I'd never known her to go out, except on our walks. Terrible doubts spiralled in my head. *Eleanor*. No, no, it couldn't be.

I remembered our discussion one day before setting out on a walk. Nora slipping her key under a plant pot, querying why I always set the alarm. People didn't lock their doors here, that was what Gavin the estate agent had said when we first saw the place. But Nick hadn't subscribed to that; instead he'd installed the most expensive lock system money could buy. I hadn't wondered why at the time. To keep people out, or to keep me in? Telling myself I was just checking something, I felt around under the pot, my fingers scrabbling in soil until I found the solid shape of the key. Then I turned it in the lock and I was inside Nora's house. Once in there in the quiet, I could hear my own breath panting, the beat of my heart.

'Nora?'

No answer, and all her lights were off. I should have left right then, I knew. But something made me stay. Maybe it was because I knew so little about my friend, when my life was an open book to her. She'd never shown me a picture of her husband, or told me anything about her own family, where she'd grown up. What if she came home and found me? I'd make up some excuse about thinking I'd seen a light in the house, I'd been worried about burglars. It was dark, and I realised what a musty smell this cottage had. Not like ours, which had been gutted to a shell. Maybe there was something indecent about that, buying up what had been a damp labourer's cottage, full of TB and mould, and making it into a gleaming middle-class palace. What had we done? Why had we ever come here?

I stepped into Nora's living room. It all screamed *widow*, as if she was forty years older than she was. Reading glasses folded on top of a book. A single mug rinsed and laid neatly on the draining rack. And the smell – damp. Hopelessness. In the living room I spun around in a circle, not sure what I was looking for. Holding a breath in my mouth, I moved up the stairs with their old worn carpet, and turned the handle of her bedroom door, thinking too late about fingerprints. Ridiculous. She'd never even know I'd been here, and even if she did find out, I could easily explain. Inside there was a single bed, like a nun's, the plain white bedspread pulled tight. A few toiletries and a hairbrush full of grey hairs on the dressing table. It made me shudder. Nora wasn't so much older than me, and I still thought of myself as young.

In the drawer of the bedside table was another book, hand cream – I recognised the brand name as an expensive one Claudia had once bought me for my birthday, which I'd promptly lost on the Tube while coming home drunk. The only other thing was a framed photo, in a heavy old-fashioned silver frame. I picked it up, held it to the meagre light from the window. Out in the country, we didn't get much artificial illumination. I hadn't understood what true darkness was until we came here. As the moon passed over the window, I saw what the picture was. A younger Nora, with long black shiny hair, bare shoulders in a white lace dress. A wedding-day shot. Her face blazing with love and joy. And the man behind her, in the black suit and white shirt, his hands sliding along her bare arms – well, that was you.

I heard a noise outside, and stumbled back, jarring my wrist against the door frame. Someone was coming.

Nora

I had learned a lot about Nick Thomas over the last few days of stalking him, and I drove home feeling invigorated. I had even bought myself a little present, so much was I enjoying my new hobby. It had been a surprising thrill, to watch him from so close and not get caught, follow him on his daily trips to the same café, and to a loud, techno-filled gym on the high street after work, and even as he walked around the nearby deer park with the trench-coat woman, coffees in hands. He had a new phone already; I saw him checking it as he waited for a turmeric latte, whatever that was. From the phone I'd taken, I'd learned that he spied on Suzi, watched her every move via cameras and Find My Friends. That he had some kind of spyware on her phone and laptop, noting every keystroke she made – the internet told me this was easy to buy, not even expensive, and I wondered if things would have been different had I known that sooner, had I used it on my husband. I learned that Nick could also control the temperature of the house, the music that played, the code to the door lock. He could leave her out on the road if he wanted to, freezing on the desolate highway, and he was notified every time the door was set or disarmed, so he knew exactly when she entered and left the house. As I drove home, avoiding the piles of slush on the roads, I turned it over in my head like an enjoyable challenge. How could I use this new-found knowledge to get what I wanted most of all? I should warn Suzi that Nick would find out whatever she was up to. But how to explain how I knew that?

When I got home that night, Ivy Cottage looked dark and uninviting. Willow Cottage was similarly unlit, and I wondered if she was out, and if so where she was. Up to no good, most likely. I bent down to the plant pot where I hid my key and felt a press of depression all over me – despite myself, I had enjoyed being in town, among people and lights and music. Perhaps it had been a mistake to come out here to live, to the silence, the smell of damp that always greeted me in the cheerless cottage. The key was not there. My fingers scrabbled in soil. To my confusion, I saw that it was in the door already, which was unlocked. Had I left it like this, distracted by my new project? Inside was dark and sad, no one home waiting for me, no lights turned on or food in the oven.

But it wasn't true that no one was there. As I reached for the light switch, a hand closed over my wrist. And a voice said my name.

'*Elle.*'

PART THREE

Alison

FEBRUARY – Two Months Later

The woman who opened the door of Ivy Cottage looked tired and lined, though Alison thought she was only about forty. She resolved to start using that night cream her mum had got her for Christmas. A pointed gift if ever there was one.

When Alison asked to come in, the woman – a Nora Halscombe – stepped back. 'Of course. I saw the vans going up and down the road. Has something happened?'

Inside was dank and not very warm; Alison could feel a draught from the badly fitting window pane. 'I'm afraid a body's been found in the snow, just up the road.'

'Oh? How terrible. Would you like tea?'

'Oh, no—'

'Milk, two sugars, thanks.'

Alison glared at Tom for cutting her off. He shrugged. He'd be gagging for his afternoon caffeine fix – usually he downed at least four coffees and no fewer than two chocolate bars from the station vending machine. Alison declined a tea herself. Something about this place gave her the creeps.

Nora twittered about, setting down a bottle of milk with bits floating in it. Alison smirked at Tom.

'Mrs Halscombe – is it Mrs?'

'Ms,' she said, with surprising firmness.

'Sorry. Ms. I need to ask if you've seen anything suspicious. A vehicle behaving strangely, perhaps.' They were working on the assumption that the body might have been flung from a van or car, or perhaps a pedestrian had been hit while walking. How else would it end up here, on this little-used stretch of country lane?

'No, nothing like that. Poor thing. Was it a man or woman?'

Alison glanced at Tom. Was that a telling question?

'I can't say right now. Ms Halscombe – can I ask about your neighbours? Nicholas and Suzanne Thomas, is that right?'

'He's Thomas. She's Matthews. They're married, but – you know how some people are.'

'I see.' Alison made a note, as Tom slurped his tea, apparently unperturbed by the on-the-turn milk. 'Do you know if they're away? It doesn't look like anyone's at home. There's post piled up in the doorway. On holiday, perhaps?'

Nora frowned. She hadn't made tea for herself, and her cracked hands rubbed over each other anxiously. 'I wouldn't know, I'm afraid. We're not very close.'

'Really? Only the three of you out here?'

'He works a lot. I see Suzi sometimes, to say hello.'

It was frustrating. They already knew that Nick Thomas had not returned to work at the local council after the Christmas holidays, that he had taken a considerable chunk of sick leave in the weeks leading up to it, and that colleagues believed him to be still ill with a serious flu, then post-viral fatigue.

As for the wife, she seemed to go nowhere and see no one. They were following up leads with her mother, who appeared to be on a round-the-world cruise and not contactable.

'I'm sorry I can't help more. I do hope you find who it is,' said Nora, seeing them to the door. As they did, Alison jumped at a sudden noise. A baby. It sounded like a baby crying.

'Oh, sorry.' Nora smiled, her face softening. 'Excuse me, I have to get her.'

The cold air hit Alison as they stepped outside, like a bucket of freezing water being chucked at her.

'Didn't look the type to have a baby,' Tom remarked. 'Isn't she too old, like?'

'You can have them at fifty these days,' Alison scolded. 'Come on. Let's go back to the station, we're not getting anywhere here.'

Eleanor

December

We always think of names as fixed, immutable. I remember that man in *The Crucible*, shouting about his name being all he has, going to his death for it. But it's not true. We can all wear many names throughout our lives. For a woman, it's easy – just get married, subsume your old self, then start using a nickname, and before you know it you're a different person entirely.

I'd been called by different labels in my life. My mother named me *Eleanor*, a stark cool name, like the woman she wanted me to be. When I escaped – when I lost her – I became *Elle*, a light-hearted fun name. For concerts, I was *Elena Vetriano*, a made-up name I'd taken from an Italian street, fitting for the dark-haired beauty I'd become, pretending I was from somewhere more exotic than the English countryside. Artists, writers, they get away with having aliases, whereas for other people it's seen as shifty. My husband called me Elle too. Elle-belle. These days, I called myself Nora Halscombe. My mother's surname. Not the one I was born with, but yet another incarnation of me. I was still figuring out who Nora was, what she was capable of. How far she would go.

When I first found that lip balm in the remnants from my husband's car, followed by the double whammy of learning that not only had he spent all my money over the years, he was also not a doctor, indeed had never been a doctor, I felt hot and cold all over. I was shaking. For a long time I couldn't figure out what emotion I was feeling – rage? Shock? Jealousy?

I think what I felt was relief. Finally, I had someone to blame. I could not bring myself to blame him, even knowing I'd been right all along, that there was someone else. He was gone, and the loss eclipsed everything else I might feel for him. I would have given my right arm to have him back, even knowing he wasn't faithful. But now I had an explanation for how he could veer off the road on a cloudless day. Of course – he hadn't been alone. The woman had been with him, and somehow she'd caused this to happen. I had looked and looked at the stretch of road he died on, staring at it on Google Maps for hours, and there was nothing for miles before it, just a country road with no pavement. Fields. She must have been in the car when it happened. That meant she had likely run from the scene. Maybe if she'd called an ambulance, he could have been saved. Maybe he would still be here with me. She was a criminal, this woman, and she'd betrayed her own husband (I was sure she was married too, much safer that way) and widowed me. I was determined I would find her, and make her suffer like I was suffering.

But how did you find a ghost? I knew nothing. No name, no description, nothing. Just that she owned a sticky tube of cheap lip balm, the kind you could buy in any high-street chemist. There wasn't even anyone I could ask, apart from Conway, who I certainly wouldn't. The 'guys' from the hospital hadn't even come to Patrick's funeral, for all the nights he spent drinking with them.

Then I realised – of course, that had been a lie too. Those were the times he was with *her*. Even when I thought I knew it all, there were still things I'd deceived myself about.

Something I had learned early on, after what happened in my teens, the fire and Uplands and my escape from it, my reinvention of myself, was that money could fix almost everything. I knew he would have used his phone to contact her. He wouldn't have had a whole different one – he liked to message her while I was there, in the next room serving up dinner. I remembered the curve of his smile as I watched him, the risk of it all.

This was the beginning of my digital education, and I discovered a whole world my husband had kept from me. I learned that there were ways into even locked phones, hacks and tricks and codes. Patrick's was tied to his Gmail account, and he had left that logged in on the home computer, which I knew the password to, though I only used it to order shopping online. The Gmail account itself was blameless – nothing but circulars, advertisements and electronic receipts, and it struck me again how impersonal his life had been. Through the account, I was able to reset the lock screen on the phone. It must happen a lot nowadays, when so much of our lives is digital, locked up behind passwords. I also didn't know the code for the air conditioning, or to adjust the alarm settings or even the smart TV. Never mind wills – this is what we should write down for our loved ones, in case we leave them suddenly.

Inside an hour, I had found the secret app, hidden away in a folder called 'tools', with the calculator and the pedometer and all that. It was called AirAse, something that sounded boring and technical. Instead, as another trip to Google told me, it was an app that automatically deleted all the data viewed on it, once it was clicked out of. There was no way to find what my husband had looked at. Gripping the chipped edge of the computer desk, I felt swayed by despair. How would I find this woman?

Then I had a thought. That last day, she had been in the car. That meant he must have picked her up somewhere – and there was a good chance he would have called or texted her, to arrange it. Maybe he hadn't got round to deleting the phone history before the accident, if he was driving. I went through the list of numbers with trembling hands. What if she answered, and I found myself speaking to her, this woman? I would fake a wrong number, though I didn't know if I might be overwhelmed by rage. I had to try at least.

The first thing I saw was that he'd made a lot of calls that day – unusual. Like most people, he mainly used his phone for texting or the internet. One of the mobile numbers went dead – abandoned. Another opened with a blare of noise, like it was a warehouse or market stall or something, then went dead when I said hello. The last – made just an hour before the accident – went to voicemail. *Hello, this is Suzi Matthews. We've no reception at the new place, so please leave a message!*

Suzi. Suzi Matthews. An upbeat, husky voice, with a tinge of Midland vowels. This was her, I was sure. The woman who had left you to die.

◆ ◆ ◆

She'd given me a clue herself in the voicemail message. The new place, she'd said. That meant she had recently moved – and we, she'd said *we*, so she was likely married, as I'd imagined. Again, by paying a bit of money, it would be an easy matter to look Suzi up on the Land Registry website. So that's what I did. I wasn't sure if it was Susie or Suzy or Susan or Suzanne (the latter, as I learned), and

I also learned the name of her husband. Nicholas Thomas. When I saw the address, isolated, receptionless, likely to get snowed in, I knew it was meant to be. And there was a cottage for rent right next door. All I had to do was give up my house, the one I'd lived in with him, and since I could no longer afford it anyway, that was not a hard choice.

A few weeks later, after I locked up the house, I drove to the graveyard. The stone was still so clean and fresh, sparkling with granite chips. It was obscene, really. *Beloved husband.* Not father. *He'll never be that now*, I thought. I left a cheap bouquet of flowers, dyed chrysanthemums in plastic wrap – I couldn't afford the good florist any more, the one with crackling brown paper and twine and fat dewy rosebuds – and then I went.

My plan at that point was to crush Suzi. Hurt her, maybe physically, certainly mentally. To ruin her life in every possible way. Not by telling her husband – that would be too easy. But by forcing her into ruining it herself.

I hadn't counted on two things. First, that she was pregnant, walking about brazenly with a bump under a jumper I recognised as Patrick's; I had bought it for him. I assumed it was Patrick's child, and she had hinted herself that she thought so. The idea of that was dizzying. He was gone, but his child had been left behind, like an unexpected gift. A little girl or boy with his dark hair and blue eyes, just as I had pictured all those years, in the pastel-shaded nursery I had ready and waiting. His baby. If I broke Suzi entirely, blew her life to pieces, I might lose my chance to be near this child when it came. To hold it in my arms. The thought crept in: maybe Suzi wouldn't even want it. Her dead lover's baby, an accident. Why would she? When I got to know her, that thought strengthened, came to life. Suzi was not maternal. She was disorganised, chaotic, unhappy. Their house, for all its mod cons, was a terrible place to raise a child. So I kept watching, and the thought kept growing.

The other thing I had not counted on was that I would feel sorry for her. What a mess she'd got herself into, saddled with that controlling, passive-aggressive husband, so worn down that she thought she couldn't leave. Not even knowing Patrick was dead, so likely she thought she'd been ghosted, as the teenagers said. Dumped, and pregnant. I knew how it was to have someone worry away at you, telling you you're crazy, you're no good, you're defective. So once I was installed as her helpful new neighbour and confidante, I made a new plan. To investigate Nick Thomas and find out what skeletons he had lurking in his past. To encourage Suzi to strike out alone, before the baby came. Then to wait until the child was born, and make sure I kept it with me, for ever.

When someone grabbed my hand in my cottage that night, I screamed. I flailed. 'Get out of my house! Get out!'

'Calm down, Elle,' said a voice close to my ear. 'Don't make a fuss. I just want to talk.'

I fumbled the switch, and saw who it was blinking in the harsh light. James Conway. I recognised his smell of stale alcohol. 'What the hell are you doing here?'

Suzi

With everything that had happened so far, it shouldn't have been a shock that I was totally in the dark. But still, I struggled to believe what I'd seen with my own eyes – that Nora, my new friend, the confidante I'd shared everything with, was your wife. Your widow. Eleanor. Nora. The same person. *No*, my brain said. *It can't be*. It must be a mistake. Why had she come here? To hurt me, clearly. To ruin me. Oh God! What was she planning? She knew I had slept with her husband, that I was maybe pregnant with his child. I couldn't stop shaking at the thought, like a bucket of cold water over my head. All the times I'd wondered if it would really be so bad if your wife knew, and here I had my answer – yes, it was awful. I was going to lose everything. Nick would find out. She might hurt me, hurt the baby. And worst of all – I would deserve it. I had done this, cold-bloodedly slept with her husband, over and over. But if she knew about the affair, why hadn't she acted yet? What was her plan? Why were the three of us, me and her and Nick, still living in this limbo?

When I heard someone arriving at Nora's house, bumbling round the back garden, testing the door, I managed to get out the front and across the road in the dark. I didn't know who it was, and was too frightened to look. There was no car that I could see. I got inside my house and stood there in darkness for a while, shaking with adrenaline, fear, shock, all of it. Nora. Eleanor. Your wife was my next-door neighbour. It was insane. What did she *want*?

I didn't know what to do. Nick would be back from work soon, and I couldn't explain why I was pacing up and down in the dark. Perhaps about ten minutes had gone by when I saw Nora's car draw up – so it wasn't her who'd interrupted me. I wondered who – ridiculous if it really had been a burglar, given the excuse I'd planned to use if she caught me in her house. I saw her glance towards my windows and I ducked, absurdly, though she couldn't have seen me without lights. Nora, who'd been in my house, whose house I had been in, who I'd walked with in the deserted country-side, was now a figure of terror. I found myself thinking of the dead rabbit. The words in the snow, the moment I'd fallen and seen her hesitate before helping me up. But then the strange music in my house – how could she be doing that?

I didn't know who to turn to. Claudia had been clear she couldn't or wouldn't help, and I couldn't face telling my mother. I could only think of one person to turn to, a virtual stranger, but one who had been kind. One who had also been a victim of yours, in a way. Maybe he would be able to help.

The phone kept ringing. Words ran through my head. *This will sound mad . . . Sorry to bother you but . . . I think someone's stalking me.*

'Hello?' My voice was too high. 'Dr Holt?'

'Speaking.' His tone was warm but harried. I was amazed he answered his own phone; my usual experience of trying to contact anyone in the NHS was a Kafkaesque labyrinth of ringing-out extensions.

'I came to see you the other day. I – I said my name was Nora.'

He seemed to remember right away. 'Oh yes, the friend of Patrick Sullivan's, my alter ego.'

It was so strange, that. Why would you, a finance clerk, even have been at a medical conference? It made no sense. Had you been trolling for sex? Or something else? 'I was thinking . . . it just seemed weird, that he said he was you.'

'I know. That's the thing, he'd have been the one to make the bookings for the conference in the first place. And I never said I was going, I'm sure of that. Also, there's – well, I don't quite know what's going on, but there's some kind of departmental inquiry going on right now. Missing chunks of budget, that sort of thing, which he would have been in charge of. Nora—'

I interrupted him. 'I'm sorry, that's not my real name. It's Suzi.'

He paused. 'OK.'

'I'm sorry,' I said miserably. 'I can explain. Do you think you could meet me for a coffee, maybe?' It was dangerous, of course. But I had to. You had lied to me, obviously, about a lot of things. This man was a link to your real life, and to Dr Conway, who clearly knew something of what had happened between us. You had once said that affair management was like filling a condom with water and looking for leaks. Dr Conway was a potential leak, perhaps the only person who could link me to a dead man in Surrey. I could at least find out how much he knew – perhaps even learn what the hell was going on in my life.

'Alright,' he said. He had a nice voice, Dr Andrew Holt. Warm and guileless, the way yours had never been. We made an arrangement to meet in Guildford the next day – I'd just have to figure out a way to get there again. I hung up, testing myself for guilt, finding less than I would have thought. Perhaps everyone has a limit. Or maybe emotions have a hierarchy, and right now I was filled with fear – jittery, mind-numbing fear.

The noise of a car outside. Nick? I ran to the window but saw nothing, just the sound of an engine fading into the distance. Perhaps Nora's visitor had parked down the road, where I used to wait for you. There was a light on in her house now, burning behind pulled curtains. I wondered if she was standing behind it, watching me as I was watching her.

Eleanor

'What are you doing here?' I said again, wrenching myself free of Conway.

I saw he had helped himself to the small bottle of brandy I kept in the kitchen cupboard for shock, and my disgust for him rose. Imagine having so little self-control. But how had he found me out here?

'You skedaddled,' he said, face twisting in a horrible smile. 'One minute it was the funeral, next you were selling up and shipping out. No forwarding address for friends. Lucky for me you gave it to the hospital.'

My heart sank. He was right. Eddie had contacted them and updated the records for Patrick's pension; meagre as it was, I needed the small amount of money it would bring in. Conway must have got into the system. I stepped away from him, sickened by the touch of his hand on my skin. 'Well, you found me. What do you want?'

'What do I want? Let's see. The money your husband borrowed from me?'

'You've no proof of that.' I took off my coat and boots, trying to show that this was my place, my home. He had no business being here.

'Don't I?' He came closer again. A man with no concept of physical space, and the idea that he had access to anaesthesia made me want to vomit. 'We can sort this out nicely. All you have to do is pay me and I'll disappear.'

'Why would I do that? You can't do anything to us now. Patrick is dead. He's dead and there's not much more I care to lose.'

'What if I tell Missy across the road who you are?'

I blinked. I hadn't even imagined he knew about Suzi.

'That Paddy's baby in her belly, is it?' Another hit for him. He knew much more than I could have thought. Perhaps Patrick had told him? I imagined him speaking tenderly of Suzi, and my heart spasmed.

'Of course not. Look, blackmail is a crime. If you leave now I won't tell the police.'

He laughed. 'You, go to the police? Tell 'em who you really are? I don't think so, *Nora*.'

I paused for a moment, working out my next move like a chess player. 'How much did he owe you?'

'Twenty k.' I highly doubted it would be that much, even if he had borrowed some. But Conway had me at a disadvantage. One word to Suzi about who I was and she'd bolt, taking her baby with her. Patrick's baby.

'You'll have to give me time to get it,' I said, as calmly as I could. 'Patrick left me almost nothing, you know.'

'Cleared you out, I hear. But there must be some. After your family died in that fire, so sad, poor little Eleanor! What a coincidence, she's alive and safe and the rest are – poof! And your swanky piano career. There must be cash.'

Ellie. Ellie, I'm scared! A white face at a window.

I had to stay calm. He couldn't know about that. No one did. 'He spent it all,' I said, the truth making me savage. 'He ruined me,

James. I'm sorry if he did the same to you, but what can I do about it? The money is gone. And he's dead, he hit a tree and died, so I can hardly make him give it back.'

Conway gave me a horrible, sly smile. I hated him in that moment. If I'd had something heavy to hand I would have bashed him over the head with it. 'You really believe that, do you?'

'W-what?' I stammered.

'Think about it. He's a good driver, right?' The present tense again. I wanted to kill him for it. 'Got a good, strong car, costs a bloody fortune. But he drives into a tree on a quiet road? And you thought it was an accident? Wake up, love.'

I felt sick, the room lurching. 'What do you mean? Tell me. Tell me what you know!'

'Money first.' He drained his glass of my brandy, and I knew I would throw it away after he left. 'Get it and I'll tell you the truth about your husband. Paddy-Sean-Andrew, whatever his name is. You don't know the half of it, love.' Andrew? What did he mean?

'Tell me right this minute what you mean, or I'll go to the police.' I tried to hold it together. I needed to know what he knew. My head was spinning, and I could feel it leaking away, all the control I'd carefully taken back, all the pressure I brought down on my memories, squashing them flat. My husband, with another woman. A house, roaring up in flames.

'Nah, you won't. Come to mine – I'll give you till Friday. Flat 7, Hereford Gardens, in Guildford. I'll be there after eight.' And he gave me a horrible pointy-finger sign, like he was shooting a gun, and stepped back towards the door. 'Bloody nightmare finding this place, isn't it? Bit more snow and you'll be stuck down here.' I wondered why I hadn't seen his car. He must have parked it up the road, around the bend. And I had walked right into his trap.

At the sound of the door shutting, relief flowed through me. That awful man was gone. I was alone. I could think, breathe, get a hold of myself. But what did he mean? Was he saying there was more to Patrick's accident than I thought? I had wondered the same. How could he crash like that, on an empty road? It made no sense. What did Conway know?

Suzi

Christmas drew ever closer. The lights and noise of town, they dazzled me as I walked through the centre of Guildford once again. I'd had enough money hoarded to pay for this trip without asking Nick, and even that small taste of freedom made me realise how trapped I was. I wandered from shop to shop, drunk on lights and music and *things*. The sheer overwhelming tide of stuff we were supposed to want or need. I'd always loved this time of year, and had even fantasised about a country cottage with holly round the door, twinkling lights in the eaves, candles in every window. Snow piled up round the gables. Now I had it, and the reality was cold and isolating. I couldn't imagine Nick and I on Christmas morning, exchanging gifts, clinking glasses (non-alcoholic for me; the fact of it being Christmas would not mean I could have a sip of champagne). And in later years, a child leaping on to our bed, hyper with excitement. I just couldn't picture it. Maybe fear was clouding the future. One word from Nora and I'd lose everything. But why hadn't she said anything yet? Why become friends with me, encourage me to talk about how much I'd loved you? I didn't understand what her plan was, and it scared me. Was it even her behind the strange happenings, the music, the dead rabbit?

I'd barely slept the night before, thinking of Nora across the road from me. Your wife. A large part of me didn't really believe it. I was learning that I was good at that, denial.

◆ ◆ ◆

Dr Holt was early, dressed in jeans and a nice navy shirt, the sleeves rolled up. He stood when I came into the Costa Coffee, pulled a chair out for me. Polite. 'Hello again.'

'Hi. Sorry that last time we met I was . . . well, a total mess.'

He waved it away. 'You'd had a shock. I'm just sorry you had to find out that way.' He asked what I'd like to drink, and despite my protests went to get it for me. I chose something laden with sugar and spices, a bucket of festive joy, hoping some of it might creep into my cold winter bones. I watched him chat with the young barista, the open friendliness of the doctor's face. If only I was married to a man like that. Not one like Nick, so suspicious and critical. Or you, as slippery as a water snake.

'Thank you.' I drank too fast, burning my tongue, a flood of sweet chocolate filling my mouth.

'So what did you want to talk to me about?' he asked.

I didn't know where to begin. 'It was just – it was so weird, wasn't it? Sean – Patrick, I mean – using your name like that.'

He toyed with the dregs of a ginger-spice latte. 'It seemed strange to me, yeah. And potentially, very dangerous for my career, if someone's going around saying they're me. I mean, I'm known in the field. I'm surprised no one questioned him, at the conference.'

'It's possible he didn't go to any of it,' I admitted. I hadn't wanted to think it, but a conference was the perfect place to pick up women. Which meant, what – I wasn't special? You'd done it before?

I didn't want to think about that.

'Oh?' He cocked his head at me, his warm brown eyes fixed on mine, and I was drowned with shame again for what I'd done, the ease with which I'd jumped into bed with you. What had I been thinking? What blank misery had driven me to do it? 'Suzi, listen – I'm not judging at all. You and him – you were close?'

I hesitated, then nodded.

'But you're married.' His voice was gentle, glancing at my ring finger, the gold biting into the swollen flesh.

'Yes.'

'Alright. Do you know if . . . did you get the sense he regularly said he was me? It's true I am a little scatty. It's possible I just haven't noticed before.'

'Maybe. He was very keen to explain he was a doctor. Successful.'

'Well, that was nice of him,' muttered Dr Holt, frowning. 'And – I'm sorry to ask you this, Suzi – do you know if he'd . . . had other friends before? Like you?'

Had you had affairs before, he meant. And I thought how good you had been at it, knowing all the tricks, the ways to get caught. 'I think so,' I said. Tears came to my eyes, and I felt a spurt of hot embarrassment. 'I'm sorry.' So stupid. How could I be upset, when you'd never been mine to begin with?

Some men panic when women cry. He wasn't one of those. He took a packet of Kleenex from his jacket pocket, and passed me one, pressing my hand as he did. The gentleness made me cry even harder. 'Poor you. What a thing to happen.'

'It's my own fault. I'm a cheater. A liar.' I scrunched the tissue miserably in my fist. 'I even lied about my name. You must think I'm awful.' Was I just as bad as you?

He was quiet for a moment. 'Suzi, you see all sorts in my job. I've kind of come to realise that we're all just doing the best we can. No one really means to mess up, or hurt other people.'

I had to say what was really worrying me, crazy as it would seem. 'Dr Holt . . . this is going to sound really weird, but I think his wife – Patrick's wife – she might be someone I know. I mean, this woman rented the house next door to us a while ago. We became friends.' I spilled out the story of finding the pill packet in your house, seeing your picture in Nora's bedroom. The weird things that were happening. He watched me patiently, trying to understand.

'You're sure it's not just a similar name, someone who looked like him?'

'I know how it sounds. I know I seem . . .' I didn't want to say the word. I thought about my visit to my GP, the fact it was now on record that I'd been hallucinating, imagining things. 'I . . . maybe it's nothing.'

He was looking at me with concern. 'Would someone really do that? Move next door to you?'

'I don't know. I know it sounds insane.' I was almost doubting myself now. Had it really been your picture in her house? It was dark, and I wasn't in my most rational mind. Was it really such strong evidence? *Nora* and *Eleanor* – were those even the same name?

'You should go to the police, if you're worried.'

I stared down at my dirty cup. I couldn't go to the police – that would be admitting I'd been in your car that day. I was trapped.

He hesitated. 'Suzi . . . the stuff with your burglar alarm, the music. Is your husband . . .? I'm so sorry to ask this, but I have a duty of care. You seem scared. And this . . .' Gently, he touched my wrist, the shading of the bruise where I'd caught it against Nora's door, and instinctively I jumped back, drew it into the sleeve of my coat. What if Nick somehow found out I was here in a café with an attractive man, letting him touch my hand? But all I could see

191

in his eyes was concern. 'Are you sure there's not something else going on?'

'Oh no, nothing like that. He'd never lay a hand on me.' But I *was* scared, wasn't I? So much that I could hardly sit still, or focus on a task for more than five minutes. I was afraid of Nick finding out, yes, but I wasn't actually afraid of him. Was I?

'Just because someone doesn't hit you, it doesn't mean you can't be scared.' I had a feeling he'd been trained in this, how to support women who were in abusive relationships. But I wasn't. Just an unhappy one. 'This is going to seem really awkward, but . . . I brought something with me.' He slid a shiny pamphlet over the table, with the NHS logo on it. *Understanding Coercive Control.* A stock photo of a crying woman, locked in a bathroom, while a man shouted at her from outside. 'Something about you at the hospital that day. You were just so jumpy. And pregnancy is the riskiest time for domestic violence.'

I blinked. 'Oh, it's not . . .' I trailed off. Nick never shouted, never raised his fists or his voice. But all the same I was under his control. I couldn't go places or see people without him knowing. He knew what I ate, when I slept, when I left the house. He seemed to know everywhere I went, as if each step was under his scrutiny.

Dr Holt's face twisted, and I could tell he was about to say something difficult. 'I get it, Suzi. I know it doesn't always look like it's meant to. Bruises, black eyes. But it can be just as bad. That case just last week in Medway, where the guy strangled his wife. Everyone said what a nice person he was, how much he cared for his family.'

I eyed the pamphlet. I could hardly take that home with me; Nick would want to know where I'd got it. 'Thank you,' I said finally. 'I'll think about it.' It was true I might need to run away, if Nora was who I thought she was.

He checked his watch. 'Oh bugger, I'm late for a clinic. I mean it, Suzi – if you need help, there are things we can do. I'll come to the police with you, tell them about this Nora woman, if you're really worried.' I could tell he didn't believe me. He thought I was in denial, ignoring the real problem in my life. 'Can I take your number at least, in case I find out more about Patrick?'

I hesitated. How would I explain it to Nick, another strange man calling me? But he was a doctor. He would help me. 'OK. Give me yours too,' I said. I passed him my phone to key it in, then dialled it briefly so he'd have my number. This was so risky.

'Please,' he said, passing it back. 'Anything you need. Just call.'

I thought about it for a second – leaving my home, all my things, bunking down in some hostel full of terrified women. Having my baby somewhere like that. I knew that I wouldn't do anything, not yet. What was I waiting for? For things to get better, maybe. Hope was a dangerous thing. It could keep you going long after any realistic person would have given up and run. He left first, looking back at me anxiously, and I picked up my phone and saved his number under *Andrea H*, the way you had taught me to do. Another deception, another step away from Nick and I ever working things out. As I went, I dropped the leaflet into a recycling bin.

Wearily, I trailed home. Another expensive taxi, my stash almost gone. As I paid the driver, and got out into the dark cold of the country lane, snow still lying in the verges, I saw a lamp on in Nora's house. I felt an absurd loneliness as the car disappeared up the road, its lights quickly swallowed in the dark. I stood there for a moment, deciding. Nora was behind the blank windows of Ivy Cottage. She knew who I was. She didn't know I also knew who she was. Should I confront her, or leave things as they were? Figure out an escape plan first?

I found myself edging towards her house. Why, I didn't know. What would I even say? *I'm sorry*, or *how dare you*, or *leave me alone, you jealous hag*? Nothing was right. As I grew closer, I could hear music seeping from the house, into the stillness of the lane. It was beautiful – a lullaby, like the one that had been playing in my house that day. It was so lovely I thought it must be a recording, but I looked in and saw, to my surprise, that Nora was playing an upright piano, which definitely had not been there the day before. I could see her through the window, as the curtain wasn't pulled. The small, damp room actually looked cosy with the addition of a table lamp and a lit candle, and Nora was playing with her eyes closed, a smile on her face. Her fingers, gnarled and raw from gardening, drifted over the keys, and for a moment I realised how little I knew of her. Nothing, really, and yet I'd opened my heart to her, shared all my secrets. I was so stupid.

She saw me. I ducked back, but it was too late, and she was walking to the door. Pure panic surged in my veins, but then she opened it and I saw she was smiling, same as she always was. 'Suzi!'

'Oh, sorry, I just heard the music,' I babbled. 'I didn't know you played.'

'Oh yes. In fact, I played professionally.'

'I can tell. It was beautiful.' I was edging away.

'I hadn't played for years, but then I just thought – why not get a piano again? They don't cost much, second-hand. It was delivered today. Would you like to come in?'

Did she know? Had I knocked something over, or left some sign that I'd been in her house? I thought of the pills I'd found, and realised I was trembling. I tried to keep my voice light. 'Oh, no, I should get dinner started.'

She tutted. 'Nick better start helping more. You can't be running about when you're in your third trimester, can you?' Something about it sounded threatening, but I couldn't put my finger on what.

'I, uh, yes, I'll tell him. Goodnight, Nora.'

'Goodnight.'

I almost ran across the road, having utterly failed to confront her, doubting all my judgement and feelings and sense. Doubting everything.

When you and I were together, those few months, the world seemed bright. Summer, and birds in the trees, and the deep-belly thrill of your emails popping into our secret account. The possibility that life could be different.

This was the other side of all that. The hangover after the party, the recession after a boom. Me at home, pregnant and terrified, waiting for the police to come, waiting for Nora to strike. Now that I'd lost you, it seemed to me the hardest thing a human would ever have to face was how to live without the person their heart was tied to. Every day I had to remind my brain and body I was never going to see you again. Remind my skin it would never feel your hands again. Remind my hands they would never touch your back as you slept. *Never*. I don't think humans are really built to understand what that means. I told myself it should have been easy. All I had to do was go into my house, and shut the door, and live out the rest of my life without you.

Eleanor

Suzi had been gone all day again, and she hadn't told me why. Obscurely, I felt angry that she was still keeping secrets from me, Nora, her helpful and understanding friend. Watching her cross the road to Willow Cottage, I pulled my laptop towards me. I was glad I'd bought it, despite the inroads it had made into my depleted finances. It certainly made all my activities easier. It was almost like a job these days, doing my research.

Conway's visit had thrown me. He too had become a threat, not just to me but to Suzi, and therefore to the baby. I couldn't let that happen. I'd already spent too much time picturing myself with it. Patrick's child. Conway had to be stopped, one way or another. My mind was consumed by what he'd hinted. What did he mean? That there was something more to Patrick's death, that it was deliberate somehow? Suicide – or even murder? But who would want to kill him? I had to know. Conway's insinuations had taken root in me, squirming like bulbs in winter soil, rootling towards the light. Was it possible he meant something else? But no, that was insane. I had to cling on to the truth, the reality of life, out here in the dark all alone. I had to hold myself together.

When I logged on to Facebook, I saw to my surprise that Nick's ex, Lisa Ragozzi (Italian, I thought, maybe her father's family), had replied to my message. Guardedly, she asked why I wanted to know about Nick.

It's really hard to explain, I answered, alone in my cold sitting room. Part of me felt sad that Suzi hadn't come in. I would have welcomed her warm and scatty presence, after Conway's visit. I typed, *My friend's with him and he's – it seems like he's been a bit heavy recently, you know?*

Heavy how? I could see the little dots that showed Lisa was on the other end, and felt a surge of excitement.

Oh, you know. A bit possessive, I guess? Asking where she's been, what she's up to. Not giving her money, that sort of thing. I decided to go for broke. *She's pregnant so not working. I'm really worried about the baby. It just seems – like a step up to something. You know?* I wasn't naming my fear, but Lisa would understand. Any woman would.

More dots appeared. Then disappeared. Then Lisa wrote – *I think maybe we should meet. You're right to be worried.*

Quickly, we arranged to meet in London the next day, on her lunch break (she worked in recruitment). It was possible she thought the 'friend' was actually me, but that didn't matter. It would only suit my purposes. I made myself go to bed early, ready for the following day. I would find out more about Nick, and then I would turn my attention to Conway, and deal with him.

Suzi

When Nick came back that night, it was to an unwelcoming house. I hadn't pulled the blinds or turned on the lamps or set the soft music I had ready for him most nights, and worst of all, there was no dinner waiting in the Aga. I had come straight from Nora's and gone on the computer.

Nick hovered in the doorway of my studio. 'Where were you? You didn't tell me you were going out today.'

'No.' I didn't answer his question. Why should I? And how did he know I'd been out – the alarm system, I supposed.

Nick blinked. 'Are you feeling alright?'

No, I wasn't. I was discovering that my lover, the likely father of my child, had died shortly after I'd last seen him, driving a car into a tree on a clear and dry day. Maybe my fault? And his wife, his widow, had moved in next door to me and become my friend, and she was in all likelihood out to ruin my life, sending me slowly crazy with music and lights and dead things and words in the snow. I shuddered at everything I'd told her. Damian. You. All the ways we had deceived your wife, who turned out to be the very person I was talking to. My burning question was what she would do now. Would she tell Nick? Why hadn't she already, if she knew who I was? What was Nora's plan?

'What about dinner?' Nick said, plaintive.

'I'm not very hungry. I had a massive lunch.' I knew Nick had meant I should cook dinner for him, but I didn't care. There was thrill as well as fear in pushing back on the rules, playing with fire. 'Could you shut the door? There's a draught.' After a moment, Nick went out, closing the door with a little too much force. Part of me was scared, but part of me wasn't. I was also going to cross another boundary by googling dangerous things while Nick was at home. Specifically, the background of Nora Halscombe, aka Eleanor Sullivan.

The piano had been a stroke of luck, because the first thing I found was that quiet, dowdy Nora had indeed once been a successful concert pianist. Back then, she played under the stage name Elena Vetriano. I found an old article about her in *Classic Times*, a sultry shot of her leaning over a Steinway in a red evening gown. Her hair was long and dark and shinier than a raven's wing, her full lips slightly parted. The article praised her work ethic, her technical skill, which was 'not surprising, given Ms Vetriano's tragic past, a past she transmutes into musical ecstasy for the listener'. My ears pricked up. What tragic past? So Nora had gone by at least three names that I knew of. There must be one more. There must have been a name she was known as when she was born, when this 'tragic past' occurred. But how was I going to find it? I was sure she'd have done her best to cover it up.

The door opened, and Nick came in, ostentatiously holding food on a plate, sliced and boiled carrots and a hunk of what looked like beef. I fought the urge to minimise the screen. 'I thought you might be hungry now. What are you doing?'

'Just a little research.' I moved the plate he'd brought – congealing meat, anaemic vegetables – to the edge of the desk. 'Close the door again, would you? I'm busy.'

Nick stood for a moment, radiating helpless resentment, then went, closing the door behind him. For the first time in weeks, I almost smiled.

I clicked and clicked long into the night. I read so many articles about Elena Vetriano, the young virtuoso pianist, that I felt I knew everything about her. I'd seen countless images of her pouting, haunted face, the grey eyes the same as those behind my neighbour's thick glasses. I learned that she had won awards, been the youngest British pianist to play Brahms' concerto No. 2 at the Proms, and then disappeared suddenly from the scene on her marriage. *Music's loss is love's gain*, gushed one piece, accompanied by a posed wedding shot of 'Elena' in a white lace dress. The same picture from Nora's bedroom. You stood with her, stony-faced in a tailored suit. I wondered if the magazine had paid for the wedding in exchange for these pictures. *Stunning concert pianist leaves music to wed doctor.*

But you weren't a doctor. I wondered how you had managed to fool everyone for so long. How often people actually checked something you told them as fact. What I still didn't know was Elena Vetriano's real name, her birth name. Around eleven, I heard Nick go up to bed, clomping passive-aggressively on the stairs. I didn't care. I googled pianist and Sussex, as one article had referred to her being from there. I googled *Nora pianist Sussex. Eleanor pianist Sussex.* Eventually, after going back years, I found what I was looking for. Young West Sussex pianist of the year. A picture of a pale, dark-haired girl in a plain grey dress, holding up a certificate by a grand piano that was taller than her. She looked so unhappy, her eyes wracked with some unknown pain. It was definitely Nora.

And her surname back then? Treadway. Eleanor Treadway, from Steepletops, Frimlington. A house with a name not a number. Nora's family must have been rich. There was nothing else online about her or her family.

The day had slipped away from me like something half-formed, like Christmas Day or one after a long flight. When we'd known each other, when you'd been part of my life, the days had seemed endless, golden light falling through the trees until after ten. I felt I had time, and love to spare. If I'd known how low both were running, I would have held on to you with everything I had.

Eleanor Treadway. Your wife, the faceless woman I had been jealous of for so long. I felt it was her stealing you from me. I got angry every time you emailed me secretly from the garden centre, or the house, or the shops. All I could think was how I'd never get to go to garden centres or Ikea with you. I got so used to it, checking my secret email account while Nick was paying for coffees or filling the car with petrol, shielding my phone with my hand or hair, always wanting something different than what was there. Never wanting to be where I was. It got to be an everyday pain, like walking around on a broken leg you don't even notice. A new lover is like a mirror, you see. One you can't stop gazing into. I was in a sort of daze of the senses – your smell and the feel of your muscles under the velvet of your skin, the shallow breaths you took as you gripped me, on those rare moments we were together – *Oh God, Suzi*. As if by saying my name you were saying: *It's you I choose, you and no one else*. That's what you tell yourself when you're having an affair – even though, of course, you wouldn't be there in that sterile hotel room if there weren't other people, Nick and your wife, that blank hot spot behind my eyelids I couldn't bear to look at but couldn't stop seeing. But those moments, when I managed not to think about the truth . . . it was that I missed more than anything.

I had known so little about her back then – a black-haired woman in her forties. In my head she was blowsy, anxious. In my head you needed to leave her for me. In my head she was a ghost. Now I knew who she was. So many names she had gone under, that pale intense girl in the pictures. I had to find out what had happened in her past. I had a feeling it would tell me exactly how much danger I was in.

Eleanor

It was so long since I'd been up to London I was surprised by the rush of energy I got as the train crossed Blackfriars Bridge, the Thames wide and silty below me, hundreds of people hurrying about their important lives. It reminded me that other people had jobs, and children, and worries about the strange drip in the bathroom and how to pay the gas bill. Not all this melodrama I was throwing myself into. Moving next door to my husband's mistress? What had I been thinking? I was deranged, by grief and anger and loss. But now I'd started on this path, it had taken me somewhere I didn't expect, and I had to keep going, because the life of a baby was at stake.

I met Lisa Ragozzi at a Caffè Nero near her work at Borough, and I was glad she'd chosen there, because it was cosy in an anonymous way, a constant flow of students with laptops, bewildered tourists looking at their guidebook maps upside down, and office workers whose main aim was not to interact with another human being for the thirty minutes of their break.

The first thing I saw was how pretty she was. She had rich dark hair touching the collar of her white shirt, and dark eyes, but her cheekbones were hollowed out and her legs thin and stick-like under her tights. 'Nora?' she faltered. A nervous woman. A woman someone had damaged, perhaps.

'Hello, Lisa. Thank you for meeting me.'

She was too polite to look me over, but I'd caught the micro-tell in her expression – *it can't be her*. So now she would believe it really was a friend I was asking for. Maybe she'd open up more. 'Please, sit down.'

I took my silly tall glass of coffee and sat looking at her, a pocket of silence among the background noise that washed against the walls. 'You must be thinking this is very strange.'

'Not really.' Her knuckles went white around her mint tea. No calories. 'I've always wondered if he – where he ended up. I had a little look after you messaged. He's married? That's your friend?'

I should have realised she'd do that, look him up. 'She'd go mad if she knew I talked to you. Totally in denial about it, you see.' Meaning: *Please don't contact Suzi.*

She was nodding. 'Of course. I was that way myself for so long.'

'Can you tell me about it?'

And she told me her story, staring into her cooling tea, while I drank down my mix of cream and sugar and felt ashamed. Lisa had starved herself to a saint-like purity. Maybe so a man wouldn't want her again. Maybe to hide in plain sight. She told me how she'd met Nick in her first year at Nottingham University, when he was in his second. How immediately she'd been bowled over by his attentions, when all the other boys she'd met only wanted to have fumbling sex then never talk to her in public. Bruised from a term-long affair with a rugby player, she'd found kind, attentive Nick – short, neatly built, a pleasant rather than sexy face – a lifeline. 'He took me to dinner! That was unheard of. I mean it was only Pizza Express, but still. I was so flattered. And he remembered everything I told him, the names of all my tutors, my childhood cat, all of that. Before I knew it, we were living together.'

'In a student house?'

She shook her head on its fragile neck. 'Just the two of us. Nick's father – I think he left quite a lot of money. I felt so grown-up. We even had a cleaner! But then . . .'

Ah yes. The *but then*. I wondered did it happen to everyone at some point, the moment when you realised your perfect, shiny relationship, your great love, had an underside, like turning over a stone. For me, it had been finding that lip balm from my husband's car. 'Yes?'

'He started getting jealous. I had a male project partner, we got on well, but Nick was so suspicious. He used to call me while I was out studying, thirty times an hour sometimes. And if I took a minute longer than usual to walk back from the library, say if I looked in the shops or anything, he'd want to know why. Then he stopped me going out with my friends. My friends, they weren't even party girls – just normal, hard-working students. We went to this gig and I wore . . .' She looked down again, the painful memory fogging her voice. 'I wore a corset top. They were all in at the time. And he went mad! *Who are you wearing that for, since I won't be there? Are you seeing someone else?* In the end, I changed into a T-shirt. It was just easier.'

By the end of her second year at university, Nick had Lisa never going out except to class – and he would sometimes escort her there, under the guise of protecting her from the violent streets of the city – and to the gym. 'He encouraged that,' she said, with the bitter ghost of a smile. 'He never said it but – he'd bring it up a lot. Once he read this article about how girls often gained a stone in their first year at uni.' I looked at the exposed bones of her clavicle, and wanted to do some damage to Nick. He had separated her from friends and family – even her lively Italian parents had given up calling, since Nick always answered and told them she wasn't home, which she would of course only find out about much later.

If she tried to call them he'd pout. *Why are you on the phone for so long? Aren't I your family now?*

'And he made me come off the pill,' she said, flushing. 'Sold me this whole idea, wouldn't it be lovely, have a kid young while I was still fertile. I had finals to take! Luckily it didn't happen.'

And starving yourself was quite an effective contraceptive too.

'I'm so sorry, Lisa,' I said, and I meant it. 'I hope things are better now.'

'I'm with someone.' Unconsciously, she touched her left ring finger, which was bare. 'But you don't just get over it. Something like that, it leaves scars.' She looked up. 'Your friend – he's done these same things?'

'I think so. It's been more – gradual. Subtle.' Because Suzi was a lot more spirited than this timid woman. It had taken longer, more devious means to break her. He had waited until she'd done something she was ashamed of, then whisked her away to her countryside prison. I wondered how long he'd been preparing the move before he told her.

I said goodbye to Lisa outside London Bridge, and watched her walk off on her thin little legs, a slow-burning anger for Nick deep beneath my ribcage. Somehow, over the last few weeks, it had begun to eclipse my rage at Suzi. Nick was controlling, gaslighting, contemptuous of her. And yet I couldn't even think what I used to, that I'd been lucky not to have a man like that. Because he had been like that, hadn't he? He'd convinced me I was crazy, imagining affairs. He'd lied to my face, for ten years. And he'd done other things. Stolen. Cheated. And maybe, as Conway was hinting, something even worse than that.

Suzi

First, I needed to lay some groundwork. A place to run to if and when I blew my life up. Somewhere to escape to, someone to take my side now that Nora had turned out to not be the ally I'd thought. I told Nick I was going to see my mother. I explained it away with some pregnancy mumbo jumbo. 'When you're about to be a mother yourself, you just want to be with your own. Besides, we won't see her over Christmas this year.'

He did his usual slow blink. 'Usually you fight with her. Won't that be bad for the baby?'

'That's sort of why I want to see her – I hope we can put some issues behind us, ready for her grandkid to arrive!' I did my happy, hopeful mother-to-be smile, and soon Nick was nodding, offering to book the train tickets for me. To make sure I was really going, probably. I was, in fact. And things had become pretty bad when I was voluntarily making the trip to rural Oxfordshire.

Mum lived in a small, pretty village near Oxford, the kind with an active parish hall and multiple busybodies behind expensive shutter blinds. We saw three people she knew on the drive back from the station, and she honked the horn each time and waved. I found myself thinking, *plenty of witnesses for Nick*, and I almost laughed, things were so ridiculous.

'You don't normally come on your own,' she said, manoeuvring the car into her little driveway. She lived in a two-storey Victorian red brick, attractively draped in ivy. My father had died when I was fifteen, and Mum had never remarried, despite many offers, but she did date from time to time. Sensible, cheerful relationships, mostly based on hiking holidays in Wales or wine-tasting at the parish hall. Usually with widowers or divorcees, who inevitably had children too. I wondered why she had the knack of a non-dramatic love life, while I seemed utterly incapable.

'He's working,' I said, lumbering out of the car.

'But you usually come on weekends.'

'I know. I just thought it would be quieter, on the train. And I wanted to see you before you go.' Mum was spending Christmas on a cruise with Nigel, her latest squeeze, and I was horrified to find myself jealous, at the idea of being thousands of miles from Nick, and Nora, and the mess I'd made of my life. Upstairs, the spare room was stacked with guidebooks, travel supplies, sun cream, ready to be packed.

'That's nice, dear.' But her keen eyes roamed over me, and I knew that the fine attention to detail that made her such a good lawyer might show her the truth. I wanted her to see it. I didn't know how to bring it up, so I needed her to ask.

As usual, she skilfully filled the silence between us with bustle. She made me unpack, though I'd only brought enough for one night, and had me peeling a mound of vegetables for stew, and then go through the programme for a local literary festival, ringing anything that sounded interesting. Mum only read highbrow authors, and had chastised me as a teen for 'wasting my mind on that trash' when she saw me with Agatha Christie or Jilly Cooper.

She fussed around me, pushing me to eat cake and cheese, so she could show how abstemious she was herself; Mum's usual MO, which had seen me weigh twelve stone at the age of fifteen. Finally, dinner eaten, washed up, leftovers carefully decanted into labelled Tupperware, we sat down by her small, old-fashioned TV. She put on her reading glasses and peered at the listings in the *Radio Times*. 'Now, what would you like? There's a Scandi drama I've been meaning to have a look at, or a rerun of *Bergerac*.' Mum did not do on-demand telly. I suspected she thought it was too self-indulgent; you'd take what the schedulers gave you and like it.

'Mum – I thought maybe we could talk.'

'Talk?' Her brow creased. She was so elegant still, her hair a shade edging between grey and blonde, her glasses stylish, her figure trim and slim. 'Is everything alright, dear?'

I paused. It was my moment to say, *no, not really*, but I couldn't just pour it all out. I could already picture her disappointment, the *oh, Suzanne, how could you?* Guilt again, so much guilt. I couldn't be in denial about what I'd done if I told her, said it out loud. 'Yeah. It's just – when you were having me, did Dad go a bit . . . funny? Like, over-protective?'

'Oh no, dear, your father was very gentle. He'd hardly say boo to a goose.' I remembered so little of him, every memory bulldozed aside by the force of my mother's personality. That was her moment to probe me, ask what I meant, but she didn't. I would have to carry the burden of this talk alone.

'It's just that Nick – he worries so much. He doesn't really like me going places without him, or getting upset, and he kind of monitors what I eat and drink all the time.'

She rustled the magazine. 'Someone needs to, darling. I know what you're like with the biscuits. And the wine! You haven't been drinking, have you?'

Disappointment made my fingers tingle. She was doing her best not to understand. 'Of course not. It's just – now I don't earn, I have to ask him for money, and I hate that. It means I can't go anywhere without asking. I'm so isolated out there.'

She sighed. 'I did say not to buy that place.' The old *I told you so* – could anything be less helpful when you were there, admitting you'd been wrong, begging for help?

'You did. Happy to be right?' My tone was sharp. She looked up.

'Darling, I think you're tired. Maybe an early night?'

'I'm not tired. I'm trying to talk to you, and you're just – shutting me down.'

She looked bewildered, and I realised she genuinely had no idea she did this. In her head she was a lovely, supportive, generous mother. 'I'm right here. What is it you're trying to say? You want your own money? You could always go back to work after the baby comes, commute in.'

Mum didn't know the reasons I could never go back to my old job – I would have to find another one, somehow explain the time I'd been out of work, cross my fingers for a decent reference from my old boss, Daphne, who I was sure knew exactly what had happened with Damian. Juggle work with a small baby. 'I suppose.' Even though Nick would give me his sad, baffled face if I suggested it. *But I brought us here for you.* 'I just feel really lonely. The cottage is so far from anywhere. You were right about that. And I can't get out during the day. I need a car but Nick says it's bad for the environment.' *Plus, my neighbour moved there to ruin my life.* Nora had been watching at the window when I left, her usual spot. I wondered why I hadn't found it creepy before.

She was nodding. 'Yes, that is the dilemma we all have in the countryside. Darling, are you sure this isn't just baby blues?'

'I haven't had the baby yet. That would be after.'

She thought about it. I could see her eyes flicker, not really wanting to get involved – she preferred people to pay her to unpick family messes – but seeing I was upset, that she couldn't just leave it. 'I'm sure Nick is just taking care of you. It's taken so long to get here, hasn't it? Is there anything that really worries you? Anything he's done?'

She meant had he hit me, and of course he hadn't. He just questioned my every move. He just said I was crazy when I was sure the house had got hotter, or music had begun to play, or I couldn't open the door to get out. He just didn't like me leaving the house. And why should he? He knew I had lied to him, most likely, about Damian. And I was still lying. I was spending his money chasing down another man, the one I'd cheated on him with, and now that I'd found out the truth, and learned who Nora was, I was still dashing about the country figuring out what to do. From Nick's point of view, maybe he was very much in the right. And suddenly I was so afraid that if I told my mother the truth of what I'd done, she would side with him. And I couldn't bear it. I had come here looking for an ally ahead of the coming storm, if I decided to leave Nick, if I confronted Nora and got outed as the cheater I was. I could see now my mother wasn't going to help, any more than Claudia would. I said, 'No, nothing like that. I guess I'm just finding the move hard.'

She looked so relieved. 'That'll be it, darling. And the adjustment to the country. Maybe once the baby's here you could join some mother and toddler groups, that sort of thing. Or take a class – Nigel speaks very highly of his bookbinding course.'

Clearly, she hadn't taken in the fact I had no access to a car. I hesitated. 'Mum. If I need to, can I stay with you for a bit? Me and the baby?'

She paused a fraction too long. 'Well, darling, of course you can, though your room's really full of junk now, all my sewing things and the leaflets for the campaign to save the village green. It would be a lot to move – but of course! Whatever you need!'

In other words, no.

'Thanks,' I mumbled. 'Let's go with the Scandi drama, shall we?' A bit of gloomily lit murder would suit my mood quite well.

The next day, I trailed back home. I felt thoroughly beaten. Mum had made it clear – this was my life now. Behind sealed glass and code-protected doors, raising my baby, making Nick happy. If that was even possible. The trains were slow, and it was after five when I got back. Nora's cottage was in darkness again, and it unsettled me. Before, she had always been there, and now she kept going out. Did she know I'd found out who she was? And once again, the question that had rarely left my mind since I'd learned the truth – *what the hell does she want?*

Nick was there, of course, ready to find fault. He was at the kitchen table, surrounded by pictures of Poppet, and I saw that he was printing up a new poster. Another thing that was my fault.

'Sorry,' I said, too weary to even make excuses. 'I just . . . it took a while. I got groceries.'

Nick got up, taking the bag of shopping I'd returned with. As I trailed round the aisles of the supermarket, I'd found myself wondering would I even be there to finish the sugar-free granola, the jar of peanut butter. If I would have escaped by then. But where to? Not to my mother's, clearly. Nick slammed the door of the cupboard. 'I mean, it's not much to ask, is it? I work all day, and when I come back I want to find the house warm and welcoming, the dinner on.'

I gaped at him. 'You came back before five o'clock! You're telling me you wanted to eat dinner then?'

Another slam. 'I want a wife who's here waiting for me.'

'I'm here every day! Where else would I go? I was at my mum's.'

He stood with his hands on the counter, his back to me. I could feel him reconfiguring his argument, as if he knew he was being unreasonable, even within the template of unreasonability we lived by these days. 'I just worry about you. You're pregnant, and it's such a long journey.'

'You were the one who brought me here.' I snatched up the rest of the groceries, a packet of noodles, a jar of chia seeds, which were supposed to be good for me, and shoved them into a cupboard. I knew that Nick would rearrange them later on, into an order he preferred.

He frowned. 'Please don't speak to me like that, Suzi.' A warning. I'd gone too far. 'And are we going to have any dinner, do you think? I'm starving, and I'm sure the baby is too.'

I waited a few seconds until I knew I could speak without screaming. Now was not the time to kick my life to pieces, not before I knew exactly what Nora was up to. 'Of course. I was going to make bolognaise, but if you can't wait there's stuff for a stir-fry.'

'Bolognaise would be good.' He was mollified. Crisis averted again.

'Coming right up. Why don't you sit down with a beer?' He'd switched to that from wine since I got pregnant, presumably to underline the point that I wasn't allowed to so much as sniff alcohol, let alone taste a smidge from an open bottle.

'Alright.' In passing, he patted my stomach, the only part of me he ever touched now. 'How's Mum, by the way?' I hated how he called her that. She was my mother, not his.

'The usual. Up to her neck in village committees, looking forward to lots of improving lectures on her cruise.'

He pursed his lips. 'I hope you told her we're expecting some support when the bub comes. Granny needs to pitch in, along with

Nana!' I could just picture my mother's face when I told her she was 'Granny'. No grandfather in sight, of course, on either side. I wondered what it was about our mothers that sent men into early graves.

As I sliced veg and wrestled mince into the pan, mildly nauseated by the pink curls of it – like a brain – I looked across the lane and saw Nora's cottage was still in darkness, the curtains open. She had gone. But where?

Nick padded into the kitchen behind me, rinsing his beer bottle to put in the recycling. Easily, as if it was no big deal at all, he said, 'I meant to tell you, the police called again today. They still want to talk to you.'

Eleanor

In the days after my husband died, I had looked through the items in his car like a historian pouring over the grave goods of some long-dead pharaoh. What did they mean? How had he been able to lie for so long about his job? It certainly explained why there were never any parties, or dinners with work colleagues. He had always said he didn't want to socialise with them, that he preferred to spend time with me when he wasn't working. I'd been pleased. Then the entire sham of my life was laid open to me and I had to find out more.

Suzi had gone away again a few days before, taking an overnight bag and another expensive taxi. Watching from the window, I'd heard Nick call, 'Say hello to Mum for me,' and I deduced she was visiting her mother. She'd told me 'Mum' was away for Christmas on a cruise, so that made sense. I felt a coldness between us – she hadn't told me she was leaving; indeed, we hadn't spoken since she heard me playing the piano. I wondered what was going on. I had even felt a brief stab of fear, but surely there was no way she could know who I was. Suzi was so wrapped up in her own grief and fear that she probably never gave me a second thought.

I kept coming back to what Conway had said. *You don't know the half of it, love.* Did he mean what I thought he meant? It sounded so ridiculous even to think it. I ran through the steps in my head.

They'd said Patrick was still conscious when the ambulance came. What had happened after he arrived at hospital? Someone would have had to treat him – multiple someones. Nurses, doctors, receptionists. It would have left a trail. If he was well enough then, wouldn't they have been surprised when he later died? Would it not have raised alarm bells? Had someone hurt him, while he lay in hospital, recovering from the crash?

◆ ◆ ◆

I drove to Surrey General, marvelling that I had never been there before. I had suggested a few times that we could meet for lunch, but Patrick always said he was too busy. Saving lives, bringing babies into the world. The more I thought about it, the easier I saw it would have been to fool me. I never came to his work – and he did work there in any case, just not as a doctor. I'd never met anyone he worked with. I never questioned what he told me. He had shelves full of medical texts, and I'd even seen a picture of him at medical school.

I parked in the car park, which was exorbitantly priced – for the first time in my life I was experiencing the unsettling feeling of worry about my bank account. The moment I entered the hospital, the noise of the place assaulted me. Lights, running feet, TVs blaring, patients everywhere. The snow had caused a rise in both accidents and flu. I saw several people with legs propped up on chairs, looking cross and tired.

I knew from Eddie that Patrick had worked as a finance clerk in the obstetrics and fertility department – that bit at least was true. The irony of it wasn't lost on me. But instead of delivering babies and performing life-saving surgeries, he had charged people for private room hire and calculated the doctors' expenses. A cashier, essentially. I walked up there, bracing myself for the soft, cow-like bodies of the pregnant women. Suzi had joined their ranks, thanks to him, but I likely never would. I told myself it wasn't a big loss. The world was full as it was, and at least by having no child I had ended my family's terrible legacy, their twisted genes. But my body didn't understand that, and wanted to cry as a toddler ran up to me, seizing my leg to hold himself up.

'Tyler!' His mother, pregnant and lumbering, came up. 'Sorry. He'll grab on to anything these days.'

'It's alright.' I had to turn away from his bright laughing eyes and starfish hands. Try to find the anger again, the thing that had sustained me for so long, living side by side with the woman carrying Patrick's baby. All I felt now was a sort of bone-deep loss. So many lies. Even more than the ones I thought I knew about. Would I ever get to the end of them?

'Can I help you?'

My aimless wandering of the department had drawn the attention of a receptionist, swinging a lanyard like a weapon.

'Oh, I'm sorry. I just – my husband used to work here. Patrick Sullivan?' Not Dr Sullivan, as I had long imagined. No wonder he wouldn't let me phone the ward. I remembered, dimly, ringing up once when I couldn't get him on his mobile. *Who? There's no Dr Sullivan here*. And his anger. *Some silly temp. They have enough to do without taking domestic calls, Elle. Don't do it again.* And I hadn't.

Her face softened. 'Oh yes. We were very sorry to lose him, Mrs Sullivan.' She had liked him, I could see. Women usually did.

'I was hoping I might be able to see his office. You know, so I can picture where he worked. Collect whatever things he had.'

She hesitated. Tears sprang to my eyes – unfeigned, as it happened. 'Of course, Mrs Sullivan,' she said. 'Just follow me.'

◆ ◆ ◆

His office was little more than a cupboard. A cheap desk and chair, a bookshelf with boring publications on it, health service regulations and copies of Sage operating manuals. There were no pictures, no sign he had been married or had any kind of life. The receptionist left me, and I sat down in the chair, imagining Patrick in this place, sitting for years at this desk. Not saving lives as I had thought, but filing expense claims and inputting data to spreadsheets.

I opened the drawers of the desk, apprehensive. In the top one were some paperclips, two used-up biros, and a coiled-up blue silk tie, left there as if for meetings. I remembered buying it two Christmases ago – it had cost £100, and here it lay in this dusty drawer in a dingy NHS back office. I took it out, running the silky material through my fingers. A tiny piece of him, left behind.

The second drawer had a bottle of whisky, almost drunk, and another of aftershave. An expensive custom-blended one. A toothbrush in an opened packet, shower gel. I didn't want to think about why he had all these grooming items in his office. I remembered how he would shower every night when he came in, almost compulsively. Washing off the smell of Suzi, perhaps. But she'd told me they only met in May. This behaviour of Patrick's, the lateness, the sneaking around, had been going on as long as I'd known him.

I put that thought aside and tried the third drawer. It was locked. For a moment I thought about going down the legitimate route, asking if anyone from maintenance had a spare key. But I didn't want to draw attention to myself, and from my experience of hospitals, it would likely take hours. Luckily, I had retained a few skills from my time in Uplands, where picking a flimsy desk lock would have been child's play to the semi-feral girls I lived with for six months. I straightened out one of the paper clips from the top drawer, and within two minutes I had the lock open.

All that was inside was a notebook, a cheap lined thing. In it were names, in my husband's neat print writing. I recognised

Conway's. Beside them were numbers, dates, scrawled facts. Things like *With girl in conference bar. Three-hour lunch break for two. Expensed for extra hotel night.* What did it mean?

As I turned the pages, something fluttered out. A piece of green paper – a prescription from this hospital, with no doctor's name specified. It was signed in an indecipherable scribble, and the medicine name was also blank. I thought of the pills he had brought home for me, my 'doctor' husband, urging me to take them. Saying I needed them for my anxiety, my mental health problems, just like my mother. And I had taken them, of course I had, because I believed he'd been to medical school. Had someone given him a blank prescription, to be filled as he chose?

The ramifications of that were just sinking in when I heard a noise, and the door into the room opened. 'Can I help you?'

Suzi

The police came back the next day. Of course they did, because I had stupidly never called them to say I knew nothing, to take myself off their list.

They were very polite, wiping their shoes on the mat and thanking me for the tea I made, in a china pot, chocolate ginger biscuits out on a plate. I apologised for them not being home-made, then kicked myself for trying too hard. As far as they knew I was just an innocent neighbour, who had nothing to do with this accident. I was obsessively running over the story, looking for holes. Was there a way to connect us? There must have been, if Nora had found me. I still didn't know how she'd done it.

There was a man and a woman, both in the same dark uniforms, radios on their belts. I knew from TV this meant they hadn't sent the detectives, that this was probably a routine inquiry. We sat down in the living room, which I noticed had an icy chill.

'Sorry it's so cold. We're meant to have that kind of holistic heating, what do you call it' – I'd lost the word. Baby brain. 'Maybe it's not working.'

'It's a struggle with the snow,' said the woman politely. 'We get a lot of call-outs this time of year, elderly people freezing. They keep the heating off so they can eat.'

I arranged my cardigan around me, ashamed of all my wealth and privilege. 'My husband said it was something about an accident?' I used the word 'husband' consciously, like a shield. *I'm married. I have nothing to do with this man, whoever he was.*

'That's right. About three months ago there was a crash on the motorway slip road, the one that runs parallel to here a few miles over. A man drove into a tree.'

I put on a frown. 'Oh, how awful. I don't remember hearing about it.' But would they know that wasn't true? Would they check the searches I'd done online, see that I'd viewed news articles about the accident? 'Was it ice? The roads don't get gritted out here.'

'No, it was before the cold snap. Still sunny and clear, nothing on the road that we know of.'

'How strange. You're still looking into it?' Why had it taken them so long to get out here?

They exchanged a brief glance. 'It wasn't high priority. Cuts, you see.'

I wanted to offer an explanation – like maybe a sudden stroke or aneurysm, or something worse, shock at the news I'd just delivered you, the veiled threat I had made – but an innocent bystander wouldn't do that, so I kept quiet.

'You didn't hear anything?' the woman said.

'Not that I can remember. When was it?'

She told me the date, as if I would ever forget it, and I made a pretence of getting my phone and going through my calendar. Would they be able to tell I'd been out of the house that day? Did the alarm system keep records of when I came and went? No, it was ages ago, no one would remember, plus Nora hadn't moved in at that point. Of course she hadn't. It must have been your death that drove her here, to find me. To destroy me.

221

I hedged my bets. 'I can't see anything in the diary, but I can't remember that far back. I sometimes pop out for a walk, but I just don't know, I'm sorry.'

They began to stir as if leaving, and my heart eased, thinking maybe this was just a routine call after all. They didn't know anything.

'Thank you, Mrs Thomas.'

I didn't correct them about my name. Then, just as I was breathing again, poised to get up and see them to the door, they said something else.

'Actually, Mrs Thomas, we noticed there was a call to the police a few weeks back, from this address.'

'Oh?' What the hell? A quick flash of panic ran through me. Had Nick told them something – did he know?

'About a missing pet?'

I exhaled hard. 'Oh, right, right, of course. Poor Poppet. I told Nick not to waste your time with that.'

'Normally there's not much we can do for missing dogs, but he's right, there are gangs operating in this area, trying to steal pedigree animals. Have you noticed anything strange, anyone watching the house?' I hadn't even thought of that. It would be ridiculous if, after all this, Poppet's disappearance was the only real crime going on here. If the strange happenings that had so spooked me had nothing to do with you and me at all.

I pretended to think. 'We did have a few dropped calls, that sort of thing. I thought someone was casing the place – but we have such a good alarm system, I wasn't overly worried.'

'Very wise.' They exchanged another little look, and my stomach dropped away like on a rollercoaster you think is over, only to find there's one more loop. How stupid I'd been, how arrogant, to dismiss them as plods. They knew something. Of course they did. This was more than just routine. 'Mrs Thomas, our system cross-references names automatically on our databases. We couldn't help but notice that, earlier this year, there was an allegation made against you. That you committed a crime.'

'*What?*' I had started to rise from the sofa, and now collapsed back into it, winded by fear.

'A car break-in, in East London.' Oh my Holy God. 'The victim gave your name as a possible suspect. A Damian Henderson.'

I gaped at them in what they hopefully saw was genuine outrage. 'Damian!'

'You know him?'

'We worked together. I knew about the break-in – but I – I was living down here already when that happened! It's madness!'

'That's what the police thought, hence they never followed it up. Can you think of any reason he'd accuse you, Mrs Thomas?' The woman met my eyes calmly over her notebook. They knew. They must have guessed why he would say something like that, what kind of person I was.

'I . . .' *Oh God, be careful, Suzi.* 'We didn't part on the best of terms, is all. But I haven't seen him since, not for months.' That was a lie. I was lying without even meaning to. Shit.

Another look between them. I almost envied that, the ability to communicate without saying anything, to be that in sync with someone. I'd had that with you for a while, or at least I'd thought I had. Not like Nick and I. Our conversations had run dry long ago, and when we went out for a meal both of us would leap on our phones, after we'd agreed not to have them out. I felt your loss in so many small ways.

'Alright, thank you for your help.'

Was it over? Had they any more nasty shocks in store?

'I hope you find out what happened,' I said, ushering them to the door. 'His poor wife, what a terrible thing to happen.'

They were out the door and at their car when I realised, with a sickening plunge of the stomach, that they hadn't mentioned a wife.

◆ ◆ ◆

Rage was coursing in my veins. Fucking Damian, telling the police that! As if I would bash up his poxy car!

I shouldn't have done what I did next. It was yet another really stupid thing, to pile on top of the last few months of very stupid things. I seized my phone and called up the secret email account, dashed off a message to him.

You never mentioned you gave the police my name! FFS Damian. I never even thought about you after I left work. I was glad to get away from you, alright? I want nothing more to do with you. So if you tell them anything more about me, they'll find out a few things about you too.

I had pressed send before I had time to realise quite how stupid it was. I was threatening him – but with what? An accusation that what happened in the alley was not consensual? I regretted that night, of course, and I would not have done it sober, but was that really what I meant? I thought of having to go to court if it all came out. Nick's face. The shame of it, claiming I was a victim, when I'd gone there willingly with Damian, kissed him greedily, flirted with him for months. Even if I hadn't wanted it to go further, who would have any sympathy for me?

A cold terror slushed through me, and I jumped to my feet, almost crying with frustration. What was I going to do? There was no one who could help me. Nora was your wife – she must hate me, even if she hadn't told Nick the truth yet. Something terrible had happened in her past, I was sure, and she was taking medication for severe mental illness. I had to get away from her, but where could I turn? Nick at least suspected I had done something with Damian. Someone, maybe Nora, was watching me, perhaps had stolen my dog. I wasn't safe, and I was pregnant, and I was fairly sure I'd made several large mistakes in my interview with the police, tripped myself up on my own lies. What if they came back?

I was trembling, standing in the middle of my expensive kitchen, listening to the house click and whir about me. Machines to set the temperature, and play music, and make the blinds go up and down, and switch the lights on. To lock the door and keep me in here for ever. I was like a bird in a cage, with a cat sitting just outside my door, watching my every move.

Eleanor

The man who'd found me in Patrick's office – Dr Andrew Holt, he told me, who ran the IVF unit here – had a kind face, I thought. I imagined it would be reassuring for the pregnant ladies to have him around. His voice was soothing, his eyes gentle. All the same, when he saw me reading the notebook in the office, he looked worried. 'Mrs Sullivan, is it? Gemma told me you were here.'

'Eleanor, yes.'

'Right.' His brow knitted further. 'I'm sorry for your loss. Is there something we can help you with? I'm afraid I didn't know Patrick all that well.'

Neither did I, I wanted to say. 'Dr Holt, I don't really know how to say this. I've been having trouble accepting it, the death. It just makes no sense to me, that he could crash like that.'

He nodded sympathetically. 'That's quite common.'

'Maybe if I understood what happened when he was brought here, after the accident. Would they have taken him to A&E? I know you wouldn't have treated him, I just – didn't know who else to ask.'

'I have a patient . . .' He looked at his watch, and seemed to come to some decision. 'I can find out, I'm sure. Why don't you come to my office? It's just along here.'

I followed him down several corridors, each painted identical shades of puce and lemon. His own office was larger than Patrick's, but much more untidy, with a jacket heaped on the chair and the desk covered in paper, half-drunk cups of coffee, medical journals with pages folded over. 'Let me see.' He pulled his chair over to the computer, and began to stab at the keys, two-fingered. 'Here we are. Your husband was responsive in the ambulance, told paramedics he'd hit his head. He was first seen at A&E, yes, then because he complained of blurred vision and memory loss, transferred to the neurology ward for observation. Unfortunately, he then worsened and passed away, very quickly. Head injuries can be like that.'

'Wouldn't I have been called, once he turned up at hospital?' I still didn't understand that, why I hadn't found out until the police came to my door. They knew it was him by then – I hadn't been asked to identify the body. That terrible moment of seeing the blue light flicker on my windows. Knowing something life-shattering was about to happen, that I would never recover from. The deep regret that had crushed me later, imagining him in the hours before, dying, while I sat at home drinking wine, oblivious.

'Ordinarily, yes.' He squinted at the screen. 'It's possible they couldn't find your number. Or if he was confused, he might have given the wrong name, even. You live in town here, I see?'

It would be the old address on the medical records, most likely. 'I've moved,' I said, distracted. 'What doctors would have seen him? I mean, who would have noticed that he was . . . dead?'

It must have been a strange question, because his sandy eyebrows went up. 'Well, if he was under observation, the neurology registrar would have seen him. Plus some nurses. If he went downhill quickly, it's possible they didn't notice. We're so short-staffed at the moment. When he stopped breathing they would have rushed in to help, but been too late. I think that's probably what happened. I'm very sorry.'

'Right.' My mind clicked and whirred. In that time he was left alone, apparently fine, that was when something must have happened. Could someone have killed him? But why? I thought of what I'd found in the office, the coded notes in the book, and the word *blackmail* rose to my mind, absurdly melodramatic. Was it even possible? If Conway was in on it, and maybe one or even two other people, could they have killed him and made it look like an accident? 'Dr Holt . . . have you ever heard of doctors in this hospital having secrets? Things they wanted to hide?'

He really thought I was crazy now.

'Gosh, I don't know. Everyone has secrets, don't they?' He looked at me. 'Mrs Sullivan . . . there are people you can talk to, you know. It's very normal to be struggling. To be . . . confused about things.'

Was that what I was, confused? Or was I seeing clearly for the first time in years?

He went on, 'You could always stay here, if you like. Have a rest.'

I frowned. 'What do you mean?'

He stood up, his shadow falling over me. 'Just that – you seem a little distressed. There are people who can help. You don't have to go home alone.'

'I'm not alone,' I lied. Did he mean I was crazy? He wanted to admit me as a patient? No way. It was just like with Patrick, and after the fire when I was younger. People kept trying to tell me this, that I was somehow unhinged, but I knew now that I wasn't. In fact, the problem was that I was all too sane. I stirred, gathering my coat and bag. 'Thank you for your time.'

'That's – if you're sure, Mrs Sullivan.'

'Very sure.'

He clicked out of the screen on his computer, and for a second I saw that his Gmail account was open on there, and in it were several messages from a Suzanne Matthews.

I walked back to my car, my head so full it felt like an over-brimming glass, like it might spill and run out of my ears if I didn't keep very still. Dr Holt knew Suzi – he must have been the doctor she spoke to when she went to the hospital in search of Patrick. But why was he emailing her? I wished I'd taken the notebook from Patrick's desk. I hadn't liked to do it with him watching me, but would I find Dr Holt's name in there, among so many others? Had he been part of whatever Patrick was up to?

On my way out I passed a doctor in a white coat, handsome with greying hair. He was on the phone by the coffee machines, a teasing, smiling tone in his voice. 'OK. But I'll only have an hour, alright?'

Arranging an affair? Meeting his mistress? He wore a wedding ring, and I thought about his wife, maybe at home wrangling children to bed, wondering why he hadn't come back yet. Pouring herself another glass of wine, when she really shouldn't. Watching some crime drama on Netflix, the kind about cheating husbands, when her own was out flirting with other women. When you hear stories about women who are married to serial killers – Sonia Sutcliffe, for example – or whose husbands turn out to have four other families stashed away, you always say, how could she not know? She must have known. But I realised now that some people were just so good at lying that you not only believed them, you actually did your best to. You so much want to believe that what they tell you is true, you do the lying for them.

Suzi

'Hello, Suzi?'

When my phone rang about an hour after the police left, my heart rate went through the roof. So many different things that could ruin me right now. I didn't understand who it was, from the name that came up. I answered with shaking hands, recognising Dr Holt's voice. Of course. I had saved him under a fake name, because that was the kind of person I was now. A liar.

'Oh! Hello.' I wondered why he was calling me, and what might have happened if Nick was here. How I would explain myself.

'Are you alright?'

'Not really.' Where to start – the police, Damian, Nora? 'You know what I was telling you about my neighbour, that I thought she was – that she'd been married to Patrick?' I still couldn't think of you by that name. 'Well, I was doing more research and I think she might have done something bad in her childhood. Something violent. I'm scared, you see, for my baby.'

'Right.' His tone was cautious. Wondering where I was going with this probably, as well he might. Then he said, 'Listen, I think you might be right. About your neighbour, who she is.' He explained that an Eleanor Sullivan had come to the hospital, asking about her husband. 'She had all these questions – were doctors open to blackmail, what happens when an accident victim comes in. Is your neighbour a dark-haired woman, lovely hands?'

'That's her. Did she say why she was there?'

'No.' I heard his sigh down the phone and suddenly, irrationally, wished to be wherever he was. I imagined a cosy bachelor flat, with some hearty food, a bottle of good red wine. I had no idea if he was married or not. Maybe he didn't wear a wedding ring, or maybe he had a live-in girlfriend, or even boyfriend. I reminded myself I knew nothing about him. 'I was worried. She seemed . . . not entirely stable.'

If Nora had been in Guildford today, she would surely come home soon. And then what? Things couldn't go on as they had. If I spoke to her again, I knew I couldn't pretend I didn't know the truth – but what would she do to me then, if there was nothing more to hide? What reason would she have not to execute her plan, whatever that was? I said, 'I want to go and see where she grew up, find out what I can. But the thing is, I don't have a car. I'm stuck out here. And I'm afraid.' I was aware I was playing helpless, appealing to his weaknesses, whatever it was in him that made him want to protect women. I felt a little disgusted with myself. But it worked.

He sighed again. 'You really think she's a risk to you?'

'She moved in next door to me! You're telling me that's a coincidence?'

'No, no, it's not that. It just seems so crazy is all.'

'I know that. I just – need some proof.' I hoped he would understand, the impulse that drove me on to find more – there was no reason he would, he barely knew me. I had no right to ask him for help. And there was no reason for him to help me – his only involvement was that you had, briefly, stolen his conference lanyard – but all the same it seemed he was in.

'You're lucky I have a rare day off tomorrow. I'll come and pick you up. What's your address?'

It was of course risky to be picked up at the house, what with both Nora and Nick potentially spying on me. I told Dr Holt, as I had once told you, to meet me up the lane a bit, where a passing place widened out the road and a car could pull up. If he found this strange, he didn't comment, and a few hours later we were driving in his jeep towards Sussex, where Nora was from.

He kept glancing over at me in the passenger seat. 'You're sure you're alright?'

'Fine.' I scrabbled to find clear floor space for my feet – the car was like a bin on wheels. Remnants of non-NHS-approved fast food littered the footwells, and the back seat was heaped with trainers, jumpers, fleeces, boxes of tissues, a bike helmet. As if he lived in here most of the time. I found it endearing somehow, after the sterile tidiness of my own home. 'The place is hard to find, I think – nothing's coming up on Google Maps.' From the old news reports, I had worked out the approximate postcode of where the house was, and we were heading there. To find what, I had no idea.

I almost enjoyed the trip. It was warm inside the car, with a slight undertone of old burger, and we listened to Radio 2 and shared a bag of wine gums, which he'd brought along with him. He asked was I alright at least four times. Was I warm or cold. Did I need water. Did I want to stop for the loo. I wondered why Nick's version of looking after me didn't feel like this.

After a while, he said, 'So what are you hoping to find out?'

'I don't know. What happened to her family – if she's dangerous.' If she might hurt me, or my baby. If I really had no choice but to run, burn my life to the ground. When I wondered what we might learn when we got there, my stomach dipped. I cradled my bump, and the gesture wasn't lost on him.

'Suzi, you don't need to go home after this. If you feel you're in danger from . . . anyone.' Meaning Nora, meaning Nick. Both, or either. He was right to think I wasn't safe at home. But I couldn't think that far ahead.

'I know. Thank you.' We drove the rest of the way in peaceful silence, me turning over my options in my head, not liking any of them.

Steepletops – or what remained of it – had been a large-ish modern house not far from Chichester. New money, not an ancestral pile, with vulgar gateposts that had once been topped by stone eagles. I guessed it would have had something like ten bedrooms back in the day, had it not been lying in ruins. The outer wall of the garden was crumbling away in places, and the fence that replaced it was sagging, neglected. A sign ordered no trespass, but it was so worn away I hardly believed anyone would care. Who owned it anyway – likely not Nora? She had mentioned a few times that money was tight for her, so surely she would have sold the land if she'd still had a stake in it. We parked in a lay-by. 'The gates are locked,' said Dr Holt, glancing at the large iron ones, so dilapidated that the padlock on them was hardly effective. 'We can't get in.'

I gave him a look and opened the jeep door, stepped down and over the sagging fence in one bound. He followed, reluctant.

'Trespass is illegal, just so you know.'

'There's no one here!' I said, and it was true. 'Come on, live a little.'

'I'll have you know I live a lot,' he grumbled, climbing awkwardly over. I found myself smiling, and quickly wiped it from my face. There was nothing to smile about here.

You could just about discern the remnants of what had been a sizeable house. Red brick, large mullioned windows (I was still upset Nick had pulled out the ones in the cottage to replace them with high-tech versions) almost destroyed.

'What happened here?'

A cold wind blew through the site, and I huddled my coat round me.

'I don't know.' Dr Holt was uneasy. 'Since we're already breaking the law, I guess we should go and look.'

The answer was clear when we got nearer. The inside of the house was blackened like the bottom of my Aga. 'A fire.'

'Looks that way, yes.' He took out his phone, holding it up in the manner of a druid divining for water. 'No reception.'

It was then that a small, yappy terrier ran up, barking round my ankles. I thought of poor Poppet, lost God knows where.

'Alfie! Silly boy, come here!' A woman ran up, puffing, wearing an expression of canine-related embarrassment that I recognised from myself. 'Sorry.'

A dog walker. She wore a gilet and sensible shoes, possibly bought from the back of the *Radio Times*. She looked between us. 'You don't mind, do you? It's the best dog-walking spot around.'

Dr Holt and I exchanged glances. She must have thought we were something official, based on how we were staring at the house. I thought fast. 'No problem. Maybe you can fill us in on a few details? We're looking to develop the site, but the info's a bit patchy. What happened, a fire?'

She assumed a gossipy look. 'Oh, it was terrible. I was only young then, just married. That poor kiddy.' She saw the looks on our faces. 'You didn't know? Well, it was a house fire. The parents, and the little boy – only eight, he was – they passed away. The place was sold after that, some company looking to build houses, but it never happened. Maybe all the bad feeling.'

I was nodding like I knew all this. 'Of course. And wasn't there a daughter?'

Her face fell. 'They said she might have had something to do with it. I mean, it was strange as anything, her just happening to be awake and out with the dogs when it happened. At two in the morning! Then there was talk, you know, about the mother. Very hard on the girl, she was. Always threatening to send her to boarding school, and she wasn't allowed friends, hobbies, nothing. But I'm sure it was just an accident.'

Dr Holt said, 'Eleanor, was that her name?'

'I think so. Only sixteen – you wouldn't believe a girl that age could do a thing like that, would you? Maybe there's no truth to it. She did try to get back in to help them – laid up in hospital herself she was, for weeks, and they said she had some kind of breakdown, ended up in the funny farm, or whatever you're meant to call it nowadays. I never thought she had anything to do with it, not after that. I hope this won't put you off? Shame to see the place empty all these years.'

'Of course not,' I said, playing a character again. A hard-headed businesswoman, like somebody off *The Apprentice*. 'Primary real estate is all that matters here. Thank you very much.'

She moved off, clearly half unsure whether she should have said anything, half puffed up with importance. I imagined her getting home, telling her husband they were developing the old Treadway place at last. So Nora's family, including her little brother, had perished in a house fire, leaving only her and the dogs alive. I remembered what she'd said about dogs, that first time we met. *They're so guileless. Not like people.*

Dr Holt looked as troubled as I felt.

'What now?' I said.

'I . . .'

'Coo-ee!' The dog-walker was back before he could answer. 'Sorry to interrupt. I just remembered – the mother didn't die, in fact. They thought she would, but she pulled through in the end. In a nursing home, she is. The Poplars, other side of town.' She looked between us, trusting, in a way I imagined I never would again. 'But then maybe you know that, if you've bought the place?'

Eleanor

'Well. I'm here. Are you going to tell me what you know?'

James Conway's flat was so squalid I didn't want to touch a single surface. I stood in front of his antiquated gas fire, keeping my Barbour away from the mantelpiece, which was smeared with the dirt of decades. An old-fashioned carriage clock sat on it, along with framed black and white photos of a boot-faced elderly couple and a small boy with sticking-out ears. I knew that he was living in his mother's old place. The décor hadn't been changed since what looked like the mid-seventies.

Conway sat on the worn velvet sofa, wearing tracksuit bottoms and an old T-shirt stained yellow under the arms. I couldn't believe this man was allowed to assist with surgery. 'I want my money first. You've got it?'

'There's just one thing I don't understand. Why would Pat – why would my husband borrow money from *you*?' I looked around me, wrinkling my nose. Did he even have money to lend?

'I had some from my mother's will, and I wasn't doing anything with it just then. He needed it.' He shrugged. 'I'm a good friend.' Or more likely, Patrick had some kind of hold over him. Again, that word in my mind. *Blackmail*. Conway seemed the type to have several misdemeanours in his past. Perhaps he was chancing his arm, trying to get back what he'd paid out.

'But . . . what did he need it for?' I was wracking my brains. I knew that the money was gone. I knew that the house had been mortgaged, when I'd thought it was paid for outright. I knew that he hadn't been a doctor after all, just worked in the admin department. But despite that series of shocks, I still didn't know why he would have needed a large sum of money from someone so obviously sleazy.

Conway laughed. He had a horrible laugh, sneery and hoarse, like he'd smoked a million cigarettes. 'That fella, he burns through cash like water. He's never had any, you know. Any guff he gave you about being middle-class, that was bollocks. Why do you think he married you? You don't think he knew you had money? You really have no idea, do you, love?'

I bristled. The idea that Patrick had only married me for my money, that any love between us had been faked, was unendurable. He hadn't even known who I was before we met, that I was wealthy – he'd just seen my picture on the Tube and felt compelled to find me.

Hadn't he?

In that moment, I really could have killed Conway. I wouldn't let him take that from me too. 'But why did he need the money now? Did . . .' I faltered, thinking of why he might have wanted quick access to cash.

Another horrible laugh. 'He wanted to go away, didn't he? Owed a lot of money to a lot of people. They're pretty slow at that hospital, but at some point they'd have noticed the cash was gone.'

'What cash?'

He looked at me like I was stupid. 'He was in charge of the money, love. You don't think he didn't dip his hand in the till from time to time?'

The blood crashed in my ears. Conway was saying Patrick had, what, embezzled money from the NHS? He'd been planning to leave me, run away with Suzi after all? He had chosen her over me? A flare-up of my old rage at her. 'It was for Suzi? The two of them were going to leave?'

'God, no.' He smiled, like a poker player laying down a winning hand. 'He wanted to get away from both of you. You, and that demanding slut, always on at him to leave you. He wanted to start a new life. And then when she said she was up the duff, well – it got more urgent, didn't it?' Then, at my consternation, he laughed again. 'Oh Elle-belle. You really are in the dark, love. You actually thought he was dead?'

The world stopped. '*What?*'

'I told you. Why do you think he drove into a tree? One minute he's fine, talking and all, next he's carked it? And he cancelled his life insurance not long before – the companies come sniffing if there's a sudden death, don't they, so better not to give them the chance. Much more careful than the police, they are.' He smiled at me, and it was horrible. 'Eleanor, love – Paddy's not dead. It's just another of his tricks.'

The life I'd thought already shattered was breaking up further, into a million pieces. It wasn't true. It couldn't be. Of course he was dead, I'd stood at his graveside. There had been an autopsy. A body buried, though admittedly I had not seen it. I hadn't wanted to. It couldn't be true. It was the stuff of lurid thrillers. Someone had been in the coffin, and I knew enough about hospital procedures around violent deaths to be sure they were thorough. In order to declare my husband dead, they would have needed a body, one similar enough to be mistaken for him. And how would he get a dead body, out of nowhere like that? It didn't make any sense. I managed to gasp out, 'Water. Please can I have some water?'

As Conway left the room, I abandoned my no-touching resolution and fell on to the horrible sofa. All the strength had gone in my legs. *No, no, no.* It couldn't be true. It was absurd.

But then, hadn't I known it, deep down, that something was wrong? That someone as strong and brilliant as him could not die on a clear country road? As mad as it seemed, something about it chimed in me, like the thud of feet against solid rock. In the swirling currents of my husband's lies, was this the actual truth?

After a moment, Conway came back in with a smeared glass half-full of water. 'You're not going to faint, are you?'

'No.' I sucked in lungfuls of the foetid air. When I could speak, I said, 'Tell me everything you know. Tell me now.'

Suzi

I had never been to a nursing home before. One set of grandparents, my dad's, were dead long before I could remember, and Mum's were both vigorously alive in Scotland, going on coach holidays to Edinburgh and availing themselves of day trips bought with Nectar points. I had been planning to take the baby to see them once it arrived, a small act of normalcy that seemed a million miles away now. I couldn't imagine a time after this, when the mess I'd made of my life was somehow straightened out.

I had worried it would be hard to talk our way into the home, but after Dr Holt had a quick word with the receptionist, we strolled right in. Perhaps being a doctor, like being pregnant, also got you special privileges.

The room was pleasant, filled with light and looking out over the sea. A few elderly people sat in wicker chairs, some with blankets, some staring into space or doing crosswords, and classical music was being piped in. I was sure there were worse places to spend your last days. Nora's mother – Diana Treadway, née Halscombe – sat by the window, staring out at the restless grey waves. My heart began to pound. What would I say to her? *Hello, I know your daughter and I slept with her husband? Also, she told me you were dead?*

'Mrs Treadway?' I faltered. Dr Holt hung back, nodding encouragement. She turned her face to me, and I saw, as the light caught her, that one side of it was almost entirely burned away.

She wasn't always lucid, the nurse had said. Good days and bad days, that common euphemism. She had lived in the home for over twenty years, since she was in her forties. Since the fire. She wasn't even that old, but her life had effectively ended on the same day she lost half of her family.

'How did it happen?' I asked her, squatting on a low stool beside her. 'I'm sorry. It must be painful.'

I had fumbled my explanation of who I was and why I wanted to know about her past, suggesting I was 'writing something' about it. I didn't say what. But she didn't seem bothered by that. I wasn't sure she was entirely following me. She seemed unanchored, drifting in time.

'There was a fire. They died – Charles, and little Sebby.'

'I'm so sorry. It was – an accident?'

She turned her gaze on me, and I almost jumped, recognising Nora's grey eyes in that ruined face. 'They said it was my fault. I fell asleep smoking. They don't let me smoke in here.' I recognised the restless tapping of her fingers as the gesture of a lifelong smoker.

'I heard maybe it was . . . something else.'

'Eleanor. She escaped the fire. Said she couldn't sleep, so she took the dogs out. She loved those dogs. I'd been planning to get rid of them, after she went.'

'Where was she going?' Nora would have been sixteen at the time of the fire, I knew.

'School. Boarding. I could do nothing with her – she only wanted to play the piano and meet boys.' The once-beautiful mouth pursed. 'She was a slut. Ungovernable.' Her voice was so emotion-less, the ugly word hit me like a slap. Same as the one etched into the snow outside my house. Was that why she'd chosen it? 'Sebby would have been a wonderful man. He wasn't even supposed to be there that night, you know. He was meant to be sleeping at a friend's but in the end he didn't. So cruel.' Again, there was no emotion. I wondered if she was heavily medicated.

'So you think she . . .' I didn't know how to say it. I was still trying to take in the fact that Nora, my softly spoken neighbour, had set a fire to kill her whole family, including her little brother.

'I'm sure she did something. I don't know what. It was her fault, not mine.' A faint hint of defensiveness. Something flickered behind her eyes, and I thought maybe she was more lucid than she let on. 'Who are you anyway? Why do you want to know these things?'

'I . . . I know Nora.'

'*Eleanor*,' she snapped.

'Sorry, yes. Eleanor.'

'She's alive, then.' She flicked something from the slacks she wore, and I saw her hands were like Nora's, slender and lovely. 'That's a shame,' said her mother, tapping the imaginary cigarette again. 'And she got what she wanted after all. The fucking piano. I shut her hands in it once, you know. Not hard enough, evidently.' In her posh voice, the curses rang like bells. 'She got everything. Success, money. I heard she even married. She should have died, not Sebby.'

I said nothing, edging away from the darkness around this woman. Nora must not have seen her mother since the fire – 1992. Her mother was sure she had caused the fire, burned the house down, killed her father and brother. If it was true – and yes, wasn't it weird, Nora being outside at such an hour, getting her beloved dogs to safety and no one else? – that meant she would stop at nothing. Not even hurting a child. My hands went to my bump again, the fragile life I was carrying inside of me. What had I done? What was I bringing this baby into? For the first time, I imagined talking to him or her. Trying to explain the terrible mess I'd made. *I'm so sorry. I didn't mean it.* Would they come to hate me, as Nora and her mother hated each other?

Dr Holt appeared in the doorway, holding a manila file. 'They let me look at her records,' he said quietly. 'She's doped up to the eyeballs. Apparently she had a full-on breakdown after the fire, and she was on some pretty heavy-duty medication before that, anyway.'

'Was she – did she have psychosis?' I whispered. I had forgotten the correct way to say it, nowadays.

He frowned in surprise. 'How did you guess?'

Maddy

People thought it was so glamorous, living abroad. Her friends back home, a few years out of uni and struggling with internships and shifts in Starbucks, regularly expressed their envy via WhatsApp emoji strings. *You live on the Costa del Sol, you lucky cow. Meanwhile I live with my mum in Walsall!!!!*

Maddy lived with her mum too, and her dad, in the English pub they'd bought five years ago in La Tornada, a small Spanish town that was known for its sizeable British population. The pub, sitting between a tapas bar and a sangria place, sold fish and chips, chicken korma, English ales. She was constantly surprised that anyone would prefer this to croquettes, paella and churros, but every day in high season came tourists complaining about the lack of burgers in the Spanish restaurants, throwing themselves with relief on the pub's laminated menus.

Now it was the down season, and Maddy's parents had pushed off on holiday to Florida, leaving her to manage the place so she could 'learn the ropes, my girl'. She didn't want to learn the ropes. Running an English pub in Spain was not high up her life goals. Of course, she wasn't clear on what was, but definitely not that. It was hardly worth being open in December anyway; no one came in, except a few alcoholic locals who'd been banned from the other bars in town, or some of the ex-pats craving their chips and battered sausage. Even after years in Spain, they barely spoke a word of Spanish, and wouldn't have eaten a squid tentacle if you'd paid them. Maddy had heard one couple complaining about the local food having 'too many eyes'.

But today, someone interesting had come in, as Maddy idled by the bar in her pocketed apron, watching the Sky Sports that played non-stop. Her dad said that was as much of a draw as the home food.

'Are you open?'

The man who'd come in fixed her with deep blue eyes, the kind you never saw in Spain. She stood up straighter, causing a breeze that wafted the cheap tinsel her mum had stapled round the bar. Still twenty degrees outside, it was hard to imagine it was nearly Christmas.

'Oh! Yeah. It's quiet though.'

'That suits me.' He took a seat at the bar, inviting conversation. 'I saw the sign for chips and couldn't resist. It's the one thing I've been craving.'

'On holiday here or . . . ?' she fished.

He played with a rugby-themed bar mat. 'More of a permanent thing, I think. Just checking it out.'

'It's a great place,' she said, moving behind the taps, selling the town though she hated it herself, and was only there because finding a flat and job in England had seemed impossible. 'The beach is lovely when it's warm, nice people, good food.'

'Fish and chips?' He raised an eyebrow at her. He was older than she was, in his forties maybe. Dark hair silvered with grey, an expensive-looking polo shirt and well-fitting jeans. Maddy liked older guys. Boys her age – and they *were* boys – were all broke and awkward, their jeans falling down over their pants.

She leaned over the bar, showing her cleavage. 'Don't tell anyone, but I actually like the local food. The seafood is amazing here.'

'I know. I just felt like a little taste of home, don't judge.' He smiled at her.

'I won't. How about an English pint to go with?'

He ordered a Newcastle Brown Ale, and sipped it with enjoyment. 'This is great. I could be back home. Newkie in my mouth, pretty English girl across the bar.'

Maddy blushed – something about the way he said it had sounded dirty, even though the words weren't. A boy her age would never just up and tell her she was pretty. It wouldn't occur to them to flatter her, or else they'd be afraid of sounding sleazy. She liked it, she decided. And suddenly her winter purgatory, minding this tacky bar in a dying seaside town, seemed a lot brighter. 'That's eleven euros fifty, please.'

He took out his leather wallet, which looked expensive. 'Damn! I meant to get cash. I've only a ten.'

'We take cards.' She didn't want him leaving, he might not come back.

He hesitated for a moment. 'Well, OK then.'

She took his card, reading the name, but it was initials, telling her nothing. 'What's it stand for?' she said, after he'd keyed in the PIN and she'd shunted the order to Geraldo, the local chef, who was incensed that she'd interrupted his fag break to make him actually do some work. His day was one long fag break, punctuated by the occasional lacklustre peeling of potatoes.

The blue-eyed stranger sipped his beer again. His gaze locked into hers, and she felt her stomach spin in a sick, pleasant way, like being on a waltzer at a fairground. Every bit of her felt alive, where before she'd been sulky and apathetic, blood thudding through her veins. Even the framed pictures of Jim Bowen over the bar looked quaint and charming.

'Oh,' he said, 'you can call me Sean.'

Eleanor

I needed proof. Everything else was just speculation, doubt, cobwebs crowding my brain. The word of a drunk, a liar. An insane story about a faked death. They say if you know a person, you know how to find them. And I knew my husband. I knew him better now than when he was with me.

After I left Conway's, I paid a visit to my lawyer, Eddie, in his cramped offices above a building society. Dimly, I resolved that when all this was over, I would find a job of some kind, and take control of my own money. Give piano lessons, maybe. I could do that. The office was overheated, strips of tinsel taped to the filing cabinet in a gesture to the season. It seemed ridiculous to me, that Christmas was so near. What would I even do for it? Spend it alone in my damp cottage, watching my husband's mistress, pregnant with his child, play happy families across the lane, or wander the streets like a madwoman as I was doing now? If what Conway said was true, Patrick had controlled me just as Nick did Suzi. Kept me medicated, afraid, terrified of losing my mind. Lied to me. Made me doubt the evidence of my eyes. We weren't so different, Suzi and I – we had both been lied to by my husband. I could feel my plans shifting again, twisting and convoluting as the world changed.

Eddie was there, in an afternoon fug of coffee breath. He was alone, no sign of the ditzy teenage assistant who answered the phone and painted her nails in the office. 'Elle! How lovely. Kathryn's gone to the dentist. Did you . . . ?'

'Sorry, no, I don't have an appointment. I just need five minutes, if you don't mind?'

Eddie never minded. He'd seen me through the loss of my family, and of Patrick. It was perhaps because of him, his office here, that I'd settled in Guildford in the first place. He was the nearest thing I had now to relations. I no longer counted my mother – she had been dead to me for decades, even if she was technically still alive. I had always paid for her nursing home from the money I'd inherited direct from my father – none left to her, which must have killed her – but I'd have to think about that, going forward. Now that I was broke. Now everything was different. 'Of course.'

'I'd just like an accounts statement. Of everything, all the transactions in the last year.'

'Well, alright. You know, you could get this yourself if you signed up for online—'

I cut him off again. 'I will. But for now, please?'

It took a few minutes for Eddie to click on various screens, turn on the ancient printer, turn it off again when it failed to work, turn it back on. I almost screamed. Didn't he know what was at stake? Finally, I had a stack of printouts, everything that had been spent from our bank accounts since I lost my husband. Because I knew him. I knew he wouldn't be able to live off whatever cash he'd siphoned over the years. There would always be the temptation to spend a little more, probably on some woman. And he knew I never looked at the accounts, that I wasn't good with technology or forms, and that Eddie was less than vigilant. He might think it worth the risk.

My eyes devoured the sheet of tiny figures. I knew I would find something, in among all the dozens of tiny expenditures I had made myself. Food, petrol, the move. And eventually, at the bottom of the tenth page I scoured, there it was.

'Elle?' Eddie sounded worried. 'Is everything alright?'

I felt the edge of the desk under my hand, and I felt the rest of my doubts collapse and fall away, taking with them Elle, Eleanor Sullivan, Elle-belle. The wife he'd duped over and over. Who he'd left to cry at his grave, which didn't even have him in it.

'I'm fine.' I found my voice, and with it my rock-bottom. Everything I had known, everything I'd built my life on was a lie. I had not known my husband at all. I had not known anything.

But that's the thing about rock-bottom. It gives you something firm to put your feet on, at last. I looked again at the printout, the figures fuzzy before my eyes. A euro transaction. A bar somewhere in Spain. The Red Lion. An English pub – really? Not even a large amount. In pounds, it came to nine forty-eight. And for a moment I was almost disappointed, that he had pulled off such an audacious plan, then ruined it all for the sake of so little.

Suzi

It was snowing again outside the cottage. Coming down silent and stealthy over my poor dead plants, bringing with it grown-up anxieties about food, frozen pipes, being trapped out here, instead of innocent childish joy in sledging and snowballs. The windscreen wipers on Dr Holt's jeep were working overtime as he pulled up near Willow Cottage. 'You're sure this is OK?'

'Yeah, it's not far.' In truth, the walk down the lane was far enough in the snow, while pregnant, but I couldn't risk being seen by Nick.

Dr Holt seemed reluctant to let me go. 'Suzi, think about this. We know she's dangerous – that she'd hurt a child. Is going back home really wise?'

'I'll be alright,' I said, with more confidence than I felt. What was my alternative? I knew that if I kept running, kept hoarding my secrets, I would turn out like Nora. And I didn't want that. I wanted to start my life again, with the truth this time.

Awkwardly, he said, 'If you . . . if you need a place . . . Suzi, you wouldn't have to be alone. OK?' For a moment, we both stared ahead, out at the swirling snow. My mind rejected what he was saying, if indeed he was saying it. I couldn't think about that now. All the same, it felt like a wrench to tear myself out of the warm car, and go out into the icy dark alone.

'I'll talk to you soon, OK?' But would I? I'd no idea what might happen tonight.

'Will you let me know you're alright? It's silly, but I feel responsible now. How's the baby?' He looked tenderly at my bump.

'Kicking like mad.'

'A good sign. Take care, Suzi.' And he went.

The snow was a worry. Nothing else could go wrong, because I had plans. When Nick got home that night, I would be ready for him. I had showered, washing out the smell of the nursing home, and brushed my hair, but put on no make-up. I wanted Nick to see me, finally, as I was. I had cooked a simple meal, one that could be eaten cold if discussions went on all night, as I imagined they would. Boiled potatoes, salad, ham. I didn't light the lamps or candles, but sat waiting for him in the stark overhead light of the living room. It was time for us both to face reality.

I heard a car outside, and my heart turned over. Footsteps on the gravel. I had half-hoped for some last-minute reprieve, that he'd work late again, but no, Nick was home. It was time.

I heard his footsteps in the hallway, and the sound of his shoes being taken off. A clear of the throat. I waited, holding my breath.

He poked his head into the living room. 'What are you doing? Why isn't there—'

'There is dinner,' I pre-empted him. 'Everything is done. But it'll have to wait.' I summoned all my courage, which I had learned was so very meagre, and got ready to crack the thin glass between us, the pretence of being just alright that could have carried us through the next fifty years if I'd let it. I said the fateful words that can end a marriage, the pebble-roll that tips off the avalanche. 'Nick. We have to talk.'

◆ ◆ ◆

Of course I didn't tell him the whole truth. Does anyone ever? Don't we reveal it by stages, even to ourselves? Haltingly, the way I described it was that I had been 'seeing someone'. 'Like a friend!' I stressed, as his face changed. 'Nothing happened. I was just very lonely. The move down here, it was so hard for me. I was used to seeing people every day, at work or at the gym or for coffee.' Nick said nothing. He was sitting opposite me on an armchair, the coffee table between us, the books on it arranged at mathematical angles. 'The thing is, I learned recently that this friend, he died in an accident. Car crash. And his wife – well, she seems to think maybe I was with him when it happened, I don't know, she must be crazy, poor woman – and she's kind of . . . after me.'

It was so cold in the living room. I didn't know why the heating hadn't kicked in. 'After you?' he repeated, finally, his voice as cold as the air.

'Yes. Nick, it's Nora. It's a long story but – basically, Nora is my friend's wife. She followed me here. I'm scared. That dead thing, and losing Poppet . . . I think she might be planning to . . . do something.'

What, I didn't know. The only thing I could think of was that she was waiting for me to have the baby. To be at my most vulnerable, and then to strike.

Nick said nothing for a long time. He was staring at the expensive hardwood floor with its underfloor heating. So much he had laid under my feet, and this was what I'd done. 'I gave you another chance.' His voice sounded strangled. 'After that fucking twat – Damian.'

My heart lurched. So as I suspected, he knew.

'I know what you did,' he confirmed. 'You came home reeking of him. Fucking *slut*.' The word made me jump. Had he seen it, written in the snow? 'Bastard got what was coming to him, anyway.'

I didn't know what he meant. But then I did. 'His car,' I said dully. 'You smashed it up.' Of course it hadn't been you. Another lie. You wouldn't have cared enough to do something so risky, go out of your way to avenge me.

Nick made an impatient gesture. 'He deserved it, and worse. But I gave you a chance. We'd move away from the city, from all those temptations, and maybe you'd behave. And now you've done it again! Jesus, Suzi, what could you even do out here? You don't have a car, and we're in the middle of nowhere! But still you managed it. You dirty little bitch.'

For a second I couldn't believe he'd said it, Nick who never cursed and hated me doing it. 'Nothing happened!' I tried the stock adulterer's approach, to be met with a hard stare.

'Don't lie to me. You can't help yourself – you're, Jesus, you're like some desperate nympho, aren't you?' I almost laughed at the seventies sleaziness of 'nympho', but managed not to. This conversation wasn't going the way I'd hoped. But really, what had I expected? Understanding, tears and hugs? How stupid I was.

'I was just lonely. He was nice to me. I know it was wrong, but you have to believe me . . .'

'Believing you would be a real exercise in stupidity.' He stood up, pacing. 'I knew there was something going on. I just hoped I was wrong. Why do you think I trace your phone? Set up the smart alarm? You know it tells me every time you enter and leave the house? You know there's security cameras I can watch you through when you're here? I see you, crying all day long. Was that for him? Starting my dinner with minutes to spare. You think I don't know? You must think I'm really dumb.'

I gaped at him. 'You trace my phone? You – *stalk* me?' Suddenly I understood. How he always seemed to know when I hadn't been where I said. When I'd gone out for hours instead of the quick walk I told him about, or vice versa. When I hadn't done each household chore exactly to his liking.

He laughed. 'Jesus, you're stupid. You did it yourself! What do you think Find My Friends is for? If you weren't so clueless, you could have turned it off. I told you about the alarm system, that it worked remotely, that we could check on the house on the cameras whenever we wanted. That you can even talk through them, if you see an intruder. You weren't even listening. You never listen to me.'

'And – the music? The temperature?' Those were all controlled remotely too. Had *Nick* really been behind all this? The dead animal, the message in the snow? It was him making me feel I was slowly going mad?

He shrugged. 'Sometimes I'd get angry. Seeing you here, with all the things I bought you, crying and moping. For another man, as it turns out.'

I felt sick. All this while I'd breathed a sigh of relief when the door shut in the mornings and he was gone, but really Nick was sitting in his office, watching me, turning the temperature up then down again, making songs play, locking the doors, changing the codes. So I'd think I was crazy. Like his little doll, walking stiffly through the rooms of his perfect house. 'Nick, this is insane. I could go to the police.'

'It's not illegal. Trust me, you signed up to all this voluntarily. Plus, I don't think you want to be talking to the police right now, do you?'

'What do you mean?' My voice wavered.

'They wanted to speak to you. Why? That man who drove into the tree, that was him?'

I nodded miserably. No point in denying it. Nick said, in a low voice, 'I'm glad he's dead.'

I made myself sound scared, which wasn't hard, since I couldn't stop my hands from shaking. 'We have to think of the baby. Nora – I'm afraid she might hurt us.' I cradled my bump. 'Our baby's in danger, Nick.'

'*Our* baby?' he sneered.

The pause between us went on too long. 'Of course it's—'

'I know you did your best to make it not mine. Suggesting the wrong times in the month. You think I can't count? You really think I didn't have my own apps that timed your cycles? That I don't know how to hack yours – it's all online, for God's sake!' Of course he did. I was so stupid. Relying on those apps, when they only knew what you told them. 'All those years with no baby, then you'd act so sad, but then you're smiling and cracking open a bottle, we'll try next month, have a drink. As if you ever stopped drinking. Then you're pregnant, after all that time? I'm not stupid, Suzi.' He stopped in front of me, and I wished I was standing, because I suddenly felt very vulnerable, my bump weighing me down. 'Is it his?'

For once, I told the truth. What was the point in lying, pretending I'd never slept with anyone but Nick? There was nothing left to save here. I could see that now. 'I – I don't know. It could be.'

'Jesus.' He rubbed his eyes with balled fists.

'Nick, I'm sorry. I never meant to end up here. But we have. So what are we going to do?'

He shrugged. 'I want this baby. I might not have another chance, and this one will at least have my name, even if it's not mine. But you – I'm done with you, Suzi. You're a whore.'

I should have been more upset, hearing this word, knowing my marriage was falling apart, but I wasn't. I had known it for weeks, deep down, and there was a certain relief that he was the one pushing it over the cliff. Not my fault, that way. Not my decision. Very calmly I said, 'Right, so what, you'll move out till I have the baby?'

Nick gave a nasty little laugh. 'I'm not going anywhere. This is my house – my dad's money paid for it. You think I'd let you keep it?'

My heart sank a little. 'So we'll just both stay here?'

I'd heard of couples in that situation, unable to separate for money reasons, and it sounded awful. Maybe I could move out, find a flat in town – it felt overwhelming even thinking about it.

'We will. But not in the way you think.'

'What?' Suddenly, I realised I had to stand up. I was far too vulnerable on the sofa and—

Too late. His fist came swinging towards me, and before I could fully marvel at what was happening, that it was Nick doing this to me, I was on the floor.

PART FOUR

Alison

FEBRUARY – Two Months Later

Alison had never been so pleased to get inside the police station. She resolved that, when she got home that night, she was going on lastminute.com to find some winter sun. Images rose in her mind – cocktails with umbrellas, warm sand under her toes, the smell of sun cream . . .

'Pasty?' His mouth full of crumbs, Tom was approaching her desk, holding out a paper bag. He'd made her let him out at the Greggs in Sevenoaks.

'Yuck.' Alison eyed the bag, the grease seeping through it. 'What is it?'

'Cheese slice. I know you worry about the poor little animals.'

'Go on then.' Shovelling solid food into her stomach helped warm up the frozen core of her. She talked as she chewed. 'It's weird about those cottage people.'

'The Wicked Witch?' Tom's dark eyebrows went up. There was a fleck of pastry in one.

'No.' She glared at him. 'The posh ones who seem to have disappeared. Two deaths near the place in the last few months, and hardly anyone ever goes there? I mean, it's the middle of nowhere, isn't it?'

Tom swallowed a lump of sausage roll. 'You reckon something fishy's going on?'

'You don't think?'

'I dunno. What are the odds?'

As police officers, they were world-weary with members of the public watching crime dramas on TV then ringing in with a vast conspiracy they'd spotted to steal all the recycling bins in their street, or insisting their neighbour was part of an international paedophile ring, rather than, say, a music teacher. All the same, Alison had an itch between her shoulder blades. A little out-of-the-way place like that should not have been at the nexus of several suspicious deaths in such a short space of time. Something was wrong.

Tom sighed. 'Alright then. Let's go to the guv'nor.' He jerked his thumb to the office of their DCI, Claire Fisher, a powerhouse in tailoring. 'It's your neck on the line if it's all in your head, though, mate.'

'Alright.' Alison wiped her hands clean. She wondered if she should tell him about the pastry crumb, and decided against it.

Eleanor

December

Police called to suspicious death.

I heard it on the radio as I drove up the A21, heading to London, the traffic already thickened and snarled. I had spent the night in a Travelodge beside the motorway, planning my next move, having bought a toothbrush and some pants in a large supermarket en route, where no one would remember me. The news was not a surprise, not really, but all the same my hands tightened on the steering wheel, and I had to focus to stay in my lane.

James Conway was dead. The short news item indicated that neighbours had called the police to investigate a seeping smell of gas, and when they broke into the apartment they found 'Mr' Conway – he would have hated that – dead from carbon monoxide inhalation. They suspected a very old gas fire in the flat was the culprit.

I didn't care that he was dead. Before I left the place, I'd made him tell me everything Patrick had cooked up. He was happy to, boasting about his expertise. 'But first the money.'

With my gloves still on, I'd laid an envelope with a cheque inside on the arm of the filthy sofa. I didn't have enough in the account to cover it, but that wouldn't matter. 'Now please. I need to know.'

He laughed. 'Not like you're going to the police, I s'pose. It's very hard to fake your own death, you see,' he said. 'Unless there's no body, because you're lost at sea or something. That's how Canoe Man did it, you know that fella who dreamed it up for life insurance. But there's no sea around here, is there? Anyway, the police are wise to that play now.' So they had to come up with something better. Something more creative. They had to wait until someone died in the hospital who was around Patrick's age.

'But why did you help him?' I'd asked, bewildered. I was struggling to take it in, a huge part of me insisting that it wasn't true. 'He was the one who owed you money, or so you say. Why risk so much?'

He'd sighed, letting me smell his vile sour breath. Memories surfaced, unwanted memories. My mother, lurching across the room. *Eleanor, you stupid slut. Get out of my sight.*

'The thing about your Paddy is, he's good at holding on to secrets, isn't he?' Present tense again. It felt so bizarre to hear that. 'He knew things about people in the hospital. Surgeries they'd slipped up in. Women they had on the side. He did the expenses, you see, filed the insurance claims. He knew everything.'

Blackmail. He didn't say the word, but that's what it was. And so Patrick had been able to lean on people to do what he wanted, and let him escape with his life. The debts that were mounting, the woman who said she was having his child. And me, pressuring him to do IVF, to give me a baby.

Part of me still thought it was insane. And yet. My internet research, carried out long into the night, until my eyeballs frazzled, had shown me there were indeed ways to fake your own death. That Canoe Man had got a fake passport, using the birth certificate of a child who'd been born around the same time as him but died

264

young. Apparently that was quite possible to do. I thought about the sums of money disappearing from our accounts, always just under the threshold of suspicion. He must have been planning this for a while.

The plot sounded so elaborate. Like something you'd read in one of those trashy thrillers I devoured on the long nights when he didn't come home. The reason for running when he did was that luck had kicked in. A man was admitted to the neurology ward in the hospital he worked at. A man around Patrick's age, in good health apart from the fact he'd been in a biking accident and hit his head on the tarmac. No one had come to claim him, and from the brands of his cycling wear, the police thought he was a tourist – American maybe. Someone with no family or close ties in the country, no one to look for him, no one who knew where he was. He was unconscious, badly hurt, but they still thought he might recover.

'You see, we had to have a body,' Conway had told me, swilling whisky. 'They do autopsies for any suspicious death, and unless we had the whole morgue on side – well. But they're busy, aren't they? Funding's so tight. They aren't going to DNA test every single body they get when it's clear who it is.'

So they had simply swapped the patients. Conway, who was in charge of the induced coma anyway, fiddled with the displays a touch, moved the man's chart around.

'You can do that in my role,' he bragged. 'A tiny flip of a switch and boom, someone's dead. The margin of life, it's so much smaller than we think.'

The autopsy had not thrown up anything strange. The dead man had no fillings or previous surgeries – another piece of luck, as fillings could quite easily be traced to their country of origin – and he was in good health apart from the head injury, probably better than Patrick was, with all his secret after-work drinks. His head injury was not inconsistent with a car crash. And so with some tweaking of records – Conway hinted that a few other people at the hospital had been implicated too – this man became Patrick, and he, as the mystery man, made a miraculous recovery and discharged himself.

'But didn't anyone notice?' I could hardly believe this tale. 'The nurses, the ICU doctors?'

He shrugged. 'They use so many agency staff now. From all over, they are. Hardly speak English some of them, and they come and go every day. No one asked.'

I thought of that poor man, dying alone in a strange place, buried in someone else's grave. Surely someone out there was looking for him? And Patrick, slipping out of the country on a fake passport. These loopholes didn't exist nowadays, surely? But to be caught would have required someone to do their job, someone to be paying attention. And no one was. Not even me. I'd been so poleaxed with grief I hadn't even thought it might not be him. Why would I?

After he finished telling me the story, I stood up, surreptitiously wiping the glass I'd used on my sleeve. I'd worn a head scarf that day, ostensibly to shield my face from the cold air, but it was also good for stopping hairs falling on to his grotty carpet – though I imagined it hadn't been hoovered in years, so it wouldn't be too hard to explain if they did find one of mine. When he left the room to get the water, with my gloves still on I'd subtly turned on the knob on the side of the gas fire, meaning it was already leaking out a small amount of toxic fumes. I'd noticed that the old-fashioned windows were painted shut, the room stuffy and unventilated. If he sat here all night breathing it in, he would die. If he lit the fire, or even a cigarette, the room would go up in flames.

'Goodbye, James,' I said when I left, now that he had explained it all and I finally believed him. On my way past, I slipped the cheque out of the envelope, knowing he wouldn't look that night, not when he was halfway down the whisky bottle already. I meant goodbye for ever. He knew who I was, and who Suzi was and where we both lived. He was an unacceptable risk to us, to the baby. And besides, I felt the world was better off without him.

Now Conway was dead, and Patrick's crime had gone with him. No one else would ever think to look for my husband, or know he might be alive out there somewhere. But I knew. And wherever he was – he would not have lingered in Spain, surely, not when he could take a ferry from there to North Africa and vanish – I wished there was a way to let him know that I was going to come after him, Lady Vengeance herself, and he was not going to get away with it.

Do you hear me, Patrick-Sean-whatever-you're-calling yourself now? You will not get away with this.

Among all the lies, his death, his affair, his resurrection, that was the one thing I clung to. He would pay for what he'd done.

In fact, I was already on his trail.

Suzi

At times of stress when I was a kid – exams, getting in trouble with Mum for poor marks at school, being caught shoplifting fruit gums that one time at the age of eight – I would sometimes imagine a sassy friend giving me advice, the kind you saw on American sitcoms. Right now, she was lecturing me, hands on her hips. *Heck, girl, what's the matter with you? Your husband has you locked in a music room! I mean, let's not even talk about why you have a music room in the first place.*

It was so hard to take in. For a long time, after I'd woken up down there, my arm crumpled under me painfully, a bruise on my forehead, I hadn't been able to believe it. Was it some mistake? Did Nick know I was here? My brain rejected the truth. Of course he did – not only had he put me here, he had planned this. It was all him – the lights, the music, the word in the snow, even the rabbit. He'd admitted the lot. Not Nora at all – I had no idea what she was up to, but it wasn't her trying to send me insane. It was my husband. Looking back, I was amazed I'd never noticed the signs. My phone, always drained of battery from the spyware he'd put on it. The way he always knew where I'd been, what I'd done. So stupid.

Among the guitars and amps and leads, there was a camp bed neatly made up with fresh bedding, a small rug on soundproofed floor. A stack of improving non-fiction books, mostly about pregnancy. Around me the empty shelves, intended one day for a wine collection, breathed dust, and I was sure there were spiders in the dark corners. Nick had left water for me, even a sandwich on a plate. He didn't want to hurt me, at least, not until I'd had the baby. He just wanted to know where I was. That was all he'd wanted! And what better way to do that than to lock me up in the dungeon I hadn't even noticed him building. It had been a while since I could climb the steps down here, and anyway, the music room was just another project I had no interest in. I'd let him build this prison around me, while I sat and brooded for another man.

I'm not stupid, he had said, before knocking me out, and he was right. I had treated him like he was blind, as if he didn't see my red swollen eyes, the repeated checking of my phone, the way I jumped when the doorbell rang or hid my face when a car crashed on television. I had assumed that, because he hadn't mentioned it, he hadn't noticed. I had forgotten that Nick didn't do mentioning. I had forgotten my earlier punishment, of being moved down here to the countryside, and now a smaller, less open prison was required to shock me into repentance.

And I did repent, really I did. If I could have, I would have gone back to the year before, never looked near Damian, never attended that stupid conference, walked right past you in the bar and gone to sleep alone in my room. I would have accepted my lot, a husband who loved me, a job I was good at, instead of always asking for more. I would never have given up work, never moved to the countryside, never met you. I would, perhaps, not be pregnant. Would I really give that up along with everything else? I didn't know.

I knew I had to get out of here – that I would not be able to stand more than a day or two alone in the dark – and that I would say whatever it took to make that happen. I knew that Nick and I were done now, done for good, that keeping me here must be a crime of some kind, a terrible violation, and that I would call the police on him if and when I got out. But all the same, when I thought about it from his point of view, it made a kind of horrible sense.

Eleanor

There were things I was good at, it turned out. Finding information. Watching. Searching for people, tracking them down. I had not known I had these skills before, and so had never thought to turn them on my own husband. Why would I? He loved me, we were happy, or so I thought. Until I learned that he was lying and controlling and keeping me prisoner with my own fears. But now I wondered, what about his past? What had he done before me? Men like my husband – liars to the bone, stamped through with deception like a stick of rock – did not change. There would be something to find. And perhaps that something would lead me to him now, wherever he was in the world.

When we first met, after that concert in the Royal Albert Hall, Patrick Sullivan had told me the facts of his life. He was a doctor, an obstetrician (not true, he was a finance clerk, hence why he lived in a house-share with three other men. I had not found that out for some time, since he never took me there, insisting he was a gentleman, and by the time it occurred to me to wonder, I just assumed he owed money on student loans). His family were dead, he said, and he had been an only child with much older parents (I didn't know if this was true or not). At university, there had been one serious girlfriend, but they split after a pregnancy scare ended in a termination. He'd told me this with a catch in his throat. 'I know it was her choice, but I didn't agree with it. It was still my baby.' How my heart had swelled at that, thinking we'd have our own soon, that I would give him a child to make up for the lost one.

It turned out the girlfriend was real, at least as far as I could see. The ex, Kathy Gilsenan, had attended Essex University at the same time as Patrick, before he failed his first year and dropped out. He had been studying medicine, hence the photos I'd seen. It was sad. If I'd known him back then, perhaps I could have helped him pass, become a real doctor, and maybe there would have been no need to lie, to cheat, to take money that wasn't his. Such a waste.

My research had led me to the fact that Kathy, still Gilsenan, now lived on the Isle of Dogs in London. So, my car eating up the miles between us, I was headed there to see her. It was a long shot that she'd know where he was, but I could think of no one else he'd ever been close to. And that was tragic in itself.

I found the address – a narrow street of terraced houses within yards of the Thames, the DLR rattling overhead. Parking was less easy – another hefty charge, I should have taken the train – but soon I was sorted and ringing her doorbell. It hadn't occurred to me she might not be in. I knew with such conviction that I had to see her, had to talk to her, that she must be there. And she was.

'Yes?' A tall black woman with braids piled into a bun, Kathy was beautiful. She must have been my age, but didn't look it. For a moment my resolve faltered.

'Hi. I'm sorry to barge in on you like this but can I ask, do you – did you know a Patrick Sullivan?'

She frowned, and for a terrible moment I thought I'd got the wrong person. Then she said, 'Do you mean Sean?'

'You're married to him.'

'I was. He – he passed away a few months back.' I wasn't about to tell her the whole ridiculous saga. I didn't want her to think I was crazy.

'I'm sorry to hear that.' Her face was impassive – I didn't think she was that sorry. 'Are you here about Jack?'

Jack? Who did she mean? 'No, I . . . I'm here because I think . . .' *Oh, just say it.* 'Kathy, I think he was lying to me. About a lot of things. Maybe everything. And I wondered if you – if you'd spoken to him in the last few years.' I had to build up to asking: *Is he still alive? Do you know where he is?*

She sat forward, toying with a mug of tea that had the West Ham logo on it. I had said no to one. Her house was spotless, but I didn't want to feel I couldn't leave in a rush if things went badly. 'It's Eleanor, yes? Sean – that's how I knew him – he did nothing but lie. The whole time. Where he was, how old he was, who he was seeing . . . He was a fantasist, I suppose you'd call it. So no, I haven't spoken to him in years, and I'm glad.'

I closed my eyes briefly. So it wasn't just me. 'I see. His parents, are they dead?'

She snorted. 'They're fine, they live in Southend.' Of course, Essex, where he'd gone to university. He'd told me he was from Somerset, a middle-class family, an orphan. But he had parents, living! What a lie to tell! Although, of course, I had also told him my entire family was dead, which wasn't strictly speaking true either. 'Far as I know, they've not heard from Sean in years, and Denise hasn't either.' She saw my blank look. 'That's his sister. She's got four kids now, Sean's never seen a one of them. Reinvented himself after uni, didn't he? I guess a working-class family weren't part of the plan.'

Nephews. Nieces. He wasn't alone in the world at all.

'And, Kathy, did you really split up because you were pregnant? I'm sorry to ask.'

She set her cup down. She seemed calm, accepting of his lies, and I envied that. 'No, that's true enough.'

'He wanted to . . . have the baby?'

She gaped at me. 'What? No, it was me pushed to keep it. He wanted me to have an abortion. Said he wouldn't give me a penny in child support. My parents are religious, and anyway, I wanted it. That's why we split. Nasty about it, he was. Tried to say it wasn't even his.'

I wasn't understanding her. 'But you – I'm sorry, you lost the baby?'

Another strange long look. She got to her feet and picked up a framed photo from the mantelpiece. I wondered why I hadn't noticed it before. She thrust it into my hands. It showed Kathy in a floral dress, beaming, her arm around a tall, mixed-race boy in graduate robes. He was a handsome lad. His eyes, in a lean, smiling face, were startling blue. 'The Sullivans are good enough to Jack. He sees them once a year or so.'

I set the picture down carefully, afraid I would smash it, my hands were so convulsed. 'He has a son.'

'Oh yes, Jack's his alright.' A shade defensive. 'He's in his twenties now – got a good job as a paramedic.'

Medicine again. His son. Patrick had a son, tall and handsome. 'And he – he knew?'

My mind was rejecting it still. He couldn't have had a son all this time, who he'd known about but never saw. He wouldn't have done that, not to an innocent child.

Kathy was contemptuous. 'Course he knew. Never gave me a penny for him, mind you. I could have got Child Support on to him, but what's the use? We didn't need him.'

'Right. I – I see.' Oh my God. All this while I had been dreaming of the child Suzi was having, a baby that was maybe his, and he already had a son. A son in his twenties.

She replaced the photo, wiping some dust off it with her sleeve. 'Did he have any more kiddies? It'd be nice for Jack, if there were. I never had another.'

'No. No, we didn't – we didn't have any.' So the problem must have been me after all, if he had fathered a child. As I'd always feared, there was something wrong with me, and no surprise, given where I'd come from.

Eleanor, you little bitch.

My mother's words, echoing through the years in my head, as if I'd never escaped her. As if fire and blood and death had not been enough.

'Oh, right. Guess he had it done then after all? I thought he was just sounding off, never thought he'd go through with it.'

'With what?' I was really struggling to follow her, my brain inching itself along, winded by revelations.

She frowned at me. 'The vasectomy? After what happened with my pregnancy, Sean was so angry he said he was going to get one, make sure he never got caught out again. I assume he did it?'

Suzi

Being down in the cellar was how I imagined being dead. No one could hear me – it didn't matter how much I screamed and shouted. The expensive soundproofing Nick had put in for his 'music room' was doing its work, and anyway, who was there to hear me out here?

I wondered where Nora was, why she hadn't come to look for me in days. Had she worked out somehow I was on to her? Perhaps she would prefer me down here, safely out of the way. In my more paranoid moments, when panic clutched at my throat, I wondered if they were in it together, Nora and Nick. A revenge pact, against you and me. If they had somehow engineered your death too. I would not have believed it, but I would also not have believed that Nick, my mild-mannered husband, had been building a soundproofed prison right under my nose, and had locked me up in it. Oh, it was nice enough, this prison. There was carpet, and a bed with soft sheets, and he gave me plenty of water and food, coming down several times a day to check on me. There was even a loo, which he'd suggested putting in during the rebuild for when we had guests, and I had agreed to, listlessly, as I did with everything. I'd been trying to wash myself in the sink, but without a proper shower I already smelled.

The first time Nick came down, I raced at him. Tried to hit him, claw at his eyes. He just held my wrists until I subsided. He was stronger than I knew – all those gym visits. Another thing I had missed.

'Stop it, it's bad for the baby.'

'You can't do this!'

'It's for your own good. The way you've been acting, running all over the country in the snow, looking for some twat who didn't give a damn about you – Suzi, it's madness. When you have time to think, you'll see how good you have it here. I *love* you. I'll take care of you – you never need to work again.'

The next time, I just cried. Big snotty sobs. 'Please let me out. Please, I won't tell anyone. I admit what I did was bad. I'll even go to therapy if you want.'

He looked sad too. 'We're past that now. This is the only way.' He was solicitous. He would ask which meals I preferred, if I liked white bread or brown, consult me on how to make certain dishes.

'Just let me out,' was all I said at first, but gradually I gave in. If I was going to be stuck down here, I might as well eat things I liked. This was how you got used to any horror. The terrible adaptability of human minds. If it weren't for the lack of windows and a shower, I could have been resting in a nice hotel, with books and soft furnishings. Just nothing I could use to get a message out. 'It'll be good for you, less phone time,' he said, as if I was a child.

I protested about the shower. 'You have to let me wash. I could get sick.'

I could see him pursing his lips. My plan was, if he let me upstairs to the bathroom, I would grab something – one of my kitchen knives, or maybe a heavy ornament – and I would hit or stab him, and I would run out of this house and on to the desolate road, and I'd keep running until I found someone who would help me. It might not have been a good plan, but it was the only one I had.

Eleanor

Finally, after all my investigations, I had to go home. Conway was dead. My husband, my entire existence, was not as I had thought. He had a son. He'd let me think all those years I might have a child too, even though he'd had a vasectomy. He couldn't be the father of Suzi's child. He was not even dead. My whole plan, to find Suzi and pull her life apart, piece by piece, had crumbled away. She might not ever know it, but Suzi was a victim too, both of his lies and Nick's control. I was sick of the narrative I'd chosen: the vengeful wife hunting down my husband's mistress. I was sick of men, pitting us against each other. Lying. Locking us up in our dolls' houses. It was time to end it. I had made up my mind – I would go to Suzi, and tell her the truth, and help her to get away from her life. Burn it to the ground, if she had to. I was good at that. Then perhaps, together, we would track down my husband, and make him pay.

It took me almost half an hour to drive down the slipway lane from the motorway to my house, normally a ten-minute journey. Snow had piled up in my absence, and the tyres groaned and slipped on the icy, powdery surface. Gritters did not come down here, I knew. I might not get out again for days. I parked near Holly Cottage, its ruined hulk almost hidden by snow. Shielding my face from the driving snow, I pushed aside its rotten doorway. The roof was so full of holes, the inside may as well have been outside.

'There, there. I'm sorry, poor boy.'

Poppet was shivering in the makeshift kennel I'd rigged up for him, his food bowl empty. I felt a stab of guilt. What had I been thinking, taking him like this? When he ran off that day in the grounds of the old house, I had quickly found him in the bushes, blazing with anger that Suzi still could not control her dog. Then the idea had come – a way to punish her, unbalance her. I had meant no harm to the dog. I could never hurt an animal, and now the poor thing was freezing because I'd left him tied up in here.

'Come on, come on.' I led him with me, towards the relative warmth of my cottage. I would make him a bed in front of the fire, feed him double helpings of Pedigree Chum. Another thing I would have to confess to Suzi.

A single lamp was burning in Willow Cottage, and I lifted the dog under my coat, hiding him. He was heavy, panting hard against me, and he stank of damp fur, but it was a comforting smell. It was 3 p.m., the light already leaching from the sky, and I decided I would cross the lane and tell Suzi what I knew. It was time.

After sorting out Poppet and leaving him in front of the gas fire, I crossed the lane, a treacherous journey given the slushy, unsalted surface. The black tarmac was slippery as a diamond. I trudged up their path, surprised that Nick hadn't cleared the snow from it, and knocked. I braced myself to confront Suzi, to both blame and acknowledge blame. At the end of this conversation, we would know each other better. Who knew, perhaps we would even come out of it allies. Stranger things had happened.

The door opened and I saw – Nick.

'Nora!' He seemed surprised. 'Hello.'

'Oh, hello. I thought I'd pop by to see Suzi.' What was he doing home? 'Not at work today?'

'I was a bit under the weather,' he said, though he seemed fine. He was wearing dark jeans and a white shirt. I recognised it as an expensive brand my husband had liked, and I was surprised, because Nick hadn't struck me as a dandy. 'Suzi's not here, I'm afraid. She went to her mother's.'

'She left when you were sick?' A woman who was almost seven months pregnant, crossing the countryside in snowy weather? It didn't make sense. And then I remembered – Suzi had told me her mother was going away for Christmas, on a cruise. *Thank God, it means we don't have to invite her here.* At the time I had felt a strange bond with her, both of us with difficult mothers.

Why was Nick lying? Was Suzi there, but didn't want to see me?

'Oh, I got worse after she went. Better she's away, to be honest. Can't have her getting ill in her condition.' He was already shutting the door and I panicked.

'Wait! Nick, I do need to tell her something. Is she contactable there? On her mobile?'

'There's no reception,' he said sympathetically. 'It's in some kind of weird rural dip, like here.'

'How about a landline?'

He hesitated. I knew I was being rude, but I didn't care. All the hair on the back of my neck was standing up. Something was wrong here. He wanted rid of me, I could tell. 'You know, I can't for the life of me remember the number. I never call her mother myself, obviously.' He did a little self-deprecating shrug. 'I can look, but you'll have to give me a while.'

He had boxed me in. I could not now get inside the house without raising the alarm. I glanced past him into the gloom of the hallway. On the wall behind, set into the expensive wallpaper, was a door, a coded keypad beside it glowing red. Did red mean locked? I remembered another thing. Suzi showing me round the cottage. *And that's Nick's music room down there, God knows who's going to steal his stupid guitars, but he insisted on this lock.* Had I seen it locked before, that door? 'Alright. If she calls, tell her I'm looking for her, will you?'

'Of course. Bye.' The front door shut with a click, its hermetic seal locking the house up. I looked at the glowing alarm keypad, so out of place on this old cottage. Nick had turned the place into a fortress, remote-locking doors and windows all operated by codes, automatic blinds and shutters, the cable of a burglar alarm snaking around the house. Of course, a fortress also made a pretty good prison.

I squelched around the side of the cottage, counting its dimensions from the few times I'd been inside. The large kitchen – a light showed beneath the shutter but no shadows moved. Suzi's studio, in darkness but for a faint blue glow. Her computer had been left on, maybe, but she wasn't in there. The downstairs loo, the pantry, all the rest of the house in darkness. If Suzi wasn't at her mother's, and she wasn't in any of the rooms, where was she? They had dug into the cellar to make the music room. If you were middle-class, it seemed you could create a virtual dungeon in your house and no one would even notice.

It was a crazy thought, but no more so than anything else that had happened recently. Was Suzi in there?

Suzi

'You can't keep me a prisoner here for ever,' I said coldly, when Nick next came down. I felt like a zoo animal. I had food, water – the large bottles he'd bought, ostensibly as snow supplies – books, a comfortable bed. But all the same I wanted to tear a hole in the wall just to get out. To have space, light. Down here, I could barely tell what time of day it was.

Nick set down my lunch, a bowl of tepid carrot soup. Perhaps he was worried I'd throw it at him, anything piping hot.

'Prisoner? Suzi, you're in your own home. You're warm and dry and well fed. I'm taking care of you! You were out of control, running all over the place in the cold. You just need to calm down a bit.'

'I'll be missed. I have midwife appointments, scans! Mum will notice I haven't called.' My mother had already left for several months of educational cruising with Nigel the bookbinder, and I tried to think if I'd told Nick the exact dates. Would she think to call me during her holiday, or just text? If we'd been closer, she might have already noticed something was up. Or, you know, actually listened when I tried to tell her.

'If she rings I can just say you're in the bath. You've told me to do that enough times, when you don't want to talk to her.'

It was true. He was so maddeningly calm about the whole thing. Almost reasonable. I had to keep reminding myself that this wasn't normal, this was a crime. *He was keeping me locked up in a basement.* I was like that girl who'd been missing for twenty years. I went cold. Surely someone would come to look for me before then? A health professional, or my mother, or Claudia even? It was a good way to take stock of your life, wondering who might come to find you if you went missing. Would Nick tell them I'd just gone off somewhere? Run away with a man? But the baby. He wouldn't make me have the baby down here?

A jolt of fear made me change my tone. 'Please, sweetheart. I'm afraid. What if I go into labour down here and you're not about? If you're at work? I could die!'

'I've taken sick leave,' he said, glancing up from wiping down the little card table he'd left me to eat at. Even imprisoned with virtually no belongings, I managed to make a mess. 'I'm always here. I told Mum not to come for Christmas, by the way. Said you didn't feel up to it, with the pregnancy.'

Things were pretty bad when the idea of my mother-in-law not coming made me want to cry. With the Christmas break approaching, it was possible no one would find me for weeks. They'd think Nick and I had bedded down, cosy and happy together in our rural idyll.

'But you can't hear me up there, if I need something.' Perhaps I could convince him to give me my phone.

'There's the camera. I'll check on you through that.'

The idea of being watched all the time made my breath stop. I twisted my hands together, trying to match his reasonable tone. 'The thing is, I really do need to shower. I read that infections can develop otherwise, hurt the baby.' I began to cry, not entirely faked. 'Poor thing. He didn't ask for any of this.'

'He?' Nick frowned. 'Did you find out the gender and not tell me?'

'No, no,' I said quickly. 'Just a feeling.' In truth, I had no feeling at all, and could barely picture the baby as a person, but I had calculated that Nick would prefer a boy. I was scared to imagine him with a little girl. The way he'd treat her dates. Smothering her in a curtain of pink.

Nick was thinking about it. 'If you promise to be good, you can have a wash. I mean it, Suzi. There's nothing to stop me keeping you down here till the birth. If anyone asks, I can say you're at your mother's. You really think the cash-strapped NHS will bother to come all the way out here? Plus, we're virtually snowed in at the minute.' He said the last words with some relish. 'You'd need a jeep to get down here.'

So no one was coming.

'Nora,' I said. 'Where is she?' What a hole I was in, when the only person who might rescue me was the woman who hated me.

He shrugged. 'I haven't seen any lights in her place. I think she's away.' He was lying; I saw his eyes flicker. Why would he lie about that? Because he knew Nora might help me? Did that mean she was around? A crazy surge of hope punched into my chest. But why on earth would Nora do anything for me?

'Well, if no one's about, you don't need to worry about me making a scene,' I pointed out. 'No one would hear.' All he'd have to do would be to hide the phones, and the house itself would become an extension of my prison.

Nick was nodding. 'Alright. You are starting to stink a bit. Smells like a pet shop down here.'

That hurt my feelings, absurdly, but I said nothing. This was my only chance.

Eleanor

I wasn't sure what to do. I was pacing my living room, rubbing my cold hands until they were cracked and red. What would the police say if I called them? *I think my neighbour's being held prisoner. Who by? Her husband. Head of local council IT. Where? Oh, in her own music room.* It was ridiculous. Suzi could well have gone away, if not to her mother's then a friend's. It was possible she'd even lied to Nick, that he didn't know about the cruise. That she'd made her escape as I'd urged her to do, just in a different way. But somehow, I felt that wasn't true. Nick had been hiding something. He hadn't wanted me there.

I had put it all together since stealing his phone and meeting Lisa Ragozzi. Nick wasn't a dupe, even if Suzi treated him like one. Far from it, he knew exactly what she'd been up to. He watched her through cameras, knew when she entered and left the house, so it was quite likely he'd also been monitoring her phone. It was astonishing how many people had Find My Friends – tracking software, essentially – turned on and didn't even know or care. He might even have cloned her phone so he could read her messages – I had read that you could do that quite easily, just by sending a link to the phone. Perhaps he'd been planning to confront her about it, her second affair, before she said she was pregnant. Patrick couldn't father a child, so it was Nick's, whether he knew that for sure or not, and a baby was likely what he'd wanted ever since he'd tried to persuade Lisa – a college student! – that she should have one.

I could see the plan clearly, as if I'd made it myself. Suzi was almost seven months pregnant now. All he had to do was keep her somewhere until she went into labour – somewhere safe and warm, no point causing distress to the baby by making it a nasty place – then when she had the child, get rid of her somehow. It didn't even have to be murder. He'd laid the groundwork so well, taking her to the doctors, reporting her anxiety and hallucinations. Documenting her panicked racing around the country, her long walks in the cold, her weeping for hours. I imagined he would have her put away, in some nice safe hospital, the kind of place where I'd stuck my mother. Then divorce her, and who would give custody of a baby to a crazy woman? She would have antenatal scans booked, yes, and appointments, but perhaps he could tell them she'd moved practices. Or scare her enough that she'd never say a word, even if he let her out and she got her chance to tell someone. There were women who lived like that for years. Even me, I had lived in a cage I thought was perfect.

Oh, Nick was good, I had to give him that. In another world, I would have admired him. I had done similar things. I too had been the eyes watching from the shadows, a victim of the relationship between my husband and his wife. I too had conspired, and sneaked, and manipulated. But only in the hot bloodlust of grieving revenge. Not this cold-blooded calculation. I wondered how far back his plan stretched. Getting her out of London, that was surely part of it. Maybe he'd even thought it would work, the move. Make her realise what she had with him, make her love him again. Or did the possibility of this plan graze his mind even then, in case she didn't comply?

I pulled aside my curtains and gazed across the lane at Willow Cottage. How well do any of us know our neighbours, what goes on behind those lighted windows and locked doors? I hadn't even known the man I shared my life with. I thought I knew about Suzi, but in truth so much of her life was obscured to me. I had tried to know Nick, to ferret out his secrets, but there he was just feet away and I couldn't reach him. More snow was falling, obscuring the cold air, fogging up the glass. Soon the lane would be impassable again, and that meant Nick might not go to work. Which meant I couldn't get in to help Suzi. She was over there, I was sure, locked up in the dark hole of the earth, her screams soundproofed away. He needn't have bothered with that. Aside from me, who was there to hear? Who would even miss her if she didn't leave the cellar for months? He'd managed to make sure she had no one even looking for her.

Oh, I had to hand it to him, he was really very good indeed.

Suzi

Upstairs, the light of the house hurt my eyes. I felt like some mole creature, pulled from the ground. The bathroom was so clean, with not a drop of water or a stray hair anywhere. Perhaps Nick wanted to show me how easy it was to house-keep.

'Five minutes,' he said, trying to sound tough. 'Just a quick one.'

'My hair takes longer,' I pointed out. 'Look how greasy it is.'

The thick red mop was already matted and dirty. I felt disgusting. Nick had marched me to the door of the bathroom, so there had been no time to grab anything, and anyway, there was nothing lying about. The hall table was empty, the vases and pots that normally sat there gone. Perhaps he knew what I'd been planning. Despair hit me – how could I out-think someone like this, who'd watched my every move for months now?

'Alright, fine. Ten minutes.' For a moment, I thought he was going to stand and watch while I changed, but I challenged his gaze, and he moved outside, leaving the door ajar. 'Be quick.'

I turned on the shower and rapidly soaped myself and my hair, enjoying the feel of the hot water despite everything. It reminded me of being twenty and spending four dirty days at the Reading festival, except this time I was inside my own house. My mind ran through scenarios. Was there anything I could use to hurt him in here? The lid of the toilet lifted off, or I'd once read a book where someone was stabbed with a shank made from the ballcock. Or there was his dressing gown on the back of the door – could I make a garrotte from the belt? Keeping the water running, I stepped out of the shower – and immediately went skidding, bashing my tail-bone into the side of the bath. 'Oh!' A loud cry of fear burst from me, and then Nick was in the room.

'I slipped.'

I was crying, from pain and from the loss of my one chance. A jolt of pure fear had gone through me as I fell – *the baby!*

'Oh, come on. You have to be careful.' He was tender, even, helping me up – I was so vulnerable, naked and wet and pregnant. 'Are you alright? The baby?'

'I don't know,' I blubbered. 'I'm sorry, Nick, I'm so sorry. I didn't mean to do it, any of it. Sean – him. The man I . . . Or Damian, I never meant – I think there's something wrong with me. I'll get help, I'll change. Whatever you want. A therapist, hospital . . . I'll do it.'

Gently, he pushed the sodden hair from my face. 'I wish I could believe that, Suze.'

He was wavering, I could feel it. As if there was a way back from this, him locking me up, me plotting to hit him over the head with the toilet lid. But in that moment, I was so afraid, so beaten, that I would have agreed to anything. Perhaps I would even have persuaded him, if we hadn't heard what was by that point an unfamiliar sound.

The doorbell.

Maddy

The man – Sean – didn't come in the next day, or the next. She realised she was waiting for him, watching the doorway of the pub, her heart lifting and sinking a little each time it was some sunburnt tourist instead, like the boats in the harbour at high tide.

Then, on the third day, it really was him. He wore a navy polo shirt, tight over his lean body, and dark-rimmed glasses that made him look smart and sexy. Maddy turned away, wiping at the bar she'd already cleaned. She could tell he'd come up behind her. She could smell his aftershave, lemony and woody. She made herself not turn around.

'Hello again.'

'Oh! Hi there.' She put on a practised vague smile. Welcoming but not too keen. She'd had to learn these games the hard way, on boys her age, and this was a man. She didn't know what games he'd want to play. 'Couldn't stay away from the chicken korma?'

He laughed, a full, throaty sound. 'No offence to your chef, but that's not really the draw here.' He didn't say what was but she knew he meant *you, I've come to see you*, and she glowed. 'Listen,' he said, stepping closer, 'do you mind if I put the UK news on? Know how it is, you come for a break then you can't keep away!'

There was hardly anyone else in, just an elderly couple who couldn't hear the TV anyway, and kept screeching at each other about the weather. 'I said it's NICE!' 'No I think it's NICE outside!' Maddy passed him the bar remote, their hands almost touching as she did. She felt giddy, high on the clean smell of his laundry detergent and aftershave. He turned on Sky News, and watched it intently, the pint she'd poured him unattended.

After five minutes, she had to interrupt. She couldn't bear the way he was watching the screen, transfixed by a story about a death back home, some ancient alco suffocated by an even more ancient gas fire. He should have been watching *her*.

'Is it not OK?' Meaning his drink.

'Oh! Course it is.' He sipped his pint.

'So what's really brought you here?' She leaned on the bar, coquettish. 'It's not the sort of place people travel to alone, is it? No backpacker hostels or that sort of thing.'

'So, why am I here then, Detective Barmaid?'

'Well, I have a few guesses.'

'Go on.'

'Number one, you're a cop. Casing out a criminal somewhere here on the Costa del Dodgy.' He laughed again. Her heart swelled. 'Number two, you're on the lam.'

'On the what?'

'On the lam.' She blushed. 'It's like, old-time talk for being a crim. Running off so you don't get caught. Costa del Crime, isn't that what they call it here? Because we have no, like, extradition treaty or something.'

He looked at her over his pint. 'You're a smart young woman. Except for that law changed in 1985.'

'Oh.'

'What was your name again?'

She told him.

'Very pretty.' And from the way he smiled at her, she knew he didn't just mean her name. 'So, Maddy, if I really was on the lam, would you keep my secret? Or would you betray me?'

She leaned further over the bar. She knew it made her cheap T-shirt, bought in the local market, stretch over her breasts. Her mother had told her this, not disapprovingly.

'I'd never betray you,' she said.

Eleanor

All day I had watched Suzi and Nick's house, through the dark of the falling snow. Poppet snoozed by the fire, providing some comfort with his smelly breath and warm fur. I hadn't put on the lights in my own house – I wanted Nick to think I'd gone out. My car was hidden further down the lane, at the passing place. But what could I do? I wouldn't be able to get into their cottage, not with all the alarms and sensors and their sturdy doors and windows. I couldn't call the police, since they wouldn't believe me, and surely they would take a look into my past and realise there was no such person as Nora Halscombe. Not to mention the fact I'd never see that baby. I couldn't try Suzi's mother, since I'd no idea where she even was or on what cruise line. Nick's mother, who sounded dreadful, would do anything to protect her son, I was sure of it. Who did it leave? I could only think of one person, and even then it was a long shot. Could I trust that person, though? Something about their behaviour had made me uneasy – too much interest, perhaps. But on the other hand, I didn't have much choice.

First, I spent some more time on my new best friend, Google, searching until I had an explanation and my mind was at ease. Then I opened my front door, stepping lightly in case I saw movement across the road. Nothing. A flurry of ice in my face, I shut the house up behind me, leaving myself in the deep winter dark of falling snow.

Suzi

Nick's tender manner vanished at the sound of the doorbell.

'Stay in here,' he hissed. 'Don't make a fucking sound.' He never swore. Then he seized a small hand towel from the rack, and shoved it roughly into my mouth. I choked on cotton and disbelief – Nick! Nick was doing this! 'Shit, shit.' He looked around for something else – what, I didn't know – and then he saw his dressing gown on the back of the door, and whipped out the belt, and I understood. He was going to tie me up. And he did, to the towel rack, my arms pulled up at an awkward angle. I was naked and dripping and terrified.

'*Uhhh. Uhhh!*'

'Shut up, Suzi! I mean it.' His voice rose and fell.

Through my shock, I had questions. Who was at the door? Nora? If it was her, could I risk calling out? Would she even want to help me? I shuddered at the thought of the two of them in league against me. It wasn't fair. You should have been here to help me with this, the fallout from the fire we'd so carelessly lit, danced around, oblivious to everything it was burning away. But you were dead, and I was on my own.

I worked my tongue against the rough towel, hearing a series of beeps as Nick disabled the alarm on the door. His voice was public, showy. 'Hello, can I help you?'

An unfamiliar voice, a woman's, said, 'Yes, hi, we're looking for a Suzanne Matthews? I'm DC Catherine da Souza, with the Surrey police?'

I began to pant very hard, unable to stop it. A mistake, because my mouth was filled with fabric and now I couldn't breathe. All I could do was grunt. Would they believe me, even if they heard me? Or would Nick, with his patient rationality, make them think I was crazy, a naked soaking-wet pregnant woman? I thought of the records they had on me, the trip to the doctor Nick had forced on me. I thought how this situation could get worse – my baby taken away, me in some psychiatric hospital, or worse, stuck living with Nick for ever, only a Nick who was even more angry with me. Peering out the gap in the door, I saw the shapes of two people. Not uniformed – not the same police as before. What was this about? I could not spit the gag out. I had only forced it deeper into my mouth, and I was very close to choking. I took small breaths through my nose, which was also blocked with tears. I had never been brave, as I'd thought. Just reckless. Not brave enough to walk away from a disastrous marriage, before it was too late. Reckless enough to have an affair, and start this chain of events that had spiralled so far out of control.

'Is something wrong? I'm afraid she's at her mother's. A pre-Christmas visit, you know.' Nick sounded so plausible. I thought I was the liar in our marriage.

A man's voice said, 'We found your wife's details at a possible crime scene. Her name, her address.'

A short silence. Oh God. Oh God, what would Nick do? What were they even talking about?

'That's strange. What crime scene?'

'A man was found dead in Guildford yesterday – asphyxiation due to a gas fire. At the moment we're not sure if there was any foul play, but we can't rule it out.'

Nick said, 'What was his name?'

I had no idea who they were talking about. Who was dead now?

'A Dr Conway, James Conway. He worked at Surrey General Hospital.'

I could almost hear Nick's wheels turning. He knew I'd gone there that time, supposedly to check out the facilities. But why would Conway have my name and address?

'That's weird, I'm sure she doesn't know anyone by that name. We looked at the hospital as a possible birthing location – we're pregnant, you see.'

We! What the hell did he have to do with it! For a moment, rage replaced fear as my dominant emotion.

'Strange that he had her details in his home, though.' The police were being very forthcoming. I wondered if they had a plan – if they thought Nick was involved in this death somehow.

'That's so odd. If I had to guess, maybe he saw her at the hospital and took a liking to her. My wife is . . . well, she's beautiful.' He almost sounded proud, when he said it. A good actor too. Why had I underestimated him so much?

The police didn't stay long – it was freezing, I could feel the cold air from the open door, and Nick hadn't invited them to sit down or offered them tea.

'Thank you for your help, sir. Can you ask your wife to call us when you speak to her?'

'I will. It's really coming down out there. Be careful on the lane, it's not gritted.'

'Don't we know it,' said the male voice. 'Almost went into a tree on the bend. It's meant to get worse tonight. Your missus might not make it back.'

'As long as she's safe,' said Nick tenderly. 'I'll get her to contact you.'

'Please do.' And they left, and the soft electronic click of the door was like a prison gate slamming shut. Why hadn't I tried harder to get free, struggled, shouted? I was pathetic. And who had killed Conway? It seemed too much of a coincidence to be an accident, you and then him, your confidant, both dying within months of each other. I heard the soft fall of Nick's feet coming back to the bathroom. When he took out the gag, I gasped in air. My mouth was dry with threads of cotton.

'I was good,' I said, almost shouting in fear. 'I didn't say anything!'

He stared at me, still naked, still tied to the rack.

'Who's this Conway?'

I knew that look in his eyes, the dangerous quietness. I had to talk my way out of this, and fast.

'I'll tell you everything,' I said, my voice shaking. 'It's not what you think. I'll be honest with you, I swear. Just let me get dressed. Please?'

Eleanor

There was no possibility of getting my car out. Even if it hadn't been stuck in five-feet drifts of snow, I didn't want Nick seeing the lights. I didn't want him to know I was about, not until I figured out what to do. Instead I hiked down the icy, pitch-dark road, wearing my stoutest walking boots. Even then I was scared with every step. A car coming round the bend would have no chance of seeing me in time; I could be thrown off the road into the ditch, dying there in the snow, without anyone realising. Because no one would come to look for me. I had no one left.

I had gone about three yards when I saw the vehicle. It swept past me, skidding slightly, and instinctively I jumped on to the verge to avoid it. A man and a woman, both in suits. I knew immediately it was the police. Coming about what? For me, about Conway? It could have been my chance to get help for Suzi, but what would I say to make them believe me? And I couldn't risk being arrested, not when she needed help. I crouched down, my dark coat hiding me against the bushes, and after they passed I staggered on in the snow.

Eventually, ice flakes whirling in my eyes and freezing my face numb, I made it on to the slip road, saw signs for the M25 ahead. And there it was – the tree you had supposedly died at. If it hadn't been so dark, I would have been able to see the marks your car had left, the damage to the bark. What a risk to take. What a stupid, audacious thing to do.

As another car came past, driving very slowly, I stuck out my thumb. Hitch-hiking – what would Mother have said? Unladylike, not to mention dangerous. But I hadn't seen Mother for over twenty years, and really, I didn't give a fuck what she thought.

I was in luck. The driver was an elderly man, bewildered himself by the snow – glad, I think, of company to help navigate it.

'Hell of a night to be out, love.' He had a local accent.

'I know. I just need to get to Guildford. It's urgent, and my car's stuck. Going anywhere near?'

He looked at me curiously. 'Just off to the shops, love. What takes you there on a night like this?'

'I have to get to the hospital – it's my mother, she had a fall last week. The ice, you know.'

'Treacherous it is. I'll take you there, don't you worry.'

'Oh, you are kind. Thank you.'

He told me his name was Bill and we chatted for a while about the snowfall, how this was the worst he'd seen since the 1950s, and about his wife, Hetty, who'd always loved the snow, but who had died five years before. I sensed he was lonely, like me. Visibility was terrible, but the road had been gritted and traffic was at least moving. After an hour or so, we reached the lights of Guildford.

'I'll drop you direct. Can't have you walking in this weather.'

I was almost sad to see him drive off as he dropped me in the car park. The hospital blazed with light, with humanity, a well of brightness against the dark. I knew I would find help here, or nowhere.

Suzi

An hour later, I sat at the kitchen table. I was dry, dressed warmly in jeans and a polo-neck jumper. Nick had served me up some stew he'd made.

'Good?'

'Lovely.' It needed more salt for my taste, but of course that was 'bad for the baby'.

'I forgot the veg box was coming, so we had all this stuff left over. I'll have to cancel it for next week.'

This was surreal. We were chatting about veg boxes, when just hours before I'd been locked up in the cellar. I had told Nick everything – almost everything. About meeting you, our affair, your death, going to the hospital, meeting Conway there. My guess that Conway was planning to blackmail me, maybe, and that's why he'd had my details. I remembered his down-at-heel clothes, his alcohol breath – I could well believe he needed money.

It hadn't been easy, telling Nick these things, but he'd nodded, as if he knew most of it already. I didn't mention my meetings with Dr Holt, or the fact I'd seen Damian again. I could still rescue this situation. Get on cordial terms with Nick, then as soon as the snow melted I could run away, far away, to my mother's perhaps, or to Claudia. She would help me, I thought, even if we'd grown apart. I'd stay in a hotel if I had to. I hadn't quite realised that the law was there to help me, to make sure I had access to the money, and above all, to let me keep my baby. I just had to avoid going back in the cellar, and after that everything could be sorted out.

'What are we going to do?' I asked timidly. 'It's such a mess, Nicky.' An old nickname for him, back from when we'd loved each other. A time I knew had existed, but which I could hardly remember now.

He sighed, his elbows on the table. 'I don't know. We could go away, maybe. Abroad, somewhere warm. Wait till the baby comes.'

'And then?'

'I don't know. Suzi, do you . . . ?' I knew what he was going to ask, and was ready with my lie.

'Of course I love you. I just – I'm messed up. I was so lonely out here, and I felt like you hated me.' He nodded, as if seeing my point. 'I'm so sorry. I'm no good – I don't know why I do these things. But it's not just about us now, is it?' I placed my hands on my belly.

His face was open and vulnerable. 'Suze, please just tell me – is he mine, the baby?'

This time I was faster. 'Of course. With him I always . . . I never . . . It has to be yours.' It was a lie, but Nick seemed to swallow it. In fact, I had always felt it was your baby, based on my ovulation apps and how hard I'd tried to avoid going near Nick in the fertile time, but it seemed he had been one step ahead of me there. Maybe the baby was his after all.

He stood up, taking away the dirty stew bowls. I'd eaten all mine, like a good girl. And it might have been alright, I might have rescued the situation, and we might have found a way to muddle through before I could safely divorce him, if the erratic mobile phone reception around our cottage hadn't chosen that precise moment to kick in. My phone, which I saw now was on the

301

counter, charging, vibrated, shuddering across the marble worktop. A text. Nick frowned.

'What's that?'

Stop, no, please. I knew with certainty it was a message that would ruin everything. But I could hardly tell him not to read it, and he did, picking up the phone, and his face changed. Gone was the tenderness, the sadness. In its place, cold, glittering rage.

'So you told me the whole truth, did you?'

Oh my God. Who was it from? Dr Holt would know not to text me, wouldn't he, so it had to be—

'Fucking Damian.'

He flung the phone on the table, where it landed with a heavy thunk. I read the message in a flash. It was a reply to the angry email I'd sent him, the one I'd known was a mistake. *Er dunno what you mean. I'm not the one who came to see you babe am I.*

Oh God oh God. I hadn't changed my number since we worked together. Texts still popped up on a locked screen – Nick would have found it suspicious otherwise. Why hadn't it occurred to me Damian might text back instead of emailing? Oh Christ.

'You went to see him? You used my money for that?'

'I – weird stuff was happening. I thought maybe it was him. I couldn't think who else – I didn't know it was you.'

If I'd hoped to guilt-trip him, that was a pipe dream. 'You lied. I asked you to tell me everything and you lied. You are a liar, Suzi. I can't trust a word you say.'

I got up, edging away from him. I couldn't go back in that cellar, breathing in the smell of dust and plastic. I couldn't. Left out on the counter was a knife Nick had used to slice the vegetables. I could see shreds of carrot clinging to it. I seized it with an unsteady hand, feeling how much I was shaking.

'Stop it, Nick. You're scaring me. The baby . . .'

He sneered. 'The baby, the baby! Poor bloody kid, with a slutty mother like you! Sometimes I think it'd be better off not being born.'

Oh shit. The murder-suicide, favourite method of angry, vengeful fathers. He wouldn't. This was *Nick*. All the same, panic was clawing at my arms. I steadied the knife with my other hand.

'Come on, be reasonable,' I tried. 'This doesn't change anything we talked about.'

'It changes everything.'

He lunged at me, and I dropped the knife. The noise of it clattering on the floor tiles was the worst thing I had ever heard. His face was very close to mine.

'You bitch, you bitch, you slut, you whore.' He said it so quietly, almost a whisper, it made it even more terrifying.

What could I do? *Girl, you better save yourself.*

My eyes darted round the kitchen in a nanosecond. There on the draining rack was the lid of my Le Creuset pot, a heavy orange thing we'd got as a wedding present. I had used it the night we had Nora over for dinner, when I still thought there was a way out of all this. I lifted it, my wrist complaining at the weight, and hit Nick hard in the face with it. It was so easy that I shocked myself, feeling the reverb all the way up my wrist.

I dropped it but Nick was staggering, turning white.

'Fucking . . . bitch . . . you fucking . . .'

My phone was on the table, the landline right nearby. I could have called an ambulance. But he was already pulling himself to his feet, and so, taking my chance this time, in a thin jumper and bare feet, I ran out into the snow.

Eleanor

'Oh – it's you.'

After Bill, my elderly chauffeur, had dropped me at the hospital, I followed the same route as before to the obs and gynae wing. I hadn't even thought what I'd do if Dr Holt wasn't working tonight. Or how I would explain myself, given that he didn't officially know I was Suzi's neighbour. In the end, there was no need to worry. He was there, sleeves rolled up, hair sticking on end, buying a Coke from a vending machine draped in tinsel. I approached. 'Dr Holt? It's—'

'Eleanor. Patrick's wife.'

'Yes.'

He looked wary at seeing me, his can rolling forgotten in the drawer of the machine. In the end, I decided just to be honest. After all, I wasn't sure how much time we had. 'Dr Holt – I need your help. It's Suzi. Suzanne Matthews – I think she's in trouble.'

Unsurprisingly, he didn't believe me at first. 'Eleanor – I know about you. You moved next door to her. You know that she . . . knew your husband.'

There wasn't time for this. 'Yes, they had an affair, but that's not important now—'

He stepped forward, laying a hand on my arm. 'Mrs Sullivan, please. I can help you. We have people here—'

'You don't understand. Suzi's in danger. Her husband, Nick, I think he has her locked up! He said she's at her mother's, but she isn't, and the music room's locked and it's never locked.' It sounded crazy. How could I make him believe me?

He was frowning. 'What?'

'You've been in touch with her, haven't you? I saw her emails on your computer. At first I didn't know why you'd be involved with her – I even wondered if you were caught up in it.'

'Caught up in what?'

'The blackmail.' I waved a hand; that didn't matter now either. 'But you weren't, were you? You just cared for her. I didn't understand why for ages – but then I looked you up.'

He went still.

'Edward Holt, Jane Holt – they were your parents, weren't they?'

'Mrs Sullivan . . .'

'Please! Please don't send me away or call security or whatever you're about to do. Suzi needs us. Yes, I meant her harm to begin with, I hated her, but it's different now. You see? It's changed. I've changed.' Oh God, I wasn't making sense. 'Your mother – I know what she did. I understand why, OK? It was the same in my home.' Jane Holt, a mild-mannered housewife who loved gardening, had stabbed her husband, Edward, to death one day in the middle of Sunday lunch. Her lawyers claimed she was the victim of decades of coercive control, but she'd gone to prison all the same, and died there a few years later.

He was shaking now. 'How do you – you can't—'

'You get it, don't you? How these things work, how someone can make you lose yourself, lose any faith you ever had in your own mind, your strength. We have to stop him, Dr Holt. Please come with me.'

I didn't think it had worked – I thought he might insist we called the police, or just refuse to believe me – but after a moment I saw him nod.

'Are you sure we'll make it?'

Dr Holt scrubbed at the clouded-up windscreen with his sleeve. 'This is a four-wheel drive. I bought it after those few bad winters a while back, when I couldn't get to work.'

We were crawling down the frozen M25, hardly any other vehicles braving the trip. I could see almost nothing, just gusts of wind that from time to time cleared the freezing fog. I had explained all I knew – my original plan, the revisions I'd made to it when I learned about the baby, my growing doubts about Nick, why I thought Suzi was imprisoned inside the house.

It turned out he and Suzi had seen each other a few times, and I detected a tenderness towards her. She was the type of woman men wanted to take care of. He admitted, 'I was worried about Suzi. The things she said about Nick, how possessive he was, it sounded like coercion.'

'You don't know the half of it.' I told him what I'd learned, that Nick watched Suzi through their alarm system, that he reset the heating and door codes to wrong-foot her, that he played music remotely to make her think she was going mad. Dr Holt's hands clenched on the steering wheel.

'Yet just because he doesn't hit her, no one would think it's abuse,' he muttered. I deduced from this he was not just thinking of Suzi.

'I think he might have moved on to more physical threats now,' I said, thinking of the cellar.

'Pregnancy is when most instances of domestic abuse get worse,' he said, glancing anxiously at me. 'Eleanor – one of the other doctors died a few days ago. James Conway – he knew your husband, I think. He knew about Patrick and Suzi.'

'He was going to blackmail her,' I said. I didn't explain how I knew this.

'Do you think that maybe Nick . . .'

I didn't answer. Now was not the time to open that particular can of worms. After a moment of silence, he said, 'I don't want to miss the turn-off – tell me when we're close.'

We almost did miss it in the gloom of the whirling snow, then had to take the turn too fast. I held on to the side handle, white-knuckled. Then we were bumping down the narrow, dark lane, the dazzle of the motorway suddenly gone, the car rocking over potholes left from earlier freezes. Ivy Cottage appeared, forlorn and snow-covered. And someone was at my door, hammering on it, desperate. Suzi! I saw she wore only thin clothes, and had no shoes on. Her feet were bare and red in the lights from the car.

'Stop!' I shouted, grabbing for the wheel without thinking. 'It's her!'

For one confused moment, Dr Holt pulled the wheel one way, and me another. That was all the time it took for a dark shape to loom up in front of us on the road, and then Dr Holt was swearing and braking, but the road was too icy to stop, and I saw a white startled face in the headlights of the jeep, and I knew what was going to happen, and there was nothing we could do about it.

Suzi

I didn't understand what was happening. I had run across the lane – icy cold on my bare feet, like tiny needles stabbing me – and gone straight to Nora's, even though the house was cold and dark. Even though I was likely in danger from her too. There was simply nowhere else to run, so I had to hope maybe she was hiding inside with the lights off. I was screaming, my voice whipped away by the wind.

'Nora! Please help – help me!' Was it mad to think she'd been helping me all along – advising me to leave Nick, telling me my rights? That she hadn't wished me ill at all?

Nothing. She wasn't there, and I could hear Nick blundering across the road to me, cursing and screaming. Terrible words, things I'd never heard come from his mouth before.

I knew it was no good. He would drag me back, put me in the cellar, keep me there until I had the baby. Maybe he'd tell the hospital we'd moved away, force me to give birth down there alone. I wondered how long it would be before anyone came to look for me. Months? Years, if he was smart. And I knew he was smart. He'd had me fooled for so long. All this went through my head in seconds, and then I saw the lights of the car.

It was swerving, going too fast for the narrow icy lane. The thing Nick had always warned me about, to look both ways before crossing. It was driving straight at him. I'd like to think I shouted to him to look out, but I couldn't say if I did. Instead, I watched the car – a large jeep – plough right into him, tossing him off the road into the ditch like a child's toy.

The jeep stopped, jackknifed across the road, and someone got out. Nora. But this wasn't her car. I didn't know whose it was, but it looked familiar. Then I saw the driver get down, run to where Nick was, throwing off a thick winter coat to free his arms. I knew that stocky, capable build. It was Dr Holt. He bent over Nick, pummelling on his chest, while Nora and I stood frozen, watching.

'He's gone.'

Dr Holt sat back after a moment, wiping his mouth with a shaking hand. Snowflakes whirled around us, settling on our cheeks and eyelashes, and on to Nick's white, still face, a spread of blood flowering on his temple.

'Oh God. I've killed him. I'll lose my licence. I'll be struck off.'

I don't know what would have happened if it was just Dr Holt and me there. I was half-delirious with shock and cold, and all his instincts were to tell the truth, call the police. We might have got off, given that Nick had come out of nowhere on a dark road. But there was the dent I'd made in his forehead, and the pot lid still with his blood on it, and the car had swerved towards him, and the police could check for things like that. Maybe Dr Holt would, as he'd said, have been charged with dangerous driving. Lost his job. Lost everything. And me – I didn't know what would have happened to me.

Either way, it didn't happen like that. What happened was Nora – *Eleanor* – stepped forward, took Dr Holt by the arm.

'Let's go into the warmth,' she said, nodding towards the house I'd just run out of. 'Let's go inside and talk about what to do.'

Alison

'That was the wife on the phone. Suzi Matthews.' Later that day, Tom leaned against Alison's cubicle wall, causing it to buckle alarmingly. 'She's fine.'

Alison had been vaguely worried for the woman, who seemed to have disappeared, and who she knew had been heavily pregnant. 'You tell her she's a widow now?'

'Nah. Said to come in. We'll need her to formally identify him.'

When they'd gone to see their boss, DCI Claire Fisher, and tried to explain Alison's hunch about the case, she had told them it was pretty much a certainty their corpse was Nick Thomas. His body had barely degraded at all under the snow, and he even conveniently had his wallet in his jeans pocket. Hit and run, body hidden in the ditch all this time. The story was clear to read.

All the same, there was still something about it that Alison didn't like.

'Where's she been all this time?'

'At her mum's, she said, and then with a friend. They had some big row and Thomas stormed off. Texted to say he was leaving her, told his own mum the same. She's got the messages to show us, says she hasn't seen him since December.'

It was very neat. Little chance of finding the car that had hit Nick Thomas, so long afterwards, and an explanation for why no one had seen him all this time.

Alison thought for a moment. 'And the link to the other two cases?'

Tom shrugged. 'Dunno if there is one. The first crash, Patrick Sullivan, that was most probably an accident. James Conway – could be an accident too, with the gas fire.'

Alison looked at him sceptically. Coincidences like that didn't really happen.

'There was a lot dodgy about that crash,' she said. 'And why was Matthews' name in Conway's flat – how do you explain that?'

'Well, how about this? He's a blackmailer, Conway. Drives the first fella – Sullivan – to top himself, steering into that tree. The hospital are being well cagey, but looks like Sullivan was nicking money from them. They have some kind of internal investigation going on. Then Conway, he moves on to Thomas – he has the wife's details so he can go to her with whatever it is he knows.' So far they had found nothing to suggest Conway and Thomas had known each other, and nothing untoward about Nick Thomas, an apparently blameless member of the public, but experience had taught Alison there would be something blackmailable. There always was. Everyone had at least one secret they'd kill for, if they were the right kind of person. Thankfully, most people weren't.

She sighed. 'You're saying Thomas kills Conway to stop the blackmail. Then who kills him?'

Tom shrugged again. 'That I dunno. Genuine hit and run? Some accomplice? How would we ever find out?'

That was the problem. They were so stretched at the moment, with all the cuts, that it would be hard to make a case for digging deeper into it. Fisher was keen to have it all wrapped up. Three apparent accidents, where at least two of the victims had known each other? Was it that rare thing, a real coincidence? Alison sighed again, eyeing the emails ticking into her inbox like the dripping of a water clock.

'Suppose you're right. Let's kick it upstairs, see what they say.'

Tom stretched. 'Who's doing the death ID, me or you?'

Alison couldn't face the thought of it, taking Suzi Matthews in to look at her husband's dead, frozen body.

She pleaded with him. 'Ah please, mate. I can't. It's been such a freezing, awful day.'

'No worries. I'll sort it. Doubt she'll be too upset anyway, if he left her.'

'I owe you one,' she said gratefully.

'One pint?'

'If you like.'

'After work, The Feathers?' Suddenly, he wasn't meeting her eyes, fiddling with a thumb tack on her wall. They'd had drinks together dozens of times. This was no different. But all the same, Alison suddenly found it hard to meet his eyes too.

'No Tinder date tonight then?'

Tom cleared his throat. 'Nah. Thinking I might knock all that on the head. You in?'

'Alright then,' she said casually, letting him walk away before she allowed herself to smile.

Eleanor

FEBRUARY

I shut the door on the police with relief, and went to pick up Isobel. She was red-faced, howling in her crib. I watched her every day for signs of who she looked like, but so far all I could see was Suzi, her fuzz of hair, her clear blue eyes.

'Shh, shh.' I jiggled her in my arms, and gradually she went limp and contented against me. 'You're hungry, aren't you? Don't worry, angel, Mummy will feed you soon.'

Suzi had looked stunned on that winter night two months back, when I'd herded her and Dr Holt into the warmth and light of her cottage. The cellar door stood open, a dark yawning mouth, and I could see that I'd been right about where Nick was keeping Suzi. It haunted me still, the little bed, the card table, the warm prison he'd made for her. Both of them were semi-hysterical, and Dr Holt kept saying we had to call the police. But I talked him round. All we had to do was move the body, drag it a bit further into the deep ditch at the side of the road, then leave it there until the snow thawed. That could have been a week or, as it turned out, several months.

In that time, I would text Suzi from Nick's phone, which he had conveniently left in the house, suggesting he had ditched her after learning of her infidelity. He hadn't disconnected it from every app since I took his other one, so it was easy to get in and reset the passcode, as I had done with Patrick's. The police might be able to tie these three suspicious deaths together – Conway, Nick, and Patrick of course – but there was enough material there to write themselves a different story. Conway had been blackmailing Nick, perhaps, or Nick had killed him to shut him up about Suzi. Or Patrick and Conway had been killed by the same person, someone else who was being squeezed for money.

Suzi didn't believe it would work. Nick's mother would notice he hadn't called. His office would wonder why he didn't come back after Christmas. But I knew it would. In the modern world, people don't need to hear your voice to believe it's you they're speaking to. A few evasions here and there, and he'd resigned by email and told his mother over text (because he'd been sick, as he'd already helpfully told her himself, he'd lost his voice) that he was leaving Suzi, going away for a while to get his head straight.

And so we'd settled down to wait. Unwilling to go back into her own house, that beautiful prison she'd thought she might never escape, Suzi had moved in with me, and then, when little Isobel arrived earlier than expected in January (hardly surprising with everything that had happened), to the hospital. It wasn't suspicious if you thought Nick had left Suzi. At least, we hoped so. Now would be the real test. The police had found his body.

I was debating whether or not to text Suzi to tell her, when I heard the sound of a car pulling up. I watched as she took her customary five minutes to extract herself from the car, tangled in headphones, scarves, cardigans, shopping bags. She couldn't seem to stop buying things for Isobel, as if making up for not feeling excitement before the birth.

As soon as she came in I said, 'It's time. They found him.'

Suzi's face, flushed from the heat of the car, went pale. 'Oh.'

'It's a good thing. Get it over with.'

'What should we do?'

'You need to call them – say you were at your mother's, or a friend's. Stick to the story. Nick left you. He's been texting, you haven't seen him.'

She took Isobel from me, soothing her in a gesture that made my heart ache. Issy wasn't mine, she never would be. She wasn't Patrick's either, and as it turned out, there could have been no child for me with him. But I hoped she would think of me as at least a kindly aunt, and I hadn't come away with nothing – I was going to take Poppet, since Suzi hadn't the first clue about dogs, and hopefully train him up to be well behaved. We could never explain the true relationship between us, Suzi and I. All the same I hoped there was one, and one that would endure, no matter what happened next. She said, 'But they'll be able to tell, won't they? How long he's been . . . there. In the snow.'

'I don't know. Even if they do, you don't know anything about it. If someone else texted you from his phone – well, how were you to realise that?'

I knew nothing as the innocent neighbour, and they'd never think to involve Dr Holt. There was no trail linking him to us, no reason they would think to test his jeep for damage, or discover that it had been sold just before Christmas. I had thought it through many times over the past two months, placing weight on each part of the story in turn. I was confident it would hold. After all, I'd done it before.

Suzi had asked me about that, as we sat in her house on that terrible night, shell-shocked. Did I do it, what the whispers claimed? The fire that ruined my home, killed my father and my sweet little brother, sent my mother further into her madness? That saw me

315

locked up in Uplands, a psychiatric hospital for teenage girls, until I managed to talk my way out, convince them I was an unfortunate victim of circumstances? I said accidents were sometimes just that: accidents. That was all she needed to know. Not about that night, when it should have been only myself and my parents in the house, when Sebby should have been sleeping over at a friend's. A friend who, it turned out, had chickenpox, and so Sebby was at home as usual. I, locked in my own room for some new transgression, for complaining about being banned from piano lessons, the boarding school they were about to send me to, had not known he was there. And Suzi didn't need to know how I had sneaked out, passing my mother's room, seeing her wiped out on her bed with a cigarette burning down between her slim fingers. Or about me moving her hand ever so slightly closer to the curtains. Nor about getting out, taking the dogs with me so they'd be safe. Considering my father, absent even if present in body, never less than two glasses of whisky in, and dismissing him. Not about realising, too late, that Sebby was also there. Seeing his white face at the window as I raced up the lawn of the house, the grass cold and wet beneath me, the dogs yelping. *Ellie! Ellie!* Trying to get in, beaten back by smoke, my precious hands burned.

Of course I didn't know he was there. He was a child, an innocent. I would never have hurt him. Anyway, I was a different person now. Not Eleanor Treadway, or Elena Vetriano, or Elle-belle, or Nora Halscombe. I didn't quite know who I was, not yet. But I would find out.

'Eleanor,' said Suzi now, hesitantly. 'I'm afraid.'

'Don't worry.' I stroked the baby's hand, and she clutched my finger in her tiny fist. 'It's all going to be fine. The investigation will be wrapped up soon, and then I'll leave.'

She went even paler. 'You're sure?'

'I'm sure.'

'Will you tell him about me? About Issy? The truth?'

'I don't think he deserves it.'

She nodded. Soon, she was going to sell the gleaming prison Nick had built for her, and move into a flat in town. When I asked her what it was like, the one she'd viewed today, I knew she'd rave about the mullioned windows or cornices, and not a word about stairs or transport links or boilers. Bless her, she wasn't very practical, Suzi. Not ideal for a single mother. But I thought that, in her usual style, she wouldn't be single for long. The places she'd been viewing were all quite near to Dr Holt's little bachelor pad. And once Nick was declared dead, she'd have his life insurance, his pension, all their savings. It had turned out pretty well for Suzi, whether she deserved it or not. As for me, I had gained nothing. I couldn't have, really. Revenge was a zero-sum game, I knew that now. At least I had some stake in Issy's future, and hopefully, a friend for ever.

But I had one more thing to do before I settled back into my life, and tried to move forward. I was only forty-two – there was still time, and now I knew that the reason for my childlessness was not me. It could happen. I had hope, if nothing else, but that small spark was enough to hold back a world of darkness. First, though, I would book a ticket to a small town in Spain, one with an English pub that served Newcastle Brown Ale.

Maddy

APRIL

With the coming of spring, life had returned to La Tornada. Tourists once again wandered into the bar, eating battered fish with obvious relief that it didn't have its head still on, standing in front of the big screen gaping at football matches back home. Maddy worked hard, scraped ketchup-spattered plates, pulled pints, smiled. But she couldn't stop thinking about Sean. They'd kept each other company all through the dead winter months, her sneaking off to his flat in the harbour every time she had a spare moment. They'd watched films, played board games, gone for walks on the beach, and of course more. Maddy blushed when she thought about the more. But then he'd gone. The messages suddenly stopping, no answer at his door when she went to knock, ashamed at being so needy.

She honestly thought he'd come back, and every day for a week she'd made an effort with her appearance, ready to be aloof but forgiving when he came into the pub, but there was no sign of him. Ghosted, by someone too old to even know what that meant. At least she hadn't told anyone about the relationship.

One day, not long after she'd last seen him, a woman had come into the pub. Much older than Maddy, like twice her age maybe, but there was something about her that made you look. She was stick-thin, lucky cow, and had long dark hair, dyed probably, but shiny and rich. She wore an ankle-length printed green dress and a floppy hat and sunglasses, and in a posh sort of voice, like an actress or something, she had asked after Patrick.

Maddy had been on red alert right away. *Wife*, her senses were telling her, even though she couldn't have said where she'd learned this. This was his wife. But the name was wrong. 'Patrick who?'

The woman had placed her sunglasses on the bar, so Maddy could see her grey eyes. 'Patrick Sullivan.'

'Oh?' Maddy's neck was prickling. 'I don't know any Patrick.'

'He could be calling himself something else. I need to get in touch with him about an inheritance. He could be rather a rich man, if I can just find him.'

Maddy had remembered what he'd told her, that he was strapped for cash, and if he wasn't he'd take her away from all this, to live in Paris or New York or even London. Just somewhere . . . better. But he was Sean, not Patrick. He wouldn't have lied about that, would he? 'Sorry.' She shrugged.

The woman's gaze was like a laser. 'You're sure?'

'Yeah.'

Ever since then she'd been kicking herself. What if it really was an inheritance? Had she lost her chance to help him, and had he somehow found out, and that was why he'd ditched her? That was stupid. No, it was far more likely the woman had found him through someone else – La Tornada was a small place, after all – and then he'd done what he'd said and buggered off to somewhere better, only not with her.

There was a rustle of the fly curtain and her dad came in, huffing and puffing in his old-man shorts, his belly rounded under his

England top. That was what years working in a pub, sampling the wares, did to you. Maddy resolved once again to get out, move back to England, find a proper job. Start her life.

'Seen the commotion, love?'

'What commotion?' said Maddy, bored stiff. It was probably a sale on grappa or a donkey stuck in an alley again. God, she hated this place.

'They found a body down in them harbour flats! Some accident with the gas stove, carbon monoxide got 'im. He's been there weeks!' Her dad seemed excited at this news. Immediately, Maddy's heart began to race. It couldn't be. No. But it would explain . . .

'Who was it?' she said, trying to sound casual. Her parents didn't know she'd been seeing Sean. They wouldn't have approved, seeing as he was so much older. She thought he was maybe even older than he'd told her, which was thirty-six. Sometimes his references just didn't add up.

'Some British fella,' said her dad, already forgetting, getting engrossed in the football scores on telly. 'Apparently his name was Patrick.'

ABOUT THE AUTHOR

Photo © 2017 Jamie Drew

Claire McGowan was born in 1981 in a small Irish village where the most exciting thing that ever happened was some cows getting loose on the road. She is the author of *The Fall*, *What You Did* and the acclaimed Paula Maguire crime series. She also writes women's fiction under the name Eva Woods.

Printed in Great Britain
by Amazon

65395806R00196